THE MEN I SENT FORWARD

CLAYTON LINDEMUTH

THE MEN I SENT FORWARD

CLAYTON LINDEMUTH

HARDGRAVE ENTERPRISES

SAINT CHARLES, MISSOURI

COPYRIGHT © 2020 BY CLAYTON LINDEMUTH.

PUBLISHED BY HARDGRAVE ENTERPRISES AND CLAYTON LINDEMUTH.

CLAYTON LINDEMUTH ASSERTS HIS MORAL RIGHTS AS AUTHOR OF THE MEN I SENT FORWARD

.

EDITED BY GAIL LAMBERT AND CHRYSTAL WILKINS

COVER BY DIDI WAHYUDI

ALL RIGHTS RESERVED. NO PART OF THIS PUBLICATION MAY BE REPRODUCED, DISTRIBUTED OR TRANSMITTED IN ANY FORM OR BY ANY MEANS, INCLUDING PHOTOCOPYING, RECORDING, OR OTHER ELECTRONIC OR MECHANICAL METHODS, WITHOUT THE PRIOR WRITTEN PERMISSION OF THE PUBLISHER, EXCEPT IN THE CASE OF BRIEF QUOTATIONS EMBODIED IN CRITICAL REVIEWS AND CERTAIN OTHER NONCOMMERCIAL USES PERMITTED BY COPYRIGHT LAW. FOR PERMISSION REQUESTS, WRITE TO THE PUBLISHER, ADDRESSED "ATTENTION: PERMISSIONS COORDINATOR," AT CLAYLINDEMUTH@GMAIL.COM. NAH, JUST KIDDING. SEND IT TO CLAYTON.

PUBLISHER'S NOTE: THIS IS A WORK OF FICTION. NAMES, CHARACTERS, PLACES, AND INCIDENTS ARE A PRODUCT OF THE AUTHOR'S IMAGINATION. LOCALES AND PUBLIC NAMES ARE SOMETIMES USED FOR ATMOSPHERIC PURPOSES. ANY RESEMBLANCE TO ACTUAL PEOPLE, LIVING OR DEAD, OR TO BUSINESSES, COMPANIES, EVENTS, INSTITUTIONS, OR LOCALES IS COMPLETELY COINCIDENTAL.

THE MEN I SENT FORWARD/Clayton Lindemuth

ISBN: 9798686282162

FOLKS I APPRECIATE:

I would like to thank the following people for their enthusiastic help and wisdom. This book is vastly better because of their ideas and efforts. All errors are mine.

STORY:
   Victor Shultz
   Dubhghlas Kraus

EDITING:
   Gail Lambert
   Chrystal Wilkins

LAW ENFORCEMENT/WEAPONS FACTS:
   Jerry Hanford

For Georgena Lindemuth. Can't wait to see you on the other side, Ma. But I will.

"You see, the problem with materialism is that nothing real is material."
—Chicago Mags

CHAPTER ONE

Corazon sat on the commode lid and leaned against the tank. She turned off her cell phone and shifted her gaze to the linoleum floor. It was clean. The bathroom reeked of bleach.

The motel where Baer Creighton left her and her sister Tathiana was an improvement over sleeping in a garage. The beds were better than cardboard on top of cement and the fireplace was pleasant.

But after reading on the Internet that regular bleach leaves traces of DNA in blood stains, while oxy bleach does not, Corazon re-soaked her clothes and knife. Everything had been dry for hours but the smell lingered.

Earlier she'd tried to relax in the hot tub with Tat. The sisters wore bras and panties but Corazon hadn't felt comfortable. It wasn't shame or fear of how others saw her. No matter how she perceived her body men and sometimes women wanted it. Instead, being in the hot tub under the stars, where motel guests walking to their rooms could look from the sidewalk and see her naked shoulders barely submerged... it felt like flaunting vulnerability.

Corazon was not vulnerable. Nor was Tat. Each concealed her weapon of choice within arm's reach.

In tactical situations the sisters wore their weapons on their belts. But for times when they weren't hunting they'd bought bags at a Navajo gift store outside Flagstaff, Arizona, not caring about how much makeup or pads each bag could hold, only how easily it would both conceal and yield a weapon. Tat carried a Sig Sauer P220 Elite .45, which she cooed at and stroked like an infant needing love. One time after Tat cleaned the pistol she stretched out on the recliner with it on her belly. Corazon shifted the Sig to Tat's breast to suckle.

Corazon also had a child — not one that she loved so much as put to work: a Microtech Navy Seal Scarab. She'd discovered it at a near-deserted pawn shop in Tuba City, Arizona. It looked cool and though she thought the shop owner was a thief, she'd asked Baer for the cash and he'd given her the hundred fifty dollars.

Later she looked up the Scarab on her cell phone and discovered it was worth three to five times as much, depending on who was selling. Hers was the anodized model, built to withstand perpetual exposure to water. The three inch blade launched instantly out the front with the a press of the button on the side. She discovered one of the knife's most endearing features while practicing with it one evening. The blade's firing mechanism was illuminated with a tritium insert.

Now, back inside their tiny suite, dressed and prepping in the bathroom for a wild night out, Corazon lifted a small spiral notebook from where she'd rested it on the sink.

Her process since departing Flagstaff was simple. First she located a wealthy part of town on her cell phone using a real estate website: Bluff, Moab and Thompson Springs in Utah; Grand Junction and now Glenwood Springs in Colorado. Homes with high sales prices always clustered together. She scribbled the address of a property close to the center of the group, then entered the address into the search field on the government *look-up-your-pedophile-neighbor* website, with results limited to a one-mile radius. The website returned a list of sex offenders with addresses and photos.

Some were young, some middle aged and some old.

In her fifteen years Corazon had been penetrated by dozens of men. Most occurred in Salt Lake City during her abduction by Wayman Graves, who drugged her and sold domain over her body in one-hour increments. Freed by her sister, Tat, and journeyman badass Nat Cinder, who were set in motion by the wandering — what do you call him? — prophet, shaman, madman, murderer — Baer Creighton, Corazon next hid in an underground end-of-the-world shelter where she spent six months learning how to speak English like a native and how to exterminate pedophiles.

Even after having experienced life as a sex trafficking victim — the daily drugging and being raped so often her resistance became less about sex and more about pain management and control of her body — Corazon saw only a sliver of the equation. That view expanded while she wintered in the mountain lair with Baer and Tat. The federal government and many states published websites with searchable lists of sex crime convicts, and these websites painted the rest of the picture for Corazon. She would have never guessed how many pedophiles surrounded her at any given moment. It seemed they were everywhere. She wanted to shrink and look over her shoulder. While some of the men's photos suggested they were young, wild and probably made an innocent mistake fooling with a girl barely illegal, the vast majority were frightening specimens and Corazon surmised from their images that sex with them by any female on the planet, — regardless of her age — in any context — could only be forced.

Remembering the men who paid Wayman Graves to experience making her weep, Corazon saw patterns. Regardless of race, they all had sallow skin. They were well groomed and smelled good. The last time she walked into a wall of strong aftershave — in a gas station — she grew sick to her stomach and her chest constricted. She hurried about the aisles until she found the cologned offender. He was young and muscled like a boot lace and Corazon's anxiety receded. The men who abused her were always older. They wore suits and their shoes gleamed. When they bared their chests their skin hung.

They were outwardly, but not inwardly, serious.

They shined their shoes but didn't do sit-ups.

They wore watches that cost thousands of dollars but forgot the mouthwash.

They were serious about appearing, but not about being: a nebulous concept Corazon wouldn't have been able to articulate. She simply knew how to identify men whose worldview told them it was okay for them to compel others to have sex with them. To take a drugged child's lack of fight as consent… she couldn't think very deeply before anger derailed her.

While scrolling the government pedo website, Corazon always found at least one man whose face easily substituted in her mind's eye for one of the demons from Salt Lake City.

She killed her first in Bluff, Utah and her second and third in Moab and Thompson Springs.

Life was suddenly exciting and purposeful. Maybe if she exercised great care, she'd be able to murder them all.

Corazon wrote an address and a name from the pedo site: Chester DeChurch. Tough break about the name. Regardless, Chester had the look. Although Corazon would provide him an opportunity to save his life, from his eyes she knew DeChurch would fail.

She pulled a zip lock from her pocket, dropped in her cell phone and filled the baggie with sink water, sealed it and placed it on the floor.

Corazon isolated each part of her process. Any reasonable home buyer might search for both new homes and pedophiles in an area they were considering purchasing, so she was comfortable assuming that performing both tasks from the same cell phone would not flag her for special attention. After her first two killings, she'd decided to search for local high schools as an added camouflage. After that her cell phone's mission was complete. If she retained the mobile phone, or used the same device to research multiple killings, or worse, carried the phone on her person to each slaying, eventually the people who ran the world from behind their computer screens would catch on. They'd track her with the phone and be waiting for her.

Corazon killed as many cell phones as men.

She opened a giant Rand McNally map book and flipped to the page with the correct grid. She searched the street listing, found her location at the motel, then Chester DeChurch's address. She pulled an orange highlighter from her pocket and traced a route, then ripped the page from the map book.

Corazon stood with her eyes closed, remembering the layout of the motel, the parking lot, the street and the interstate highway. She imagined the map and the correct orientation, then opened her eyes. Outside the motel door she would turn right, then right, then left and on the road left again.

She folded the torn page, tucked it in her pocket and exited the bathroom.

Tat rested under bed covers with Stinky Joe curled at her feet. She'd bunched pillows to the headboard and was watching the fire. She turned her head toward Corazon.

"Again?"

Corazon nodded.

"Want help?"

Corazon shrugged.

Tat threw back the top blanket — she hadn't been between the sheets — and dropped her booted feet to the floor. She wore the black outfit given to her by Nat Cinder, the very clothes she wore when she had rescued Corazon. Tat pulled her Sig from her hip holster, held it aloft and made a face.

Corazon strode to the door and turned. "You can come."

Tat grabbed her coat, dragged her hand across Stinky Joe's head and kissed him on the nose.

"You have to pee?"

Stinky Joe stared.

"Time to poop?"

Stinky Joe sighed. Curled.

"You haven't pooped since this morning." She looked at Corazon. "Do you think he has to poop?"

"He said no."

Tat reached into her coat. "Aren't you going to wear anything more?"

"We're running."

"How far?"

"Six kilometers. Do you have the room key?"

Tat patted her pants pocket. "Got it."

Corazon knelt at the door and retied her boot laces. "You should leave the key outside where either of us can use it. In case we get separated."

So far she had not experienced any close situations with law enforcement, but she knew if she continued her path, encounters would be inevitable.

Corazon exited the motel room and Tat followed. Corazon looked around, heard a giggle from the direction of the hot tub and a low-toned voice. The hedge row blocked her line of sight. Corazon nodded and Tat tucked the plastic room key under the door mat.

Corazon led. They jogged along the access road parallel to Interstate 70. She turned at an intersection and removed from her pocket the plastic baggie containing water and the cell phone. She opened the bag and dumped the mobile into a runoff drain.

Navigating from memory, Corazon stopped a short distance from a street light and opened the map so her shadow hid all but the section she consulted. She turned the map and looked up the street and back.

"Let's go."

She folded the map as she jogged, taking in every light, every motion, every sound. Aside from a rare car on an adjacent street, they were alone. The evening was late and most of the houses with lights on were dark downstairs.

That was okay. She'd wake Chester DeChurch if necessary. He'd be thrilled, until he wasn't.

She stopped at the last turn and after a moment, Tat stood beside her.

"It's up there. Third."

Corazon unzipped her jacket and pulled a travel-size plastic bottle intended for shampoo from her pocket. She unscrewed the cap and dumped the contents — Wild Turkey whiskey stolen from Baer Creighton — into her mouth. She swished the alcohol until it numbed, then spat it to her hands. She splashed the Turkey on her face, hair and top.

She said, "I don't know how he drinks it."

"If you swallowed it you would know."

Corazon knelt at the edge of the sidewalk and jammed her fingers through melting snow to the soft ground beneath. She curled her fingers, withdrew a clump and wiped mud across her cheek, getting some in her hair. She dropped and ground her knees through the snow until the cold numbed her skin, then standing, wiped mud on her elbow.

"When he comes to the door, run past so he sees you."

Tat said, "And then?"

"Wait behind his house. Ten minutes."

"And then?"

"I'll be out."

Tat shook her head. "I don't — "

Corazon sprinted a diagonal path across three snowy lawns and slammed into DeChurch's house. A dog yipped inside. Corazon knuckled the side window then raced to the front. She bounded across a wood porch and beat the door with the sides of her fists.

"Please! Help!" Corazon pounded the door. "Please!"

The door opened. "What's this? Who — "

Corazon looked back to the lawn as a dark figure ran halfway across the lawn and stood, pistol in hand.

"Oh God! Help me! Please!"

The figure slowly pointed the pistol toward them.

"Oh shit! Get in!"

DeChurch grabbed Corazon's shoulder and dragged her inside. The figure on the lawn bolted. DeChurch slammed the door and locked it.

His voice conveyed surprise and fear but his hands were steady on the deadbolt.

DeChurch's face was normal size, but it rested atop a body of such size Corazon wondered a moment if she'd best back away.

But...

Life was in or out and required volition. She had to engage on one side or the other. She was either for child rape or against it. And just as there was no middle ground between evil and good, there was no way for her to know how to do something good and not do it. Maybe experiencing rape made her an absolutist, but the only result that mattered was whether there was a girl out there who would have a normal life because she wouldn't be raped... because the man who would have done it showed his true self to a girl who said *no more* with a sharper edge than the women before her.

Would Corazon's action right now save a girl or not?

She'd stay a minute and get a deeper sense of the situation. A large man wasn't necessarily tough, wily, or especially dangerous and she'd already learned a million ways to use a man's size against him. More size meant more to use to her advantage.

It seemed like something Baer would say.

DeChurch stepped into another room and jerked open a desk drawer. The dog that had been yipping trotted down the hallway and turned around and came back. A little nuisance pet, it pranced to Corazon's feet and began yipping again.

Corazon looked around the room and said, "Wow, thank you. You saved me."

From the other room DeChurch said, "Who was that?"

"I don't know. He attacked me. I was walking home from work and he just attacked me."

Still in the other room: "You're lucky to have found me."

Something about Chester DeChurch was off.

Corazon said, "I'm lucky you were still awake. Thank you for letting me in. I'll just wait a minute and go."

DeChurch stood in the entrance to the other room with a revolver loose in his hand and pointed at the floor.

"Like I said, you're lucky to have found me. You're safe here. Wait a few minutes. Do you smell bleach? Is that you?"

CHAPTER TWO

Corazon looked at the short black revolver in DeChurch's hand. The chill of his eyes didn't match the warmth of his smile.

"Like I said, you're safe here." He held the revolver so she could see it from the side. "It's a thirty-eight like Michael Corleone used to whack the police chief."

Corazon watched.

DeChurch held her look and parted his lips with a wet click. "Great movie. Yeah… Well, aren't you a cutie?"

DeChurch lowered the revolver and gestured toward the sofa with his other hand. He turned on a lamp. The sofa was brown leather, the lamp copper and cowhide. The floor was shiny wood in a zebra pattern. DeChurch was rich and single. He stepped to the sofa and placed the .38 on an end table that looked new and beat up at the same time and sat.

His knees popped.

DeChurch patted the cushion beside him.

Corazon tingled. With his body angled away from the gun he would have to twist his shoulders and extend backward to reach it.

In a moment of alarm his grasp would be prone to error. Given his size and age, Corazon thought she could cut him first.

She sat on the right side of the leather sofa with her blade in her front-opening right jacket pocket. She arched her back against the oversize armrest, rolled up her pelvis and barely — just barely — widened the gap between her knees.

"Wow. Bleach and alcohol," he said. "Have you been drinking?"

Corazon flashed a smile, looked away and then met his eyes. "A little."

She eased her hand to her chest and unzipped her top a few inches. The cloth was snug. She wore no bra.

Chester looked.

She said, "I'm sleepy. I should go now. I am grateful to you, but I must go."

"You can go if you want."

She waited.

Chester looked straight ahead.

She smiled. "You're scaring me with your gun. I think the man outside is gone. You should put the gun away."

"I like it nearby."

"I see how you look at me."

"How do I look at you?"

"Like a man."

He smiled. "That isn't strange, is it?"

"You know…"

He waited.

"Sometimes when I need a little money…"

"Yeah?"

"Sometimes when I feel safe…"

"Uh-huh…"

"You know."

"I'm not sure."

"Sometimes I make men happy."

DeChurch's mouth fell a little and the corners turned up.

Corazon grinned, but she sensed a look of calculation remained in her gaze and she wondered if that was how DeChurch felt earlier when his eyes didn't match his grin.

She'd seen men clumsy about sex, but this man was not. The situation reminded her of when her father taught her to play chess; the face of an adversary — even one who loved her — was not the same as the face of a friend. DeChurch didn't look like a man scrambling to find the words to close a sex deal. He looked like a man engaged in a game of strategy, dealt a hand he knew would win.

But if he perceived something strange about her being there, why didn't he dismiss her? Should she bolt for the door?

He said, "That could be interesting. Where are you from?"

"Las Vegas."

"You might have passed through Vegas, but that isn't where you're from."

"You won't tell?"

"Tell who?"

She stretched her left arm to the top of the sofa. The back was too tall so she lowered her arm to the cushion, fingers stretched toward DeChurch.

Chester placed his hand on hers.

Corazon tingled. All her dead so far had been armed only with superior size. DeChurch's revolver changed things — but did it? He might be a little on edge but like all men, he was mentally weak. His constant desire for gratification made him gullible, and that negated the advantage of his greater physical strength.

Corazon imagined the face of a random girl who would no longer be in danger from DeChurch, and slipped her hand from below his and placed it on top.

She thought through her next moves: She'd lean toward DeChurch and slip her hand to his wrist. She didn't have to restrain him, only slow him.

No.

First, she'd unzip her top another few inches and drag her hand between her breasts. His eyes would stop there and he'd misinterpret her hand on his wrist as if she'd placed it there to pull him on top of her. Men thought that way. She'd lock eyes, extract the Scarab from her pocket and whip it toward him.

No...

She'd wait until he was in motion of his own volition, then attack, firing her blade open midway to her target the way she'd practiced. Overshoot, jerk back and the blade would be positioned at his neck. Ripping toward herself, she'd destroy his left carotid artery and windpipe. Dechurch would spurt blood before his heartbeat quickened.

Ready?

Corazon had killed men with both firearms and knives and found comfort taking life with a blade. Sure, using a pistol in close proximity, the bullet punched meat so quickly after pulling the trigger that the sounds compressed into a single, oddly satisfying bang-smack. On the road she'd used Tat's Sig Sauer and the instant explosion and spatter followed by the man's raspy wheezing and choking was quite a reward. She'd watched his fear blossom and fade like time lapse photography. His death was really nice... but it wasn't like watching a pedophile's life bleed out from his neck and thighs.

After the first kill she'd felt a tiny pang of conscience afterward, even though she'd taken great care coming to informed opinions.

What if he'd changed his heart?

Corazon had studied pedophiles while holed up in the mountain lair for six months. English was a second language but it came easily. She'd read news stories and blog posts and even medical research, and views disagreed. Pedophile recidivism was high or low depending on the research a writer chose to cite, but the bulk of the papers expressed what Corazon had seen — pedophiles were plotters — and from that kernel sprouted her understanding.

Normal people found it difficult to knowingly cause harm to another. They required the heat of an impassioned moment to deliver the will to use violence. But pedophiles sustained their willingness to harm a child for sexual gratification throughout planning and execution. They didn't need a moment of peak frustration to put them in an aberrant mental state. They were already there. Always.

Pedophiles were wired differently.

There was no other way to think about it. They were defective and whatever part of them that malfunctioned didn't somehow get fixed in prison or during probation. Therefore, if a man was on the pedo website and he looked like the men she'd experienced in Salt Lake City...

Fair game.

So long as he failed her test.

Corazon's first kill asserted her in a world that didn't care if she existed. The man had proved his rottenness. Executing a death sentence that she ordered using self-asserted law founded on her own moral experience proclaimed her an authentic being. It celebrated her agency and justified her, but she didn't need to kill to feel good about herself.

Her motive wasn't revenge. Her sister Tat had already killed all the men who had harmed her in Salt Lake City.

Nor did she desire to punish pedophiles whom the government had already returned to society. Punishment was a rehabilitative tool used on redeemable people.

Since she acted not for revenge or punishment, but only to protect the nameless innocent girl, Corazon needed to ascertain if her target was still a threat.

After her first killing she stood before the mirror cleaning blood from her skin. She realized her face still recorded her years accurately. Her soul felt a hundred years old but her face was fifteen. Perhaps, instead of running up and shooting men, she might give each the opportunity to prove he no longer desired fifteen year old girls.

Her next pedo had been a whitehair and he failed. He'd struggled but Corazon had spent months inside a cement mountain practicing knife moves learned from *YouTube*. Nothing changed when she started using the Scarab except pressing the mechanism to fire the switchblade. Her hand was fast and even if he had expected her to slice his femoral artery, he wouldn't have been able to throw her — not with her hips on his shoulders and his trousers bunched at his knees.

Corazon smiled again at DeChurch. She tried to twinkle her eyes but a nagging feeling that the house didn't feel right kept her from slipping into the moment.

"Okay. Here's the truth. I need the money. I will make you very happy."

She pressed her tongue against the inside of her cheek and pulsed it outward, mimicking a blowjob, knowing it looked junior high but that would be a plus to a pervert.

"Oh, really. Uh, wow." DeChurch shook his head. "I don't know. You just showed up from nowhere."

"Of course. A man was chasing me."

She looked at his groin.

"And now you want me to pay you for sex. You police or something?"

"Do I look old enough to be a cop? I'm fifteen."

That explained why he seemed on edge.

Didn't that mean he'd otherwise have sex with her, if she gave him the chance? Was the logic sound enough to kill him, *now*?

She needed harder evidence.

"I have a confession," Corazon said.

"What?"

"I'm traveling to New York and I ran out of money. I looked you up on the government website. You're like my regular clients. I'm passing through. I'm clean — "

"You looked me up?"

"The website. It's how I find all my clients."

"Fuck off, cop."

Corizon stood, unbuttoned her pants and wiggled them down her hips. She wore no underwear.

DeChurch stared.

"Would a cop do that?"

"Uh. I — uh — you."

"I'll call you *Daddy* if you want me to."

"No. Stop. I didn't expect …. You said you looked me up on the Internet? Is that what you said? On the government website?"

Corazon squinted. "I'm fifteen years old, Daddy." She covered her crotch with her hand. "It's like a vise."

"I don't know. This feels like a setup."

"Me, setting you up?"

She jerked up her pants and buttoned them then rested her hands in her jacket pockets with her right on the Scarab.

"You're fifteen?"

"I think you saw I'm a woman."

"Hypothetically — how much money?"

"A thousand."

He waved his hand. "I don't keep that kind of cash."

"Yes you do. Men like you always do because you all fantasize about the same thing. A hot fifteen year old girl showing up breathless on your doorstep, wanting to fuck. You have the money, but if you don't, I'll come back after you go to the ATM."

"You uh, sound like you've done this before. Uh, how much time with you would I get? Speaking hypothetically?"

"One hour or less."

"What if I don't — "

"One hour or less."

"What if I don't need an hour?"

"A thousand dollars. One hour or less. Don't be *estupido*."

"Okay, so let's do this. I want you right here on my favorite sofa."

"You don't mind that I'm fifteen?"

"Like you said. You're a woman. Why don't you start by taking off your top? Then bring that pretty little mouth over here."

"Okay, but first... would you mind putting the gun away? I'm not really comfortable with guns."

He smiled and the moment was broken. "I have to decline. I am comfortable with guns. And since the clock is ticking and I bought the hour, take off your top and bring me your mouth, like I asked."

Ha-tchou!

Corazon jolted. A sneeze? From one of the back rooms?

"Who's here?"

Corazon leapt from the couch and batted away Chester's grasping hand. She darted toward the door and, looking back while she twisted the knob, saw FBI agents stampeding the hallway behind her.

"STOP!"

"FREEZE!"

"FBI!"

She yanked open the door and shadows from the yard raced toward her. Motion-sensor lights flashed on and the shadows became a man and woman in blue jackets with bright yellow letters. Did they already have Tat? They pointed guns at Corazon with faces as blank as their barrels. Her nerves flashed. She shoved toward a gap between them but one of the agents inside the house grabbed her shoulder from behind and spun her.

Corazon stumbled. The agent shoved her into the siding and her face bounced. Her front tooth chipped and she pressed the fragment to the roof of her mouth. Another agent pressed her neck to the wall and she felt vertebrae shift. Someone wrenched her arms behind her. Handcuffs ratcheted tight on her wrists. Hands smacked and jabbed all over her front, sides, crotch, legs. Someone removed her blade. Another found the bottle she'd used for alcohol.

"You have the right to remain silent. Anything you say can and will be used against you in a court of law. You have the right to talk to a lawyer for advice before we ask you any questions. You have the right to have a lawyer with you during questioning. If you cannot afford a lawyer, one will be appointed for you before any questioning, if you wish. If you decide to answer questions now without a lawyer present, you have the right to stop answering at any time."

Corazon said nothing.

"Do you understand these rights as I have explained them?"

Corazon looked forward. The man speaking to her was to her left.

"We heard you *hablo* English the entire time you were inside the house."

Another agent spun her to face the man addressing her.

"You are under arrest."

CHAPTER THREE

Three FBI agents placed Corazon in the back of a new-smelling sedan, seated behind the front passenger. They joined her in the car and she studied them in turn as passing streetlights illuminated the interior. Each agent was a different color. The one next to her in the back seat slouched and his head still touched the ceiling. A man sat in the front passenger seat. A female drove. Did that mean anything about her or the men?

During their scuffle on the porch, Corazon had noticed the woman's best feature: a thin knife scar on her cheek.

Corazon's father had overseen police for the Mexican government. She'd been in his office and had seen his name badge on his desk and the family photo to the left, turned so he could see it when seated. She never saw a piece of paper that was out of place. Her father's office was sterile and quiet, a place of repose and strategy. He never spoke about his work but one time when he came home in a bad mood, she noticed blood on his cuffs.

One evening the family had watched a cop show on television. Her father had leaned into the torture scene and later as the credits rolled, he dismissed the program with an arm wave; they'd gotten it all wrong.

Corazon steeled herself, knowing when the car stopped and the FBI led her inside, torture would follow. They would use a specialist, not the three arresting agents. The agents were firm and cold, but it took a special kind of villain to be the torture guy. Cops and FBI agents seemed capable of living by the golden rule, but torturers — and pedophile killers, for that matter — had to determine themselves separate from the rule-followers in order to claim the authority to do bad in the name of good. Corazon had watched documentaries about torture techniques online during her stay inside the mountain lair. Government researchers had discovered how to manipulate human beings so their responses were almost automatic: carefully curated suggestions, drugs, surgically applied doses of horrendous pain and at just the right moment, friendship and redemption given as reward for unburdening her soul of the truth.

Of all the dangers she'd faced, she'd never been up against a man with as many advantages as the torture guy. She would not be able to resist completely, but every second she held out, every lie she told that the government would have to track down, bought more time for her sister to get away.

More likely Tat would get herself caught or killed trying to save Corazon.

Corazon blinked.

Her duty was to escape or die bloody.

Maybe they would wait to see what information Corazon divulged in questioning before deciding to torture her.

Corazon looked beyond the agent beside her to the window and into the Colorado night. The man beside her was young and his features seemed androgynous. He was black with a shaved head, neither handsome nor ugly with very black skin, full lips and huge eyes.

Could she kill him? What could she do with her hands fixed at her back?

Escape seemed impossible, yet each minute her situation worsened because if breaking free of the back seat with three agents seemed impossible, soon she would be inside a police station that was probably fortified and guarded with multiple levels of security. If Glenwood Springs ran their law enforcement anything like her father had, if she entered the police station she would never leave government custody.

Corazon inhaled deep and let the air flow from her lungs to her muscles. She would remain nimble minded. She would search every avenue for opportunities. She had advantages and though none seemed useful in the moment, she would remain watchful.

She'd asked her father about the blood on his sleeve.

"Transitions," he'd said in Spanish, "are the most dangerous."

An answer that had said nothing useful in the moment but spoke truth several years later.

Transitions...

Eventually they'd have to take her out of the car and walk her inside a building. It would be her only chance to disappear.

Corazon's thought-world moved at light speed. Meanwhile, the FBI sedan passed where she'd pitched her cell phone in the runoff drain as she and Tat walked to DeChurch's place. She glanced, but didn't allow her gaze to linger, in case police cameras harvested clues. It was difficult to guess where technology might be lurking.

Had she allowed her clothes to soak long enough in the oxy bleach?

Her blade?

There!

Across the road, through the window of a parked car, Corazon observed an oval face surrounded by black hair.

Tat.

Corazon placed her hand on the glass and caught her breath. She forced herself not to look at the tall one in the back seat with her. He lowered his head to the window.

Had he seen her reaction?

Corazon watched street corners for landmarks. The names on the signs were small and most times not illuminated by headlights or streetlights, so she memorized their path by studying buildings and committing their features to memory.

Minutes passed but no escape opportunity presented.

Corazon shifted in the seat and reduced the pressure on her handcuffed wrists. The agent watched her face. Corazon warmed her eyes toward him and twisted on the seat, lifting her right thigh. Her leg folded at the knee and her foot touched his leg. She lowered her head, slitted her eyes and allowed the barest smile.

He pushed away her foot.

She twisted forward and leaned to him. Slid her tongue between her lips, locked eyes with his and felt along the seat with her cuffed hands. Without changing her gaze, she located the opposite door latch, flipped her hands so her palms were close to her back to get them high enough to reach the door release.

Her fingertips reported something cold and smooth as Toyota chrome — and with her hands upside down and backward from how she normally experienced them, she pressed to confirm it was a door handle.

She felt a soundless click. The door shifted. Road noise seemed a fraction louder.

Loving her agent's pupils, desperately communicating lust, she wondered why the dome light hadn't triggered.

Sometimes, Corazon thought, she just had to trust things would turn out okay. She'd introduce a little confusion into the FBI agents' night and perhaps discover a route of escape.

Sharing a deeply committed gaze with the backseat FBI agent, Corazon flashed her teeth and directed her stare toward his crotch a long moment, then returned her look to his face.

The man's mouth twitched.

Corazon heard Baer Creighton's voice in her mind. *Fella look like a fish doin' trig.*

Why think of Baer?

Her hands still contorted behind her, Corazon pulled the chrome handle.

The door vanished and Corazon tumbled outward as the dome light flashed. The agent's eyes popped white as she rolled onto nothing. She shoved with her folded leg first, then with both, driving herself backward out the door. Her thighs, then calves and feet slipped across the seat. Cold wind blasted her face and her hair tangled in her eyes.

CHAPTER FOUR

Corazon tucked her chin to her chest and hit the pavement with the back of her shoulders. She tumbled and her left elbow flashed incandescent pain.

Tires squealed.

Corazon threw a leg, stopped her roll and with her elbow nestled to her ribs, lurched to her feet.

"Stop!"

Corazon shuffled; her feet were free but she waddled without her arms for balance. How could she free her wrists in seconds? She had to run faster. Her only hope was if Tat or some other benefactor interfered with the agents. Baer Creighton? She had to create more distance…

A car door slammed.

Agents shouted.

Her lungs burned and her breath blasted from her mouth. She lurched into a run and a mountain tackled her from the left.

Corazon's shoulder crushed to the cement and her head bounced. Hands smacked her butt then pattered along her legs to her ankles and crushed them together. Pebbles cut the skin on her head. The three agents manipulated her body and returned Corazon to her feet. Her eyebrow seeped blood into her eye.

"That was stupid," the giant agent said.

"Must have hit the door lock with my elbow," the woman agent said.

She looked into Corazon's pupils and Corazon wondered at the blankness she observed. The female agent shoved Corazon toward the car but not in anger, more like when Tat and she used to mock fight.

The giant agent stopped her at the door. He turned her shoulders and positioned her face under a streetlight, then peered at the cut in her brow.

"The bleeding is slow. We're a few hundred yards away. We'll get you patched up."

Pain stabbed her mind and Corazon's ears rushed like an amplified ocean. The skin on her face and neck tingled with a million pinpricks. The place where her head hit concrete throbbed. Corazon's vision blurred as the world receded. Blackness rushed from the edges of her awareness and she waited as it consumed her.

Corazon's knees buckled.

The giant agent swung his right arm around Corazon's shoulder and pinned her to his hip.

"Easy. You're all right. Steady yourself."

His sweat stink brought her back. It must have been a long stakeout. Maybe they'd been waiting the entire time Corazon and Tat had been at Jubal White's place, enduring long shifts by pounding down Red Bull, while frustration and nerves burned stink into their armpits.

The bone of her brow hurt.

The agents loaded Corazon into the car and this time Corazon heard the lock switch activate inside the door.

"That was a stupid thing you did," the woman said from behind the steering wheel. She shook her head. She sounded like Tat.

Corazon didn't know exactly what she expected but the process so far didn't fit. From her father and the movies, she understood being under arrest to mean she would be beaten when taken into custody, tortured during questioning, possibly drugged during trial and ignored to death in prison.

But her experience diverged from her expectation.

The agents didn't strike her. Didn't curse her or cast evil looks. The giant one reminded her of a cartoon she couldn't place: an ogre careful not to allow his unwieldy body to smash things. The female seemed at times reluctant to participate, as if she was distracted or Corazon wasn't worth the Bureau's trouble. The man in the front passenger seat was senior to the others, given their behavior around him, but he didn't give them orders. He spoke quietly and then things happened, but it wasn't like he was bossing people around.

They parked in the lot and waited until all three agents exited the car to open the door and pull out Corazon. The female agent closed the door behind her and said, "Take it easy, girl. All right? You're in better shape than you think."

"Don't," the white agent said.

The female agent, unseen by the white man, patted Corazon's shoulder and the confusion lifted from Corazon's mind. It was all part of the trick.

Maybe the two male agents would be her torturers and the woman would show whatever warmth Corazon required to unburden herself of her crimes.

Except each killing was a badge, not a burden.

The two male agents each took an elbow and guided her to a building that seemed too new to be frightening. A trick, designed to increase the shock value when they turned on her behind closed doors.

Inside the building they steered her around a couple of corners then the two male agents stopped by themselves at the end of the hallway and spoke. The white man's step seemed more crisp than before, reminding Corazon of her father when he was angry. Too disciplined to lash out, he channeled his frustration into his posture and step.

The female agent stayed with Corazon while a uniformed officer received Corazon's personal items and placed them in envelopes. He spent a moment writing on a form and slid it across the counter.

The female agent stepped behind Corazon and removed a handcuff from one wrist, turned her and with her wrists in front, re-cuffed.

"Sign it," the man said.

One more man telling her what to do.

"You speak English?"

Corazon stared through the plexiglass to the wire mesh cages.

"She speak English?" the officer said.

"She did earlier," the female said.

"Did anything happen that would affect her language skills?"

"Bump on the head?"

The cop in the cage looked at Corazon's brow and said, "Wait a minute." He stepped away.

Corazon tensed as the female agent came close to her ear and whispered.

"The only word you say is *lawyer*, got it?"

The evidence-room officer returned with a Kleenex and passed it through the slot. Corazon looked at it. The female agent blotted blood from her face.

"You need to sign the form, miss," the officer said.

Corazon heard the whisper of rubber soles on linoleum. The giant agent stood beside her.

"Mark it as refused to sign," he said.

The female agent stepped away and the power hierarchy became more apparent. The white man was in charge, then the giant man, last the woman.

The giant agent took Corazon's arm and steered her to another hallway where he pushed open a door. Inside the room he moved behind the table and pushed back the chair. He removed Corazon's right handcuff and snapped it to a metal loop on the table. He left her hunched and standing, but with the chair behind her legs.

Stooped, Corazon noticed pain from her backward fall from the car. She hurt everywhere: elbow, hip, side of her knee and her brow. She sat.

In all the movies she had ever seen the questioning room was larger than hers. There was no two-way mirror, just a video camera on the wall with a red dot illuminated.

The giant agent closed the door. The female sat on the short edge of the table and the giant stood opposite Corazon. He pulled a chair from under the table, looked around the room, and stepped back out.

The camera's red light turned off.

Corazon glanced at the woman.

"Protocol," she whispered. "Nothing to worry about."

The giant returned and as he threw a leg over the back of the chair began speaking.

"We have you for murder one," he said. "The switchblade we took off you... Pretty high tech for a kid. Where'd you get it?"

Corazon sat.

"Keeping it a secret. Okay. We're testing it for DNA and unless you're the smartest person we've met in a long time, we're going to find human blood that matches one or more of five murder victims."

He watched her.

"We've been following you," he said.

Corazon made a game of breathing so smoothly her chest neither swelled nor collapsed with each breath.

"You might wonder how we found you," he said.

Corazon's mouth was dry, but she reminded herself that even if they offered water or soda she must ignore them.

"Okay, that's fine. You're going to prison whether you talk or not. Even without the DNA that knife shows intent. So worst case for Uncle Sam is — "

"Uncle Sam is the US Government," the female agent said.

The giant smiled too broad and taut. "Yes, thank you. But we both know you speak English like a native." He waited. "Are you sure you don't want to know what we have on you, so you can make an informed decision about talking to us? Help us out, things go better for you."

Corazon swallowed. She looked at the female agent who was again stone faced and her countenance confirmed that in giving advice she went against her superiors. The stony look calmed Corazon.

"Lawyer."

The giant agent locked eyes with Corazon, broke away and slightly dipped his head.

"You sure you don't want to hear what we know?"

The female agent turned her head toward him.

"Let me rephrase that, since I can't question you. We lifted your fingerprint from a gas station in Moab. Video too. The video shows you walking quickly with blood on your clothing. The gas station is located less than a mile from a murder scene and you already know this, but the time of death was fifteen minutes before you appear bloody on the video. Does that interest you?"

Corazon looked at the camera.

"I'm sorry. I withdraw the question. I was making conversation. The other thing is your fingerprints. We found a match. Your prints place you at a crime scene in Salt Lake City last fall. Maybe you remember? What, nineteen dead?"

Corazon's voice started in her throat, but she froze.

"What were you going to say?"

"Lawyer."

"I thought so. You see, we know you were one of the girls that guy — who was it?"

"Wayman Graves," the female said.

"We know you were one of his girls. We know you have all the motive in the world to hunt down men who look like the ones who attacked you. You might get a lot of sympathy for that in the courtroom."

He stared at her and clamped his jaw.

"I have sympathy." The giant tilted his head and looked away. "I know girls who experienced something like you experienced. It's the only reason we're talking like this, after you asked for counsel. But laws are for everyone. Add in your escape attempt, solicitation, and maybe jaywalking when you rolled out of the car... That's a lot of prison. I'm just letting you know, this won't go well unless you cooperate."

Corazon ran her tongue over her molars.

"Solicitation means prostitution," he said. "We have you on that, too."

He leaned back in his seat. Corazon fought her desire to glance toward the female agent.

"Lawyer it is," he said.

CHAPTER FIVE

Corazon lay in a holding cell. After the giant agent and the female departed the questioning room, Corazon was left hand cuffed to the table for what felt like hours. She dozed with her forehead on the table, woke to reposition her arm which had also fallen asleep and shortly after, an officer marched her to the tiny cement room where she now stretched on a bench.

One wall was bars, which was nice because she felt connected to the rest of the building. She'd be able to hear them coming. But otherwise the silence left her feeling as if she'd been abandoned in the basement of a large building.

At least she was alone. How much time had passed? The sun could be shining on a new morning for all she knew. Six months in a cave and she still had no innate sense of time.

She closed her eyes but sleep would not come.

They would torture her in the morning. The female agent was a trickster who had been turned by the government against her kind. And the giant agent with his fake concern… She would give them nothing.

The most likely scenario she foresaw was they would leave her to worry in the cell for either a very long time or short time. They would wake her when she slept and drag her to whatever place they used for torment. They would reduce her autonomy any way they could, even refusing to allow her the dignity of walking or toileting.

She would soon meet the man with the needles and pliers.

The outcome would be the same regardless of their tactics. Remove hope and other nonsense from her mind and only the truth about her fate remained. If she didn't escape, she would suffer whatever pain the government cared to serve. She would eventually confess everything they told her to confess, and then she would die.

Tat's fate was tied to hers, and only two outcomes would spare Tat's arrest as well. Corazon must escape — or die trying — before the torture man began his work.

Seen so clearly, even the rashest attempt made sense. And because the very next time the police opened her cell they might lead her to doom, the best opportunity to attack would be the next she saw, possibly in the holding cell. The police and FBI would have procedures put in place to eliminate her odds of success, but rules had a funny effect on the people who followed them. They ceased to think critically. They were blind to the walls that contained their views and somewhere outside of their boxes Corazon would find an angle to exploit or a weapon to wield.

Corazon waited for sounds outside her cell.

She'd learned more from *YouTube* than just slicing people with knives.

Corazon positioned herself with her head pointed toward the wall made of bars. Just a regular teen uncomfortable on a concrete bench. Its width allowed her to fold her knees close to her chest, and that meant she'd be able to kick against the wall and launch herself horizontally at anyone within a few feet. A thigh-level attack would be difficult to defend, and all Corazon needed to accomplish was to get one hand on the grip of a police officer's pistol. The power dynamic would tilt. There were guards and checkpoints along the way but with a pistol in her hand she would prevail.

They chose this when they interfered with an act of justice.

She tensed as voices arrived from far down the hall. The eerie feeling of being in a basement returned. The air was cool and dank. Quiet sounds echoed and though they were quieter still, the echoes remained audible. Keys jiggled and two female voices volleyed back and forth as the voices drew closer.

Corazon placed her hands against the cement wall and tilted back her head as far as possible while remaining on the bench, seeking both to look asleep and learn which of the approaching women might most easily yield a firearm.

"Time to get up," one said.

It wasn't the female FBI agent. This woman's voice had a southern pace, as if she dragged each syllable through molasses before winging it toward an ear.

Keys jiggled and the lock mechanism clicked. Corazon tensed.

In Mexico or in almost any other place in the world they would have made her put her arms between the bars to be handcuffed before unlocking the door. Maybe her luck was changing.

"I said you need to get up," the woman said.

There was no sound for a moment, then Corazon noticed a moving shadow as the door slid open. Feet sounds. Thighs rubbing cloth. The women were in her cell.

Still lying on her side on the concrete bench, Corazon rolled her eyes until she saw four legs: two in blue trousers and two in pantyhose. The woman in panty hose carried a briefcase.

Corazon trembled. With both hands and feet on the wall, she would launch backward, stretch straight as a missile and swipe a pistol from a holster in midair.

The moment was now! Corazon exhaled. She swallowed. Every sense tingled.

Who carried a briefcase?

Corazon twisted her neck and lifted from the concrete slab. The woman wore a blue blazer and skirt. Her hair was long but piled on the top of her head. It looked hideous. She had leathery skin about the neck and wore reading glasses like from the five dollar bin at Wal-Mart.

Her necklace was pearls.

Pearls?

"You wanted a lawyer," the female cop said.

They wouldn't let a lawyer observe torture, would they? But why should Corazon assume the first person to show up with a briefcase was an attorney? It could be yet another ruse.

"Hi, I'm Margaret Duke but you can call me Daisy like everybody else. I'm your public defender. Sit up, we need to talk."

The woman police officer said, "How'd you get nicknamed that? You're... blonde."

"Oh you're bright spot aren't you? Been a long time since this ass fit a pair of Daisy Dukes, that's for sure. But I'm not a Daisy because I married a Duke and I'm damn sure not a Daisy because I know how to stop a car when I want to hitch a ride."

"Oh?" the woman cop said.

"I'm a Daisy because my real name is Marguerite, which is also the French name of the oxeye daisy."

"I did not know that."

"I get that a lot."

Corazon sat up on the concrete bench. Daisy Duke would not be her problem.

They sat in the same questioning room as the night before. No handcuffs on Corazon. The giant agent and the woman agent were not there, nor was the white man who seemed their senior.

Instead, Corazon and Daisy Duke sat opposite an unhappy man in a charcoal suit and red tie. His briefcase stood on the floor at his side and his hands were crossed on the table. He stared a lot.

Daisy and Corazon had spent time alone in her cell before being led to the questioning room. Daisy asked Corazon's name, why she thought she was being held, her age and where she came from. Daisy placed her hand on Corazon's shoulder briefly, with a firm and friendly clasp, and described reading Corazon's file and learning about her experience in Salt Lake City.

Daisy spoke about being abused by her cousin on the farm growing up, in the milking house and again in the orchard, right out in the bright sunshine. It was strange, she said, because she'd never thought it could happen in the daylight. She hadn't understood. She described her warpath through college and then law school. She recounted her history as a prosecuting attorney for the US Justice Department for fifteen years, her last assignment in New York City. She mentioned, but provided no details, about her years of internal struggle culminating in forgiveness toward her cousin, who died in a bar fight while they were both still young and long before she'd ever processed anything. That led to her examining her role as a prosecutor and wondering if she'd run up her flag up the wrong flagpole.

"When you're in a hole the first rule of escape is to stop digging. So, I quit the Justice Department and moved to the mountains and hung up a shingle, as the saying goes. So? What do you think of all that, Sugarplum? Do you trust me enough to shake hands and tell me your story?"

Corazon said nothing.

"That's okay. I got enough to tear these guys a new asshole if they're dumb enough to charge you with what they have. You watch."

Now they sat in the questioning room. The prosecutor had thin lips and a sickly complexion. His suit color brought out the blueness of the veins on the backs of his hands.

The silence between Mr. Charcoal and Daisy Duke seemed a sort of war, with body posture changing on opposite sides of the table like soldiers moving in formations on a soon-to-be-bloodied battlefield. He tilted his head. She crossed her legs. He exhaled long. She smirked. He cleared his throat. She crossed her arms at her chest. He looked at the table and then the wall and as if addressing the concrete said:

"We aren't prosecuting."

"You're damn right, Mitch. Juries don't like folks being arrested for crimes that wouldn't exist without the police setting people up to begin with. And did you read her file? What the hell, Mitch?"

"Please don't call me that. Not here."

"Mr. Ford? Really? You can still call me Daisy. Are we done?"

"We're done."

"Okay, what happened?"

"We're done."

"What brought you to your senses?"

"No DNA means no murder charges for the bodies in Utah and Colorado. And the arrest was so screwed up.... Prostitution? Really? Fleeing arrest? Not this time. Not without an actual crime to flee."

"So why'd you keep her overnight? And bring me into it? You just wanted to see me again?"

"We were waiting on the DNA. I see you enough as it is."

"Thank you, Mister Ford."

"Ms. Duke."

CHAPTER SIX

Corazon stepped out of the front door of the police complex with Daisy Duke's card in her hand. She hadn't seen the building earlier because the FBI had escorted her inside at night from the western entrance which was off to the back near the parking area. The Glenwood Springs Police Department occupied the building to her front right. The building she departed held both the county sheriff and the county jail.

Her skin tingled with the crisp late morning air; the sun had only been above the mountains an hour or two. Her stomach tightened as she stood looking but she barely noticed. Since fleeing the cartel with Tat, she'd several times gone many days without eating. The tightness in her belly was no more uncomfortable than a fuel light going yellow on a car's dash. It was information.

Corazon's only experience in Glenwood Springs had been in the motel resort and at Chester DeChurch's house, neither located in the original town that lay south of Interstate 70 with Main Street almost perpendicular to the freeway. The motel where Baer had paid for a few days for Tat and Corazon was on the access road that paralleled north of the highway, which along with the Colorado River and the railroad tracks split the valley. Without the FBI having chauffeured Corazon across the interstate last night she never would have known that Glenwood Springs was anything more than a few gas stations and motels along the freeway.

But what a town! The grass seemed more vibrant than grass had a right to be. She looked up and the colors everywhere were delicious. The sky was so blue it threatened to haunt her if she dared close her eyes. The buildings looked clean and happy with the mountains behind them.

She walked almost dreamily and recalled her memorization of the FBI car's turns and the second-counts between them, but reconstructing her path from memory in reverse, and orienting from her present, unknown position… as Baer would say, was fuckin' stupid.

Plus, Tat at some point would reveal herself.

Corazon walked from the Sheriff's department and in the middle of the courtyard stopped and turned a circle.

She was free — but she didn't rotate slowly with her palms out and her lungs full to express her overwhelming gratitude to the heavens. As she rotated she searched buildings, cars, pedestrians. Maybe the overcome-with-joy look would make it less obvious she was on to them.

Her release had to be a trick.

Seeing nothing but modern buildings and trees, she crossed the remainder of the courtyard and turned left onto the sidewalk. Ahead were the main drag and all the businesses.

Corazon stopped. A car she hadn't been aware of rumbled past sounding as if the muffler had fallen off. A memory flashed — she and Tat and their mother had been on a Mexican dirt road when the muffler dropped off their Nissan Tsuru and her mother stomped the gas and cried out in glee.

A year before the cartel killed her.

Corazon blinked herself to the present.

Ahead was town. She turned around and walked the other direction, continuing straight where 7th grafted onto 8th and a hundred feet later read the sign: Roaring Fork River. She stopped in the middle of the bridge and looked over the edge at the roiled runoff from the storm that forced her to stay in Jubal White's garage.

Through the corner of her eye Corazon searched behind her from the direction she had come. The road was empty all the way back to the law enforcement campus.

Beyond, up in the town area she'd seen from the police campus, Corazon noticed a figure walking across the street toward the Colorado River and Interstate 70. The person wore tan clothing and appeared average in size.

Girl?

The figure stopped and turned square toward Corazon.

Tat owned tan clothes, but she was not blonde.

Had Corazon just spotted an FBI agent who didn't expect her to look back?

After a moment the figure walked behind a building on the corner of 8th and whatever.

The FBI letting her go didn't make sense. They'd taken her Scarab. She was there to kill DeChurch — they knew that. They'd seen a pattern in the bodies she'd left behind and used that pattern to predict he'd be her next target. They returned her knife before releasing her. Even without the needed DNA evidence to arrest her, why return the blade if they knew how she intended to use it?

Only one conclusion made sense: They didn't get her this time but were sure they would the next. That could only happen if they followed her.

She needed to find Tat.

Eighth Avenue departed Glenwood Springs roughly parallel to Interstate 70. Every time Corazon turned, she spotted her tan follower, as if the person hoped a mere zig-zag path might disguise her gradually nearing proximity.

Passing around a bend, Corazon spotted a wildlife trail through the dense grass and brush. She shot behind a creosote bush and hid on her knees, Scarab in hand. With the grip reversed so the blade pointed down with the sharp edge forward, she was ready for slash work.

The figure approached so quickly around the bend Corazon considered allowing her to pass and then following at a distance. The efficiency of the woman's stride was a signature, however, and though her follower was blonde Corazon recognized her and leaped from behind the bush.

The woman squawked, leaped aside and instantly manifested a Sig Sauer five inches from Corazon's face.

Corazon smiled. "Miss me?"

Tat lowered her weapon arm and stooped with heaving lungs. "Didn't you recognize me?"

"I wasn't sure." Corazon tugged a lock of blonde wig. "This from a dumpster?"

"I took it right off the rack." Tat stood erect and shook her head. "You shouldn't have made us meet like this. Now if they're watching they know we're together."

"Unless we fight and run away from each other."

"You should have gone back to the motel."

"No. They're watching. They have to be. But going to the motel would have only shown them where we are staying."

Tat stepped away and her face changed. "Why did they let you go?"

"What, you think I'm wearing a wire or something?"

"Why did they release you? It doesn't make sense unless it's a trap."

"I know."

"A trap for me."

"And me," Corazon said. "They didn't find DNA on my knife and I didn't do anything with DeChurch. One of them sneezed and I knew it was a trap. I tried to get away."

Tat nodded but her eyes seemed unconvinced.

"I can't believe you would think I would try to trap you for the police," Corazon said.

"I don't."

"You do."

"They're probably watching us right now," Tat said.

"You want to search me while they watch? Then everyone can be satisfied."

"I just don't understand. This isn't what police do." Tat looked ahead down the road and let out her breath. She glanced at Corazon's chest.

"I hate the law," Corazon said.

"They pit us against each other."

Tat stepped to Corazon and hugged her but brought her right hand between them and patted down her chest and sides.

"Satisfied?"

"Yes. You should check me."

"I trust my sister." Corazon yanked Tat's wig off her head and tossed it.

"You should trust the fact that you don't trust, instead."

They walked arm in arm.

"I was afraid I would never see you again." Tat nestled next to Corazon's ear and whispered, "We need a Jeep and we need to leave."

"Okay," Corazon said.

The sun radiated warmth on her face and her lower back was damp with sweat. Her bones felt like steel and her muscles like giant rubber bands. Corazon closed her eyes while they walked and felt a drifting stupor from the night's lack of sleep combined with giddiness at her unexpected freedom. She giggled and pressed her forehead to her sister's temple.

"But I still want to kill Chester DeChurch," Corazon said.

"We need to get away from here. We need to lose whoever is following us."

"Have you seen anyone yet?"

"No."

"Maybe there isn't — "

"There is. There's no other way it makes sense. We need to find a car."

"How much gold did Baer leave with you?"

"A few coins."

"Pfff."

"He said each is worth eight hundred dollars, if you don't let the dealer cheat you on the price. So, we are going to find a car and get away from here?" Tat said.

"That's not enough money for a car. But I'll get one."

"How?"

"YouTube. I learned in the cave," Corazon said. "Pretty sure I can hotwire one if we find an old car."

"Like how old?"

"From the sixties?"

"Do cars that old still run?"

"Probably like people that old," Corazon said.

"We need another Jeep."

"No, we need a Mustang. Cherry red, so we can go fast."

"We don't want to get pulled over."

"They won't catch us and by the time you get the Jeep two miles into the woods you could be two states away in the Mustang. Then dump it and get your Jeep."

Tat walked.

Corazon matched her stride. Looked at her and smiled.

"Okay. That's a good idea."

"We should split up in case anyone is following us," Corazon said, "then meet up and find a car tonight."

"I don't want to split up."

"Me either."

"We should wait until dark."

"What do we do until then?"

"Look." Tat pointed to parking lot.

Corazon stood on her tippy toes and looked at the sloped parking lot of a health food grocery store.

"Is that one?"

"One what? It's a salon. We should get our hair colored. You didn't recognize me as a blonde."

"I knew it was you." Corazon pointed at a Mustang. "And I thought you were pointing at that."

"The car?"

"Uh? The cherry red Mustang?" Corazon said.

"It's old, right?"

"Let's steal it now! Get on the road and find someplace to — "

"Hide."

"Hunt pedos."

"You just got out of jail and listen to you. We'll take the car tonight."

"It won't be there. The owner's buying soy milk."

"There's a sun deflector in the windshield. And look at all the dirt and garbage around the wheels. That means the car was sitting there through the last snow when they plowed. And we can't leave without Baer."

Corazon stopped and turned. "You dumped him."

"We have his dog. And he said he's coming back."

"So you can say goodbye again. We should just go. He'll understand. He's Baer."

CHAPTER SEVEN

Move the Jeep to the back of the lot, aim at the yard 'tween this parking area and the next. Someone come with flashing lights, I got a shot at freedom. Though I don't mostly care.

Ain't slept but a few hours in two day. Pull the seat lever and ease back. Let the brain settle in the head and the neck go long on the cushion. Close my eyes and wonder how I done it agin. How I let Stinky Joe get lost or stole.

Eyes shut, sun come through the window and I got to shift this way and that, get some shade. At last the bright's off my lids. Thought I'd mope later but I guess I'll get on with it.

Ain't fit to keep a dog.

Ain't fit to have a woman.

Hell, ain't fit to father a child neither.

But I can live in the woods and make shine. Go back to what I'm good at.

Time works like waves in the head. Come and go, dreamy, hear myself snore and don't care nor rouse. After long bit the back hurt and the neck's jammed and I twist in the seat sideways. Don't muster 'til water drip on my hand and after checking the ceiling I see it's drool. Was dreaming on them cheeseburgers. Keep sleeping… wipe the hand on my leg and twist the other way. Sun's behind the mountain so I maybe got seven hours under my belt. Feet's cold.

Think on days long gone. How I come to the path I'm on.

Sit with eyes closed and see those days working on Brown's farm, fixing lessons in my mind about men and women. About giving hurt and learning to fight so others can't give it back.

Other days in the cave with Günter Stroh, hiding from the world. Drink myself stone drunk 'cause hiding from the world don't cut it.

Time works like waves in the head.

Come and go.

Dreamy.

Screeching tires!

Look out the glass — cherry red Mustang convertible slide sideways, ass wheels churning.

They got the top down. Smokin' gorgeous blonde and a red with her. Cram fists in the eyes. Jam the bleary out and look agin.

Tat dye her hair blonde. Corazon red — it suits.

Stinky Joe in the back seat, looking to maybe jump out.

Save me from these crazyass women!

Tat waves behind the wheel. Corazon got her arm out, beating the door. They lips is moving but the Jeep glass turn the sound to noise.

Tat look back the way they came — like jackboot thugs is around the bend. She search the dash and press a button. Look back. Look front, up top the windshield. Mash another.

Convertible top start coming up.

I got the gold in back. What the skippy fuck? I dunno.

By shit I don't know.

Unlock the door. Stumble out the Jeep and rub the eyes. The girls is still there.

"Get in!" Corazon say. "We must go now!"

"Hurry!" Tat say.

Look at Stinky Joe.

He look back, drop the tongue out the side. Grin.

Well?

"I got a bucket in back the Jeep. Pop the trunk!"

Race around, unlock, shit this bucket heavy. Lift it by the edges and heave. Waddle like I swapped nuts with a woolly mammoth. Spring a back muscle throwing gold in the trunk.

"Hurry! They're coming!"

Fetch my pack out the Jeep. Feel for Glock. Good to go. Dump the pack in the trunk and slam the lid.

Mustang's a two-door. Corazon pop out and fold the seat forward…

I stop.

"What you doing? Get in!" Corazon say. "We must hurry!"

"Baer, come on!" Tat say.

Stinky Joe cock his head.

Man, don't leave me alone again. Not with these two…

Deep breath and dive to the back seat. Throw an arm over Stinky Joe.

Corazon jump in the car and Tat's already spinning wheels.

"I won't, Stinky Joe. No I won't."

CHAPTER EIGHT

Since we left the motel I spot the black sedans and suits everywhere. Helicopters next, jackboot thugs. Got this claustrophobe pressin' in and Stinky Joe sit up in the back seat with eyes peeled like mine. Tat can't drive for shit. They jacked a '68 Mustang with four hundred and twenty-seven cubed inches and all Tat's ever drove was a Jeep with the four-banger lawnmower engine. Slammin' this side to that. How the fuck she manage to stall a V8 Mustang with an automatic?

"Who we runnin' from?"

"Don't know, we haven't seen them yet."

"What? All this skullduggery's prophylactic?"

"What, like a rubber?" Corazon say.

"Yeah, like a fuckin' rubber. Does that sound like me, what I'd say?"

"Sorta."

"What the hell's goin' on?"

"Corazon was arrested."

"For what?"

"Murder."

Fuckey fuckey. "What?"

"Attempted murder."

"Who she try to kill?"

"Nobody. That's why they let her go."

"They up and let her go? Who?"

"FBI. And police."

"Nah." Sink in the seat. "It was a good run, Stinky Joe. We's fucked."

Why are we fucked?

"They don't let nobody go."

I scrunch down in the seat and look up and out the rear window for shock troops rappelling four-inch ropes. Like Chicago Mags said, just 'cause you can't see em don't mean they ain't there.

"Get off the town roads and out in the country. Too much shit around us here. Can't see if we got a tail."

"Yes. I think there might be two. A blue minivan and a tiny pickup truck."

"Those is just people driving behind us."

"They are following us."

My head needs a good scratch so I give it one. Maybe a good beatin' agin the glass…

"They follow every turn," Tat say.

"Sound like a tail. Turn left up here."

Tat turn left. Minivan go straight, tiny truck turn left.

"Take that next right."

Tat turn right.

Tiny truck go straight.

"See? If they was a tail that minivan'd be back on us. Didn't you watch TV six months in a cave?"

Houses thin out and the mountains bunch up tight around us. Road squiggles left and right and Tat brakes when the wheels squeal. Look down and it's hundred-foot cliff to boulders below.

"See! Look!"

Tat jabs her finger to the front left. Adjust the rearview mirror. They's nothin' but a mile of air where she point so I look behind.

Minivan.

"Yeah, see. That's just what I meant. That minivan's a tail. Next place you see a mountain or crick, pull over like a tourist, nice and slow. And put your signal on. We'll let 'em go by."

I keep an eye out the window so I can see death comin', summoned by Tat's drivin' or the government's lack of humor. I'm 'bout to throw up yesterday's cheeseburger and Tat hit the turn signal and pull over on a thirty-foot patch of dirt on the right. I twist. Minivan come 'round the bend and the nose dip.

Corazon hold up her cell phone.

"Wait here. Maybe get out and stretch the legs."

"Got them," Corazon say.

"Got what?"

Corazon pass a cell phone to me. Got a picture on the screen, man and a tig bitty bleach blonde inside a blue minivan.

"Good thinkin'," says I.

Give her back the phone.

"If that truck is following us, the minivan probably told them to pull over," Tat say.

"Yep. Let's go back the way we come and soon's we get off this cliff I want you to haul ass. See how hard this Mustang'll kick."

Tat's eyes grin in the rearview.

"Try and don't kill us."

Got this empty I'm-gonna-die feeling in my balls. Woman, Speed and Cliff might be too much temptation for ole Fate to cope with, all at the once. Stinky Joe give me a look… but he don't know the plan and I can't tell him.

Need some separation…

Tat cut the wheel and stomp the gas. We jump. She hit the brake and I bang my noggin on Corazon's seatback. Gas again.

"One or the other."

She choose the gas pedal and keep the wheels churnin' dirt. Ass end swing around 'til it burps on macadam road. Gas, brake into the turn and raise hell comin' out. A couple mile and Tat got the feel for it.

Corazon squeals.

"Shut up!" Tat say.

"Give 'r hell!" says I. "What's death anyway?"

Engine roar out the bend and we zip by a skinny pickup tucked in a tiny turn.

"Okay, up here take the next right, left, whatever."

"Shit," says Corazon, lowering her phone. "I missed them."

"It don't matter if we never see 'em again."

She look over her shoulder, struck dumb with the wisdom.

"You should have your seatbelt on," says Tat.

"Don't wear 'em."

"Not you," Tat says. "Her."

"I don't either," says Corazon.

Brace myself on the door. Stinky Joe tumble into me and I hold him close. He press his head agin my shoulder and let his eyeballs roll up. Terrifyin' times for sure.

Tat stomp the brake and cut the wheel hard. Slide 'round and we got us a new road headed into the mountain pass. Boulder's right there blockin' the view. Engine blast wide open, throw us back in the seat.

"Yes!" Tat say.

"Doom," says I. "Repent."

We rocket up the road. I watch out the back window and after the bend the road we come from disappear. Now it's luck alone if they nab us.

"You know," Corazon says, "With two tails and two turns for choices, all they have to do is — "

"Tat! Need you to scare up another couple turns. Go straight on the next and take the one after."

"Where?" Tat say. "You see any turns? It's just mountains."
"That's what I said. Scare 'em up."
"What's that mean?"
Turn appear.
"Good job. Take the next. Hit it hard on this straightaway."
"This?"
"Yep."
"It's ten feet."
"You missed it."

She swerve into the next curve and stomp the brake. Head smushed into the seat I see it. She conjured a new road and cut the wheel. Bounce through a ditch, hit the rear quarter on a rock.

"Okay, slow down just enough we don't die."

Stinky Joe say, *Maybe pad it a little.*

Mush his head back into my shoulder.

We're through the tightest of the mountain and the terrain unfolds, got some grass wishes it was green and a house way the hell up the side hill.

Tat's got the Mustang wide open, faster and faster 'til I doubt she got the skills to keep it in low orbit. We go a mile then ten and I don't see the vehicles after us. "You know where you are?" says I.

"Colorado," Tat say.

"Uh-huh. I meant which road. Where's the highway from here and all that. You know. It's called knowin' where you are."

"Glad to see you too."

"Ahh, shit."

CHAPTER NINE

Dust float from the Mustang roof. We bounce and wiggle and I got a seat spring wants to get fresh with the stink chute. Trees and rocks flash by so fast the belly's sick. Things is outta hand.

"Hey, lookit that! Slow down! Lookit that up ahead!"

"What?" Tat screams.

I lean up close and cup the hands. "SLOW DOWN."

Roarin' engine go soft. We start a hundred mile an hour coast. Corazon let out a long breath like she been holdin' it two mile.

"What are we doing?" Tat say. "Why'd you tell me to stop?"

"See that comin' up?"

It's a gold Cadillac Eldorado. Maybe '78. Sign say:

4 SAIL

"Tat, pull over. Law people know this Mustang. Time to make the switch. Pull over right here."

"You don't want me to drive to the car?"

"Stop here so these people can't get a look at the Mustang. All you know they own it."

She swerve to the dirt like to win an Oscar.

"Corazon, lemme out. And next time maybe steal a four-door with less engine."

She look at Tat like to get permission from the warden. Tat nods. Corazon busts out the door. I wrestle the seatback and gravity. Spring gets one more poke at my ass.

"Stinky Joe, you come with me and mind your manners. Tat, pop the trunk."

Latch clicks and I find the gold bucket never toppled. Must be the trunk lid held it in place. Fill my pockets with coin. Look at all my worldly wealth, product of a life of stillin' shine and livin' simple. If Tat takes off with the gold, I'll survive one way or the other.

Nah, fuck that.

"Tat, gimme them keys."

"What?"

"What I said. Hand me the keys."

"No."

Reach in, elbow past the titties and they's no key.

"I hotwired it," Corazon says.

"We came back for you," says Tat. Under her breath, "Such a dick."

"And I come back for you. But just tellin' the truth, I ain't exactly sure why and I bet you ain't neither. Right?"

"I don't know."

"Yes you do."

"I don't know what we are doing," says Tat.

"I ain't set on one way or the other. I figger'd you'd holler if anything change and you ain't hollered yet."

She folds her arm out the window like to sun her elbow. I touch her arm and she let me work it into a stroke then a caress afore she put her arm inside.

"I got to see 'bout this car up here."

Got the old FBI Glock tucked in my ass crack. Give it a feel. Pull down the shirt, cinch the belt and reseat the Glock as I walk.

Gold in my pocket I stop at the El Dorado. Kick the right rear tire — sure as shit it's a tire. All good there.

Gander along the trunk edges and the bottom quarter panel, then feel up in under like Jubal White taught me on his Pasadena car. Zip on rust. Paint got a polish shows off the trees 'n clouds.

What do you want with a new car?

"Tween me and you, Odiferous Joseph, this little travel party's 'bout to bust and we need some wheels. Maybe head somewhere else."

Chicago, you mean?

"Dunno. You thinkin' we ougghta go see Mags up there?"

Mags who?

"Just a woman. She's a genius."

That doesn't sound very promising for you.

"Help you?"

Screen door slams and I look up. Granny from *Any Which Way but Loose* tromps across the porch. Got a yippy dog in the house gone berserk.

"You stay here, Joe. Let me do the dealin' with this woman."

Step to the front right, closest part of the car to the house and Granny. Wave. Dip the head.

"That's a pretty set of wheels."

"Ten thousand."

"Sheeeeit."

"Eleven. And the bigger dislike' I take, the higher it goes."

Most these old girls like a toothy smile so I crack my best.

"How much for a feller pays in cash?"

"Now we're back to ten."

"And a fella pays in gold specie?"

"You one of them kooks?"

"Nah, I ain't with 'em."

More toothy smile. Hope it works 'cause I used all the teeth I got.

"Real gold?"

"Most is Canadian Maple Leafs. Last spot price I saw was $800. Like to be more, with the Treasury printin' paper all these months. I shoulda checked afore I called but I just saw the Eldorado and thought — "

"Who are you? Jimmy's boy?"

"Uh, well, not I know. 'Less he spread the seed wide."

"You sure as shit look like him."

"Where he from?"

"Where you from?"

"Gleason, way. East a here."

"Gleason. Where the hell's Gleason?"

"Right agin Swannanoa."

"Ah, piss," says she.

Woman after my heart. I pull out a Maple Leaf and offer.

"Put it in your hand. Get a feel of real gold and think on what it'll mean to have money that go up in price, 'steada down."

"Don't hardly sound American."

She take the piece. Bite it. She wince. Me too when I spot the tooth mark at four feet.

"Now, you said the price for fiat money was ten grand and what I got to know is the price for real money. Gold. Given all the satisfaction and peace of mind you'll have knowin' your wealth ain't a piece of government paper."

"Now look here, Gleason. The price is ten grand. In dollars."

Smile winsome. Wink. "Maybe if we drink a jug of sweet tea it'll brighten your mood a little."

"My mood's none of your concern."

"All right. We best find the spot price on gold, you want things accurate."

She nods. "That's the way we deal in Colorado, Gleason."

"Be right back."

Tramp to the Mustang. Make the rolly motion and head for Corazon's side. Approach the window and say, "You want to grab that cell phone for me."

She already got in her hand.

"I appreciate you, Corazon. How about lookin' up spot gold on that gizmo."

"What?"

"Price of gold."

"How?"

"I dunno. Turn it on."

Tat punch her leg.

Corazon smirk. Thumbs press the phone. "Here." She hand me the cell.

I carry it back to Granny and show her.

"Shit."

"That's right. Nine twenty-five. You'd a done better to dicker at eight hundred. But Southern men respect old folk so I'll give you eleven coin and you'll come out a little ahead."

"What's the math on that?"

"Nine times eleven? That's ninety-nine. Eleven times the twenty-five is two fifty plus twenty-five more. Two seventy-five plus nine hundred-ninety is one thousand two hundred and sixty-five."

"Pretty quick with the numbers. You want to give me twelve of those gold pieces, the car's yours."

"Shit. I might could give you six, or seven if you threw in one hellacious bushel a cabbage, but I don't know the car even runs."

"Seven! What kinda horseshit *lies* — !"

"Whoa now, that's a mean accusation. Don't tie your titties in a knot, Granny; tie 'em in a bow. Eleven coin is top dollar and we don't know which dollar this old Cadillac is. Might be bottom dollar. Might be no dollar."

"I'd appreciate if you leave my tits out of the negotiation."

"By all means you can keep 'em. You say the vehicle runs?"

"What? Look mister... you're a vexin' somebody. Accourse it runs. Look at it."

"I seen rocks that shiny but couldn't drive 'em. You got the — "

She toss the keys.

I glance up and down the road. They got the one house per two mile rule in effect. She was quick out the front door with me only walkin' and no sound to cue her... means she's watchin' close. Shingles on the house got a bit of rot. Weeds up the side. Dealin' high on the price right out the gate, this woman needs every dollar but wants the quick sale.

Open the driver side door and Stinky Joe trot 'round the side. "Don't get in just yet."

I scoot onto the seat, slippy like snot on glass. Twist the key and the Eldorado roars.

Granny's at the driver window.

"What year is she?" says I.

"'79."

"Ah, see, that'll shave some digits off the top. '79's got that sissy little three-fifty and not the four twenty-five."

"That sound like a three-fifty to you?"

"Why no, it don't at that."

I pull the hood release, slip out the car and take a gander. "This ain't a '79."

"Ervin bought it in '79."

"All kindness, Granny, but that don't mean shit. This is a '78."

"So, it got the engine you want?"

"Indeed."

"That puts us back at eleven gold coins."

She beams.

I could go another three rounds but I'll give it to her here. "You win. You got the title?"

She whip a piece of folded green and black paper with the government zigzags on it.

"Let's see them coins."

I fetch 'em out the pocket and drop 'em one by one in her hand. Eleven.

"What's your name, Gleason?"

"Uh, Günter Stroh. But you don't need that for the title."

She pull a pen from behind her back and rest the title on the car hood.

"I'll press light so I don't mar the paint."

She writes.

Car door slams. Another. Granny look at the Mustang.

"Who's them girls up there?"

"Ah, see, them girls and me, we uh…"

"Yeah. Günter Stroh. That's German?"

"Uh-huh."

"Whereabouts in Germany?"

"Gleason is all."

"Uh huh. Them Mexican girls find you in Germany?"

"How you know they Mexican? Blonde and red?"

She study me like I'm daft. Fold the title. Hand it to me.

I shake her hand. She pulls a little. Squint and grin.

"Pleasure doing business," Granny says.

"All mine. Git up in there, Stinky Joe."

He spring to the seat and I shut the door. Step 'round back. Notice the plate got the sticker says EXP 09 DEC. Good to go.

I hop in the seat and wave Tat and Corazon to stay put while I show off for Granny.

Brake, cut left, reverse cut right, forward cut left and stomp the gas. Stinky Joe slides this way and that. Me too. That monster V-8 sprays rocks out the ass like the front's fixed to a stripper pole.

Damn if it don't feel good to have nuts 'tween my legs agin. We roar past the girls and this time, no three point. Just brake, cut the wheel all the way and stomp the gas. Line up behind the Mustang and while the dust floats and Stinky Joe sneezes I look about for the trunk button.

Old Granny still in the yard, hands balled on hips.

I pop the latch.

Step to Tat's door and she release the Mustang trunk. I lift out my gold and back pack and set 'em on the ground.

"Great," says Tat.

No woman wants a man to feel free. Ain't in her makeup.

"I'll follow you 'til we figure out what's next," says I. "Maybe ditch the Mustang where you stole it? Or keep it if you want, I guess."

Corazon sicks her black eyes on me. "My phone?"

I pull it out the pocket and toss.

Back at the rear I heft the gold to the Eldorado trunk and it's so big and deep, even with the back-pack jammed agin the gold they's no way to be sure the bucket don't spill — less I put one the girls in there with it. Reckon the fun's over for now. Slam the lid, slip behind the wheel and flash the headlights. Let's get on, Tat.

Let's get on.

CHAPTER TEN

Tat drive on the straightaway like she got the pedal stuck and slides through the first curve, right wheels in the dirt. I had better eyes I might could make out which finger she's wavin' out the window.

I float along behind in the Eldorado. On a dirt road the car drive like some boats swim. Stomp the gas and the rotor spins, and after a good churn the nose lift and alla sudden they's a breeze.

If Tat drive so fast I lose track, I'll understand it's the Almighty set me free.

Granny coat the seat in Armor All and Stinky Joe slide to me on the first turn. Slide away on the next. I drop his window and he get back to his feet and fill his mouth with air. He look so happy I drop my window too, stick the head out and gulp wind. Tongue wag in the air and I'm grateful the bugs ain't so thick in Coloradee as North Cackalackee.

"We got a good thing, Joe. Any time you got good times, just remember they's a shitstorm 'round the bend. So don't enjoy 'em too much."

He pull his head back inside the window. Give me a sober look.

Always keep the disappointment handy.

"I know I bitch and moan one minute and — "

Bitch and moan the next.

"It's on account the women. Always and evermore. Women is doom."

So let's go visit that one you call Chicago Mags.

"That's exactly what I was thinkin'."

Sun's deep in the mountain and I can't get the feel for twilight, these parts. Seem like a good three hour. Funny Joe mention Chicago Mags. Don't recall I said her name.

So how you gonna do it?

"Do what?"

Leave Tat and Corazon.

"That ain't a done deal. But things turn out that way I reckon we'll drive."

I mean how will you end relationship?

"Relationship? I don't know it was all that. We poke on and off, but all kinda critters poke on and off and don't got a special word for it."

Maybe give it a full think.

Stew a minute. Try and recollect. I ain't been with but three women and two was Ruth. I didn't leave her 'til she left me twice — accourse, thirty year back — but partin' ways with Ruth in Flagstaff didn't feel like leavin' a woman so much as sayin' goodbye after a holiday supper turn sour. I bounce into her so many times, deep down I expect it'll happen again. So why make a fuss? Just drive. But I see what Stinky Joe is sayin'. Tat like to feel she got a claim on me, since I poke her and pay her way. Ladies understand the economics. Man like to believe he don't pay a woman for love but they's always economics to the obligation and no escape. My gold's in the trunk and Tat's is 'tween her legs. We trade pieces — and after so long doin' good business, folk get stuck in the expectation. I end the here and now, I also end the future... and that's where the expectation waits.

"Guess I'll hafta say goodbye. Somethin'."

Yeah. Keep thinking.

"What? You wanna stay with the girls?"

Stinky Joe look away.

"Hey. What?"

Got his head back out the window, low, like he's sortin' through six kind of disgust.

"Come on Stinky Joe, shit. I don't know your mind."

He look at me.

You got your flaws but I've been loyal. You left me to winter in Flagstaff snow, but I was loyal. You left me with the girls for your little road trip, but I was loyal. You drank that poison so much you didn't know your name or mine... but I was loyal.

"Shit, Joe. I know it. I ain't been precisely wonderful."

So no, I don't want to stay with the girls. Or I didn't until you asked.

Scruff his neck. Joe sinks into the seat and drops his head to paws. Just two minute ago he was happy as a lark and now on account my nonsense his ill humor's won the match.

"I'm a far sight from perfect and you're what the yuppies call a self-actualized dog. Just want to respect your volition, is all."

I'll stay with the one that saved me. But I'm still waiting on you to stop calling me Stinky.

"If I called you Loyal Joe?"

Then I would call you Patronizing Baer. You know, calling out the fact that you're trying to placate me at little personal cost.

"Yeah. Now you say it."

Rub his shoulder, along his back. Feel the old bullet wound from that kid pimp in Williams, Arizona.

"Sometimes I think you don't say a word. It's just me out here alone, got a dog and a brain fulla guilt."

Can't be. I know more words than you.

While me and Joe been talkin', Tat pull outta sight but I come 'round the bend and see she's holdin' back like she don't want to lose me. Longer I drive with the wind clearin' cobwebs from the cranium I get to thinkin' maybe Joe's right, and I owe Tat more'n a smack on the ass goodbye. Like we oughta have a sitdown and a couple solemn notes afore we call it quits. We had some good times. Some nice words don't cost nothin'. Maybe I oughta end things right, if I can puzzle what's right. Maybe we get Corazon to take a walk and give us fifteen minute for a partin' poke. So while Tat's in sight I press the gas and keep the Caddy inside the rails. Mustang disappear at the next mountain bend and shit if I ain't worried she'll disappear afore I get to call quits the right way. Then I'd got one more regret loose in the head, rest of my days.

More gas to the V8.

Joe sit up in the seat.

Easy, Alden Boone. I got a feeling.

"What?"

Slow down. Something ain't —

"Joe, it's like you said. I gotta do this right."

Go easy...

Brake a little and follow the turn. Red and blues — shit — everywhere — like they was already there. One, two, three, another on the side road, what's that sound? Head out the window — a helicopter?

Ohhhhhh... shit...

Take the foot off the pedal and drift while chaos storm the brain.

Mustang's mostly off the road, rear wheels spinnin' loose in the air and nose over a gulch. If the girls had any speed...

And Corazon never wears a seat belt.

I ain't felt this sick in the belly in a long damn time.

Think. What to do?

Up ahead is every lawman or woman in Colorado and no way I'm like to bust out the girls without a shootout, and nah-- This ain't the time. I won't go in guns blazin' 'til I want to be dead. Got to preserve the self... so how exactly I preserve the self? Already see a couple coppers lookin' this way. If I three-point on the road and haul ass, they wonder who's that in the gnarly Eldorado, and why he want outta Dodge City so quick?

But what's the odds I make it through?

Shit.

Shit.

Damn.

Try the glove box.

I bend 'cross the seat and drop the box. Pull out a bright orange ball cap says Denver Broncos. Slap it on the head. Twist and pull and get it half situated. Need a lid with a bigger brainpan. This one's made for NFL fans.

"You think that'll throw em, Loyal Joe?"

No. And don't be a dick.

I take off the hat.

But the hat is better than turning around. That would draw attention. Normal folks would rubberneck, you know?

"I hear you."

Slap on the cap and stick my head out the window. Creep the Eldorado close and put the transmission in park with the engine runnin'. I get out and lean on the door with my elbows crossed, takin' in the sights. Meanwhile thinkin' on Tat or Corazon tangled up with busted limbs and blood, and who know what other damage... And I can't do shit to help on account the law. Once a fella's in the book no moment's too low but they'll grab his ass anyway.

I scout the terrain, lest I gotta hop back inside the vehicle and cut a hard uey. Feel the Glock in my back — very same one I liberated from an agent in Flagstaff who want to place me under arrest while I crap in a knocked-down tree. It's a warm and fuzzy feelin' knowin' I can shoot bullets, but it'd be a blessin' if I never had to agin. In particular not with six divisions of police close enough I could chuck a dead frog and hit one.

Wait.

Long enough.

Turn and look back the way I come thinkin' I'll seek an alternate route but a Silverado pull behind me and the muffler rattles to silent. Rifle in the window. Fella in a cowboy hat gets out. Got a shooter on his hip and wear a flannel shirt. Big man. Clean cut. Now he's out the vehicle I spot the special white stitchin' high on his leather seat, maybe got a heartbeat or some other Chevy nonsense. He pull up his britches and wiggle his seat and once he got his mess situated, eyeballs the gold Eldorado.

"You bought that off Myrtle?"

"I dug the shit out her in that Eastwood flick. Hard as nails."

He sniffs like to arrest a runny nose and fishes a tin of Copenhagen from his front pocket and thwack it with his thumb. Offers me a dip.

"Nah. That shit'll rot your teeth."

"Good thing I quit," says he, as he fill his bottom lip.

I lean on the Eldorado and he look like a feller likes to lean too and if they was a tree nearby he'd prop it up. Car's here but some folk don't get close to another man's property 'cause they understand property's the foundation of civilization. A man's body, his land, his vehicle. His animals. And most of all his labor. All property. A man with no rights on property's got no rights on himself. And if he don't claim his property and defend it they wasn't no right anyway, 'cause that's all a right is. When you say I'll fuckin' die for it, it's a right. And if you got nothin' you'll die for you got nothin' anyway. A man like Copenhagen here is just the sorta feller what knows all this without another man needin' to say it. He's a kindred spirit and I like this son of a bitch right now, just on account he won't lean on my Cadillac. He won't mess with nobody else's nothin', and that's the highest respect he can pay.

Copenhagen cross his arms and lean back 'til he find a spot in the air that's comfortable.

Says I, "Looks like a red Mustang over the ditch there, maybe hit it hard. Ain't happen but five minute ago."

"Did you see it?"

"Nah, I was 'round the bend."

"What was it? A roadblock? And they got a chopper here inside five minutes?"

"Nah, they's no roadblock. Just a car in the gulch. That bird just come up. Or maybe was followin'. I dunno."

"Crazy things going on," Copenhagen say.

"How so?"

"You didn't hear about the hubbub in Glenwood Springs?"

"How the hell'd I miss a hubbub?"

"Hell yeah, cop died in shootout with some pothead hippies this morning. Got our own Waco situation. 'Cept it was over 'fore anyone heard about it."

"Waco? Like Janet Reno brung in the Abrams tanks? Flame throwers on the babies?" says I.

"Nah, not like Waco. Maybe like the Ruby Ridge."

"FBI snipers shootin' pregnant wimmin on the doorstep?"

"Nah, hell. Just big government shit is all."

"The Feds?"

"No, the local."

"That ain't big government."

"Well you know. The dirty sons a bitches — "

"Mmmm. Way I see it we need more government. That'd solve everything."

His mouth puckers like it want to take a shit. We ain't friends no more.

I grin.

He tilt his head.

I grin hard.

"You fuckin' with me?"

Hardest grin I got. "Accourse."

"Whoee. Damn. You look scrappy but I thought I might hafta kick your ass from here to the next right turn."

"Well I'da shot your dumb hillbilly self, so it's a good thing you held back."

More grin.

He offer his hand. "Abraham Church."

"Günter Stroh."

Shake.

"You from around here, Günter?"

"Passin' through."

He tap my shoulder and point. "Look."

Ambulance come from the other way, no lights or siren.

"That don't look good," I say. Got the ache in the chest like I run a mountain. "Shit, Tat. Hang in there."

"What's that?"

"What's up ahead? Where that ambulance come from?"

"Glenwood Springs."

"Wait. Behind us?"

"Uh-huh."

"What's ahead?"

"Carbondale."

"They got a motel? Someplace a stranger could hole up?"

"Well, sure. We're coming in on a back road but you work in a general northward direction, you'll find the 133. Take that north to 82 and you'll find all the motel-ery you'd ever want."

"You're one them fellas knows every road and number."

He smile.

"And it's a point of pride."

He smile more.

Men in uniforms open the back of the ambulance and I see right in. Get the stretchers out and I spot Tat's blonde hair as they hustle her inside. Another two minute they carry Corazon on a board — no wheels — and slide her on the inside right. Outta space so they use the seat. Two fellas in FBI jackets stand stiff backed and firm and talk at the paramedics. One paramed wave his arm and the FBI boys climb in the back.

Ambulance turn on the lights and blast off.

Holy shit. Are they dead?

"I dunno, Joe, I dunno. If they was dead I wouldn't expect the ambulance would turn on the lights and burn so much gas."

"What?"

Abraham Church study me.

"Dog ask a question," says I.

"Oh."

Another two vehicles behind the Silverado. Both trucks. One got a horse trailer and the next is filled with dirt bikes. Alla sudden I understand somethin' big and true and not much use knowin': Men like to ride things. That fella in the truck with the motorcycles got the wife inside too, and looks like another woman in the king cab. If he'd a brung the sheep, they'd all been there handy.

Up ahead the law enforcement boys and girls all get in they cars and zip after the ambulance, save one. He pop the Mustang trunk and empty out the backpacks. See him come back after stowin' 'em in his trunk and he look to half dive in the trunk, got his legs in the air and wigglin' 'til he right himself and study somethin' shiny in his hand.

Wonder if that's a gold piece stamped with a maple leaf.

Wonder if it got Baer Creighton's fingerprints… like maybe a hundred other places on that car.

Or Mrs. Jubal White's, since she handled so many gold pieces.

If that cop leaves, I got to wipe down the Mustang.

But he drop the coin in his pocket and face the string of waitin' vehicles and motion us through. So now I got to either get placed in that Mustang with them girls and all they done, or I got to circle back and handle that copper so I can wipe the vehicle.

"Looks like time to go," Abraham says. "Holler at you later."

"Was good sayin' hello."

Get in the Eldorado and think quick.

You better get going if you want to know where that ambulance is going.

"They can't be more'n a hospital or two in town. I got bigger fish."

What fish?

"Fingerprints all over that vehicle."

So what?

"I leave em, they know I was there."

You won't be here when they figure it out.

"Stop talkin'. Last thing I need is a cop wants to see the miracle pit bull."

Put the Caddy in gear and creep respectful slow. Wave. Stop.

"Howdy, officer. Them people in the accident. They live?"

"They're alive. One's not so good."

"'Preciate you."

His eyeballs say he can size a man to the nearest sixty-fourth.

"I was thinking I'd buy that, if no one else did."

"Come agin?"

"The Caddy. You bought Myrtle's Eldorado."

"It was that or marry her, so I ponied up the cash."

He smile.

I smile.

"Be safe, sir."

"Indeed, officer. You too. We need you on the line."

I drive.

When he said the one girl was alive and the other not so good, they wasn't no red nor juice.

Ride easy in town and work north as Abraham Church say. Find a mess of motels and stop in a parkin' lot with the engine off and wonder how I'll live if Tat and Corazon's in jail the rest they lives and I squeak away 'cause I spot a chance to buy a Caddy and ditch 'em high and dry.

Wonder what kinda asshole let his companions go down like that.

These girls go to prison the rest they lives, and all I do is run and hide… I don't want to carry that.

I guess morals and decency is worth the trouble.

"Joe, you got any thoughts on the subject?"

I appreciate you calling me a miracle.

CHAPTER ELEVEN

Tat and Corazon stay in the hot tub resort. I imagine they made use of the water them days I was on the road to North Carolina after the gold to try and buy Jubal off from goin' to war on the organic dope family.

Other hand, I ain't soak my ass in a tub or crick since I left the mountain lair what? Three week ago? Now I wash, accourse, but sometimes a fella want to settle and soak the dingleberries 'stead a rippin' 'em off with a soapy sock.

Plus, motels got televisions and televisions got news. I want to know what happen to Tat and Corazon. Maybe find a morning paper.

So, I stay at a motel last night.

I watch the news and the pretty girl talk on the accident and the hospital, but says the girls is unknown.

First order of business is check out the motel.

Since I didn't kill Jubal White nor anyone else I remember the last two week, I got a vision of me as a new man — but just a vision. Like maybe with the Eldorado and a skippy set of duds, one them bolo ties from Flagstaff and some genuine snakeskin shitkickers, maybe I'd be that somebody I saw myself as, if ever I was West.

Sometimes back in Gleason when the hand was cramped from five letters and the fire was oak embers with wispy flat paper blankets — and ink glowed darker even with the paper turned to ash — sometimes I'd ponder on the big skies I saw on the TV Westerns as a boy. *Shotgun Slade, Rawhide* and *Gunsmoke*. Even watched the *Little House* and crushed on Mary — the skies was nothin' to the size of her smile. But watchin' the embers glow I'd think on what it'd be like to be a new man with no curse and no history, just a regular fool with a shit ton of gold and no shortage of amusement. See the Canyon and the Rockies. Maybe shoot stick every day for six seven week in some dusky bar 'til I get the skills back, then go take mac and cheese money from the college boys. And some them college people'd talk worldly things they got from books and I'd soak it all in, not so gullible as they, but thirsty for some of the experience I'd never had, some of the innocence.

I got the vision of all that bein' possible if only I had the balls to turn ninety degree and put one foot in front the other.

But same time I got the certainty that without the ninety-degree turn, my path was set. All them men I sent forward is out there wantin' a pound of flesh from my soul, and not just them but the ten hundred men I'm bound to send after 'em afore I go myself. So much, when I get there, they won't be nothin' left of my soul for the eternity. Make no sense, but them men is there 'cause I put 'em there. One man harm another, the harm don't disappear when he die.

His bones carry the debt.

And since I got so much can't be repaid in gold specie, but only in the next life, I don't want no more, and I want to maybe grab some enjoyment outta whatever days I got left. After that it'll be the damnation I got due.

Muse on all that after the news woman say Tat and Corazon was in the hospital near dead and surrounded by law folk want 'em the rest of the way dead.

Part of me want to find the local DMV and see 'bout makin' this Eldorado legit with the plates, insurance, all that. Back of my mind I wonder if it's 'cause I want to put some space 'tween me and Baer Creighton's murderous past and all-but-set future. And the rest of me says I got no choice but stay and bust them girls out and set 'em free afore I get on about my solitary business.

Take Joe outside to do his business and the sun's happy and the air's cool. Make a man forget himself. Bust into song:

Does yer tits hang low
    Do they jiggle to and fro
    Can ya tie em in a knot
    Can ya tie em in a bow?

While Joe wanders to the back lawn for a squat I open the Cadillac and get into the glove box. Pull the title and see if they's instructions.

Joe havin' trouble with last night's Taco Bell.

Sam Hell?

Granny wrote Günter Stroh on the title as the buyer!

Joe look up like to pinch if I say so.

"No, handle your business."

This is hind tit but maybe not the emergency it first seem. I close the eyes and look straight ahead. Think. Günter Stroh on the title. No way I'm gettin' plates and registration without me bein' Günter Stroh. Need all new documents. The birth certificate. The driver license. Social Security card.

But…

Just sayin' I did come up with the way to be Günter, I wouldn't be Alden Boone. I'd be twice removed from Baer Creighton.

Fact is, I don't know what documents I need for a good registration. Maybe I can do this. Turn ninety degrees and put one foot in front the next.

"Pinch it, Puppydog. Lessgo."

I glance up from one more look at the title and Stinky Joe's already here.

Bag packed, I drop off the card for the door lock and consult the paper map in the Eldorado. Backroads took us from Glenwood but the 82's a better return shot as it's paved the whole way.

Navigate this turn and that. Find the 82 and juice the rear wheels 'cause the growl sound pretty. I recall just a little time back thinkin' on that 90-degree turn. Just made one, but somehow right back where I come from. I'm lookin' to find the girls and when I do it'll be back to the moral considerations. Exactly how much killin' can a good man do?

Zero?

All?

It ain't about whether killin' an evil man's good. That ain't the predicament.

Presidents, police, judges and soldiers kill people on government authority, and if the citizen let the government do it, he share the benefit and the guilt. They put down the murderer, the raper and I don't know who all gets the death penalty, but they remove them folk from society and every man woman child reap the reward. Less crime. Folks got manners. Troubles is met and friends abound. Each them people got a part, see? Each said, go on government, whack them people. Get 'em the fuck outta here. They ain't no good and we don't want 'em. They did it with they votes and they got the blood stain on the soul, same's the hangman.

I was a murderer long afore Larry stole Fred. Every citizen's a murderer. Consent of the governed.

I don't give a rat fuck shit about that. Them people need to die.

But they's a difference...

When my brother Larry stole Fred and Stipe and his boys put him in the ring, I didn't want the killin'. But the evil was in the law and it was me or nobody. To hell with sharin' the blame, I'll take it on myself as justice is more dear. I got little qualm with killin' dog fighters. But the lawmen after… to tell it straight that FBI feller in the woods. If I had to do it agin….

If I had to kill him agin I would, but it's a damn shame he'd make me do it twice.

Now I'm out on the limb. These men didn't kill Fred, but they want to jail me and maybe kill me on account I did the job they didn't. Police is a cartel. They want the exclusive on upholdin' the decent relations in society, just same as the doctors want to be the only folks with a drug and the plumbers the only people can swap a pipe. Cartels. Guilds. All good so far, 'cept the doctor got to fix people and the plumber got to fix pipes.

This whole clusterfuck the last six months is on account the lawman sometimes don't hold up the law. They want the exclusive on justice. We give it to 'em. Stand the fuck up, or men like me got to instead.

Glad I don't pay taxes.

But what'll the Almighty say?

Can't wrestle these thoughts out my head.

"Good Lord Almighty, it's Baer. I don't care which way You settle it, but I'm lookin' some resolution here."

You think that'll do the trick?

"Doubtful. But a fella want to try."

I don't get it. They wanted to kill you. Tried to kill you. You killed them. Is there a rule or something that says you can't defend yourself? Who came up with that?

"Well, see here, Magnanimous Joe. The Almighty ain't charged you with bein' a moral creature, strictly speakin', and that's why you can't cognitate the higher matters."

Fart along the speed limit. By and by the mountains and dirt and trees give way to business and other assorted human artifacts. Cars like to get up on me. Drive close. Got the big city feel and make a fella want to loose a couple nine millimeter bullets in the air. Ask for some room.

But they'd say I was wrong.

Keep the eyes peeled and soon as I think I missed it, they's a blue H sign pointin' right. Brake and cut the wheel.

Signal.

Think on the gold in the trunk, wonder if it'll spill. And what to do 'bout it? Problem with bank safe deposit boxes is they ain't mobile. Limits a man's options, he got to carry a hundred-pound bucket everywhere.

Tomorrow's problem. Meantime very few folk would imagine a 1978 Eldorado got a bucket a gold in the trunk. They more like to steal the tires.

Stop on the road and see the Cancer Center sign on the roof of a building dropped from the old country, somewhere. Rock walls and beige walls and dark trim. Look like high end apartments more'n a hospital, but I swing to the lot... and see it ain't so much a lot as maybe five six spaces. They must be parkin' elsewhere, but while I'm here and they's spaces... Back in with the windshield at the building. Give it an eyeball through the windshield. Don't like where I park. Move the car under some shade at the end. Let both windows down so Joe can jump out on grass if he want.

"You gotta whiz or number two?"

I'm good without, thanks.

"Magnificent. I be back when I learn something 'bout the girls."

Stinky Joe nod his head slow, recognize my virtue.

I step out the car and freeze. Didn't even check the roofs for rifles. TV news say they got police-guarded murderers in there. I scan the windows but they's no cops nor soldiers. No cop cruisers in the lot. Just Mercedes, Range Rover and one shiny gold Eldorado lookin' better'n all the rest.

I'm about as fool as fool can be. What with the highway cameras and all the rest, they maybe by now've deciphered my image and located the file. Summoned the resources to take me down.

Swing my ass back in the seat and turn the ignition.

"Got the shave last night. Need the haircut."

They won't let you in without a haircut?

"It'll soon come to that. For now I need the disguise."

Ah.

Back to the main drag. Spot a tourist-looking joint with clothes in the window. They'll overcharge by twice, but I got more gold 'n time so I'll avail myself of the goods and spare the clock.

"Be right back, Joesemite Jam."

Lock the doors with the windows down. Go inside. What fellas is shoppin' got the fluffy boy sweaters and canvas man purses. Swallow down a little burp o' bile. And I got the longish hair. Someone see me think I'm one these people. Shoulda got the haircut first. Full nazi on the sides.

"Can I help you find something?"

Her voice says pretty but I wince afore I turn. Shit. Pretty.

"Uhh, yeah. Need some trousers look like money, you know. Shirt. Maybe a suit coat goes with pants."

"You mean, like, a blazer?"

"I ain't a woman. I want a suit coat."

"A sport coat."

"That's the thing. But it got to look like money, you know? I'm headed for Aspen and I hear they arrest poor folk."

She wrinkle her face.

"Joshin', is all."

"Oh. Uh. Okay. Well umm. I have like, a boyfriend."

"Took a long time, did it?"

"What did you say to me?"

"With your personality..." Her face's so tight a rock band could drum it. "You strike me as the choosy sorta woman, I guess is the way to say it."

"Oh. I guess. The pants are on the racks behind you and some are on the wall. Shirts are just farther down and the umm, sport coats are over here."

She walk.

I follow to a rack.

"What sort of look do you want? I mean, other than money? What material?"

"Shit. You may's well ask me the girl's name that sewed it."

She blink. Again. Blink. Jaw down three-quarter inch.

"What I say wrong?"

"The *girl*?"

"That hit the nerve, did it?"

Most sewin' machines in the history of the universe been run by women, but sayin' it hit the nerve.

She glance at the wall, high close the ceiling. "Nevermind. It's nothing."

I look at the wall, high close the ceiling too. One them black oval globes with the camera.

"You might should open your own shop."

"Why?"

"No camera. You could take offense to anything you want."

"Yeah. Help yourself to the pants."

She walk away with the best fuck-you strut a woman ever strutted.

"But you'd need the startup capital, accourse. And maybe some customers offended by the same shit."

I spend better'n ten minute findin' trousers, shirt and coat. Maybe longer. She see me comin' and go in the employees-only room but a fella with a wart on his neck takes my money.

I step out the joint so spiffy people's like to think I own a strip mall. Drive the street and park at the first barber I see. Go inside and it's a wrinkled bald guy lookin' through coke bottles. He arm me to the seat. I drop my ass. Lean back. He install the apron and snap close the neck.

"Just a trim?" he say.

"Nah. I want the full high and tight."

"Joinin' the service?"

Man got humor.

"Summer 'round the corner, is all."

He buzz and zip and I think on Mae, since she's the last one that buzzed my head while we was on the run in Kentucky, was it? Recall the dirt lot. Wonder how she doin' with Nat Cinder. Can't recollect her assumed name. Wonder if she's the Mrs. Cinder now? I miss her whole life and now she tie the knot and I miss that too.

Barber hit a bump. Gouge the skin.

"You a bleeder?"

"Not usually at the barber."

He keep buzzin'.

Three minute, maybe five. Vacuum. Mirror. Shit I'm old 'n ugly. But I look like a regular asshole so even if I don't blend, least I won't be recognized.

I nod and the barber remove the hair gown. Pass him a twenty thinkin' I get ten back and he say, "Come again."

Guess I look the high roller.

Stinky Joe stand on the seat an study me up and down. Wag his tail. That's encouraging.

What you need is a cowboy hat.

"I was thinkin' that too. But not one of them tourist-to-cowboy conversion models. I need a lid with some miles on it."

Spotted sixteen thrift stores last mile. I pull out headed for the hospital trustin' one'll manifest on the way, and sure's shit they's three in a cluster. Two on the hospital side and another 'cross the road. Park. Windows down, lock Stinky Joe.

In back they's a wall with baseball caps and knit hats but nothin' cowboy. Turn around and spot a mannequin wearin' a hat look 'bout right. I swipe it off his head and the tag say ten dollar. Drop it on mine and if I hadn't cut off the hair it'd fit.

I buy the hat.

Outside the thrift they's a newspaper rack for the real estate flyers. Grab one.

Inside the Eldorado I tear and fold a strip of paper. Tuck it inside the headband and now my hat fit. And it'll adjust for when my hair grow back.

Sometimes a man can outsmart the little things and feel like he outsmart the big ones too.

Hospital.

Come in on a different street and see they got parkin' scattered here and there. Building that size must got more but I don't see it. Place feels closed in like the mountain didn't want to give up the territory. I grab a space and sit facin' the building. Watch. Lookabout.

See a man on a sidewalk got a brief case and the way his suit jacket lay, he's carryin'. Black shoes need a shine. He walk brisk but easy, maybe a little more strut 'n I want to see in a lawman.

He stops like to enter a vehicle I can't see and alla sudden a uniformed man's standin' next him. Musta got out a car already there.

They talk and the suit man step 'round to another vehicle and disappear. Now a dark green sedan back out.

I hunker.

Dumbass. I got the duds but act like a man with somethin' to hide. Scooched low and nothin' but the dash to see, I think on Chicago Mag's chicken legs in the yellow stockings and realize if not for the yellow, hell, she mighta had good legs. Might be the yellow put the chicken in mind. Maybe a good look at her ass and I'd a not even thought about her legs.

All kinda ways a fella could approach the subject.

Get to speculating and it don't take the mind's eye more'n three second to get her in the sack. But I slow things down, even just in the imagination, on account the woman's honor. I think up a good three-week courtship then scramblescrew her with my new boots on.

And here I am ready to risk my freedom on account these knuckleheaded girls don't know how to lay low for three days without huntin' down some pervert? I didn't sign up for it. I was headed away, to safety and quiet. Lookin' for the place to lay low and let things settle out. Searchin' a way to live a regular life, unknown and camouflaged out somewhere the people don't get up in each other's business. Thought the girls was on the same page…

Well that ain't the truth, I didn't neither. I saw Corazon goin' out clean and comin' back bloody. She wasn't volunteerin' at the meat store.

One side of my mind I got Chicago Mags appropriately courted and claimed, and other side I got two young girls been dealt a hand of shit, so they pull fury from the marrow to fight the war they never sought. And just as I hear Chicago Mags whisper *let me do something for you* and see her disappear under a pile of poofed up covers, I spot Corazon with her head bandaged and tubes in her arms and nose, but both wrists cuffed to a stainless steel bed.

Duellin' imaginations.

Mags, how 'bout you keep doin' what you're doin' while I noodle this.

"Magniferous Joseph, I be back when I know something 'bout the girls."

Get out the car and reseat the hat. Cinch the bolo. Now I'm standin' in the open I wonder if maybe a couple turquoise rings mighta been just the right touch. Without, I wonder if I still look too North Carolina for these parts. I don't got the walk yet. Still got the lope comes from twenty years steppin' five mile to town and back. Close the eyes and think a minute. Try agin. Short arm swing, stiff shoulders and head back.

All right. No sweat.

"Howdy."

Copper sit in the car with the window down. They's three more copper cars adjacent, none occupied.

"Morning," he say.

Don't give him more'n a nod. Folk who ain't wanted in fifty states don't look twice at coppers, so I won't neither.

CHAPTER TWELVE

Coppers all over the hospital grounds and I feel like a silver screen hero behint the enemy lines. Hold my jug a minute while I make this look easy.

Glass doors slide and they's a woman in scrubs breezin' left to right, walk with an arm trailin' like she left a conversation afore the words finished what they was sayin'. But they's no one there she was talkin' to. I knew a woman once, like to put her forearm to her forehead. In the wild, it's only the animals watched *Gone with the Wind* does it.

I can't recall the last time I was in a hospital. Feel the punji wound in my leg; empathy for all the sufferin' souls herein.

Poke about the lobby. Men, women, only one kid. They got a ruddy rainbow in skin; even the white folk is pretty well charred, like the sun and wind extract the hope and leave people lookin' tired at they fates.

Back when my days was spent gulpin' hooch an tendin' fire I don't recall bein' quite so ornery all the time. But I never passed a week stone cold sober in North Carolina. Alcohol go a long way toward tampin' things down. People like to say it's the booze makes men fight, and I say the booze makes twice as many say fuckit, let's sit here comfortable tellin' lies.

Closer I get to the elevators, someone use Clorox recent.

Blast over the loudspeaker, lady wants Doctor Frenshaw right now.

Next second the space is so quiet I hear the squiggle of a rubber wheel on linoleum. While I nose about and find the cameras a uniformed cop enters and I'm next the elevator. He hold the door. Look at me. Raise the brow.

Grin like I'm half nuts. My usual demeanor is sane and kind and humble and I want to throw him off.

"No thank you. I'm just looking for good coffee."

Two steps he's got his ass blockin' the elevator gate, arm out, pointer finger straight at the coffee vendor across the way.

He grin like he half nuts too, and I wonder.

"Thank you, officer. We appre — we uh. Shit. Obliged. Is all."

Just glad Stinky Joe ain't here to witness. Then think on it and I never once was so tongue tied when I derived most of my daily nutrition from a clear liquid.

Elevator door closes and I step back and watch the numbers. Stops at two, three and four.

I can't say for certain this copper's here for Tat or Corazon, but what I seen, Glenwood Springs ain't accustomed to the violence we brought it and I bet they ain't cops at the hospital every day.

So as not to be a liar I visit the coffee gal and buy a cup. Black with a pack of sugar though it ruin the taste. Them 16 calories'll be handy if I need to run.

Elevator opens and a nun walk out. I likely got a better grasp of the electric eel than a nun.

Drink coffee and watch the elevator lights. Four's lit.

Ding.

Door opens.

Another cop in uniform.

That puts the girls on four. Or one of 'em on four.

Wish I knew the regular goin's on at hospitals; I got no sense of how to not look like a hick. In the woods I walk easy, but get me in one of these four story skyscrapers where I got no exit and no ken of the ways, the scrotum's tight as a mushroom cappin' through the dirt.

I get into the elevator and the door closes. I wait. Nothin'.

Press the floor button.

Stinky Joe ain't even here and I hear him.

I press 4 and wait.

My weight change, the door opens and the space in front is empty. I step out and do a quick turn to get my bearings.

I'm lost.

To the left the hallway just goes. They's black squiggles on the linoleum. Seems dimmer that way, like a florescent or three is out or the bulbs is twenty years old. To the right the hall corners left, and I go that way 'cause it's brighter and people keep the bulbs fresh where they work.

Around the corner up ahead is a long desk station where nurses can sit and talk to people like me, 'cept they's no nurses. On the right is the doors to the hospital rooms, all open.

Anybody looks at me, all he'll see is a man who knows in one minute he'll be at the other end of the hallway, where he belong.

Hands in the pockets, I stroll. Ambient juice on the arms dissipate so I notice the lack.

Empty floor?

First three rooms on the right is unoccupied but a sound like a chair drug on the floor clue me to the next room. Slow the pace and half-turn the head. I pass and keep walkin', take a mental picture from half of one eye.

Tat's eyes is closed. She got tubes in her arms. Machines and monitors with lights. Cables and tubes make a mess of the wall behind her. Right wrist in a handcuff locked to the bed frame. Sides of the bed is like a crib so she don't roll out.

Next the door is a uniform cop. Two-days' hair since his head shave. Skin so pale the blue veins make him look smart and go with his uniform. If his eyes is blue they'll stick this starch-pressed rookie on the recruitment poster.

He don't have to look at me; His head's already swiveled with the right hand loiterin' next his hip. Saw all that just glidin' by.

Stop.

I step back to the room and stand in the entry. "That ain't my daughter."

Cop says, "No."

"How you know?"

"Pardon?"

His eyes stay narrow.

My first thought was they put the rookie on the job nobody want. Now I suspect they put a hotshot rookie on the job who won't fall asleep. He ain't the average donut eater.

"Nevermind, I was lost in thought. Say... This the girl from the accident on the news, other day?"

Tat rolls in her bed and the handcuff rattles on stainless steel crib. She opens her eyes.

I hold my breath. Hairs rise and tickle. The cage gets tight on the heart and I wait her out.

Tat's mouth is froze. She's just come out a good knockout — fear flash in her eyes — they flit to the handcuff and then the cop and I get a voltage on the arms like to fry a circuit and Tat's eyes shift red like to menace a demon. She see me and the eyes narrow and the red fades quick. I can almost feel her heartbeat settle as the glow dissipates and once her pupils is black the juice is gone and I take the conclusion she was set to panic but her soul settled on sight of me.

Don't even give her a wink. I just love her with all I got, like one time we was foolin' around and she said, "pretend you love me," and I let go all the shit what's usually in the head while I'm screwin' and pressed my forehead to hers and damn near cried I loved her so much.

Any more thinkin' like that I'll be hand cuffed too.

Cop never answer if she's the girl from the accident. He got me in the gaze and the man with the state-given authority to shoot people runs his next steps through the academy training he just got, while it's fresh in his noggin.

He lifts his look from my snappy snakeskin boots and holds my eye.

"Who is asking?"

"Me."

"I'll need to see some I.D."

"For saying hello? Make perfect sense. You want to get yours out too?"

Fetch my wallet and hope that skizzy Mrs. Jubal White ain't had occasion to utter Alden Boone to the law since I left her on the hill with her man dead on the driveway below. Give the officer the fake license Cinder acquired on my behalf. "Alden Boone."

Cop study the plastic. Looks at the fluorescent. "Got a glare."

"I'm like you," says I.

He looks. "Pardon?"

"I'll take an incandescent bulb any day of the week."

Youngblood Cop holds my driver license to the light. He study the picture then me. Turn the card edgewise and run his thumb over the trim. Study the back like it's penned in Morse and he forgot which letter the dot stand for.

He flips the license in his fingers so it lodges 'tween pointer and index and reaches it to me, but not all the way. This boy's bounced the local bar. I step closer and take the license easy like I don't give a shit. Slip it to the pocket without pullin' the money clip — though if he saw a bunch of green maybe he'd buy the duds and presentation.

Money clip got a bunch of hundreds. I tuck the license on top a grocery store card. Let him see the green a long second.

"Yes, sir," the young cop says. "That's the girl from the news. Are you family?"

Money made me a sir.

"I said she ain't my daughter. I'm lookin' my daughter."

He's silent.

Most men, you say some nonsense and let it hang, most men'll fill the silence after. Not youngblood. He watch 'til I wonder whether he's off a forty mils on everything or if I'm pickin' up the signals of a man can use his head.

"I saw a girl with a law officer on guard and thought she was the one from the Channel Five news last night, is all."

Youngblood don't change his look but give a slight nod.

"She's the one from the news. One of them."

"Don't look too bad. Why ain't she in jail?"

"Give it time."

"Wasn't — didn't the accident have two girls?"

"The other had significant injuries. I think she's coming out of surgery."

Tat's eyes flare.

He turn his head back to looking past Tat at the wall.

"You know officer, and all due respect, you understand? All that's due. If this was my daughter and she had a young man in the room. I dunno. It's just you got the athletic look and like I was saying'. If it was my daughter and she was alone and handcuffed to a bed. I dunno, is all. You know?"

"No, I don't."

"I'd worry you was pokin' my daughter. Not that you was, accourse. But the appearance of impropriety, and all… You got to mind the appearance. Now I said that with all the respect you got due. Full and total, you see? And I'm lookin' out for you as much as her."

"I would ask you to direct your concerns to the department's public relations officer."

I never seen such a cool kid cop.

"Ah, heck. It ain't no big deal. I was speakin' for your benefit not mine. Like I said, this girl ain't my daughter."

I give Tat another glance. Her look says if Baer Creighton can't calm her, she'll lead an assault soon as she can find a pair of hospital socks with the rubber treads ironed on.

"You can go to the desk right there, down the hall, and ask about your daughter. Is that good, Mister Boone?"

"Yessir. Sounds good."

Turn.

Stop.

Turn back to the cop. "It's the other one was messed up from the crash? You said surgery. How bad is she?"

"Is the other one your daughter?"

"No."

"I would direct you to the department's public relations officer."

"Thank you kindly. We appreciate the blue line, yessir."

He nods small like he don't want me to see it. Now I got to get a message to Tat.

"Sometimes officer, you know. I ain't talk to nobody in weeks it seem and you bein' a cop I guess I feel I can open up. Shit. I miss my girl and when I find her, she'll know I'm gonna take care of her. I'll get her home safe and healthy. She got to spread her wings like any young girl, but when times is dark, people that love one another as family does, why they pull together and fight together so they can keep what they got. In dark times, is all."

Officer nods, slow, real slow.

"Just miss my girl."

He frowns. "Good luck."

"Take care, y'hear?"

I stand at the desk with nobody 'til I spot a nurse's reflection on the corner mirror. Turn and get back to the elevator afore she get to the desk.

Door dings open like it was waitin' on me. I step inside and wonder at my heart. Tat looks to be in good shape. Ten seconds with a bobby pin on those handcuffs and I could walk her out the front door.

I was a kid in school I didn't have a dad around and one day I heard some of the girls talkin'. One said if you had to choose 'tween your ma and father, like one had to get sick and die, which would it be? I remember thinkin' that's easy.

With me and Tat together then apart, and me not knowin' which girl had the worse injuries, I confess I thought maybe things'd be really bad, such as to deal a true blow to my heart. I would've expected Tat be the one in critical care 'cause all the evil I done, I deserve it. But seein' her all in one piece, that means little Corazon's the one.

I wouldn't a seen it comin' in a thousand years.

Leave the main lobby and shit if they ain't more cops headin' in from the parkin' area.

I head back to the Carbondale motel but in the parkin' lot I realized I don't stink at all, the El Dorado's got a back seat better'n some folks got beds and I say fuck Carbondale and Glenwood Springs too.

I drive south toward this snowcapped peak sittin' out by itself. They's so many places with beautiful views the road keeps goin' wide so folks that pull over don't interfere with the locals. I park and kill the engine.

Stinky Joe ain't said a word.

Get out the car and open his door. He sniffs a trail to the river and I smell up the cool wind, some far off rain in the air, some dirt and exhaust.

We never writ words together but me and Tat got a contract, of sorts.

A man don't sign with his name. He does it with his character and he don't know how big he commits 'til later.

But he signs.

CHAPTER THIRTEEN

They's a old timey restaurant I saw back in town and I wake with a hole in my stomach wants flapjacks, butter and maple syrup.

Stinky Joe spend the night on the front seat and after I let him search a swath of grass to do his business, I return him to sleepin' and depart feeling better after a night under the stars breathin' cool air. Got the blood pumpin' and what pains I got I'm used to.

Time to find some breakfast.

Accourse they's problems to solve. Gotta get the girls and I'm thinkin' maybe a midnight run to Chicago to get my coffee back from Mags. It's hard bein' a killer without a philosophy of killin' and since I give Mags a lift a few days back I spent equal time marvelin' her mind as ponderin' her other assets. Some of her thinkin' in the Jeep that early mornin' was unlike any I heard afore; ideas sit so square and flat and perfect, such as to stack one on the next, I can't help but think she'll make sense of the world or me, one.

And the one other problem ain't so big but it aggravates heavier'n its weight.

Alden Boone.

I ain't Alden, is all.

Boone's all right.

I can't get a title for the Eldorado 'til I ain't Alden Boone.

And with Mrs. Jubal White still out there knowin' the name and able to tie it to Baer Creighton from North Carolina, who killed upwards of ten thousand men with the jaw bone of a pit bull and called down the bears on teenage ruffians and last, spent all the time in the cave half mad jawin' at the Almighty — maybe it'd be wise to get some room 'tween the sinew and gristle of the mortal man and the lie they got projected all around him.

Got to drop Alden Boone and pick up Günter Stroh, with papers.

Waitress bring the hotcakes and syrup in one to-go box and a second got the eggs, hash browns, sausage, bacon and ham. Next got the biscuits and gravy. Last box is filled with taters and toast. She put the grape jelly packs in the bag, and I ask for the strawberry.

"We're out of strawberry. We have peach, how would that be?"

"Peach is fine as water."

Back at the car we sit in the shade by the trunk and I split the grub with Joe, give him a fair portion given his size and overall duties in the operation. He finish while I butter my toast and spread jam from the plastic square.

Look at me. Over here. Still hungry. Hey! Look at me!

He nudge my leg with his nose and I'm a softie so I trade bites with him 'til the fast is broke and it's time for step one in the big plan.

I got to get me a new name, and the only way to do that is with someone knows fake papers, and not knowin' the guy in town that does the fake papers I figger to find him at the bar.

Bar ain't like to be open at 9am but the good news is after three pound of cakes and syrup I need a nap.

Splash water on my face in the restaurant restroom and find breakfast already's built up the back pressure.

Which I mitigate.

I saw a bar while cruisin' Glenwood Springs yesterday. Park on the gravel lot and leave Joe in the Eldorado with the windows down.

Go inside in my skippy duds and these boys is workin' class, not a high falutin' desperado like me. Eyeballs turn. Couple heads dip howdy. I dip howdy back. Feller give a half wink and half nod the same time. Don't know the code on that so I say, "Yep. Morning."

"Afternoon. What'll you have?"

"Seven Up."

"Sprite. What you want mixed with it?"

"My dog made me give up the likker."

He stuff his tongue in front his upper teeth and think on it.

"All right, Sprite. You ain't from here."

"Nope."

I find a place at the bar on the right so I can look left easy and see the entrance, and they's no doors nor windows behind. No one gets behind without I see him — standard precaution.

That Sprite taste sweet after the syrup and jam this morning. I sip slow and listen to the words floatin' all 'round, thinkin' one these boys'll say somethin'll let me know he's the feller or knows the feller that gets shit done. Surprised we got seven men plus the barkeep, but none look up to date on printin' technology past Gutenberg's day.

Fella next to me says, "So my brother in law said my sister won't — "

"I don't care," says I.

"Let him tell the story," says the man on the other side.

"Didn't know it was a story."

"Yeah, so he said he found the new thing. You know."

"The best way to get a blow job if you can't get a lady," says the man on the other side him.

"Gentlemen," says I, "Y'all talk too much."

"Dick fishin'," says the storyteller.

"Listen," says a man on his other side.

"Yeah it's like this. My brother in law says you put the lawn chair in the river where it's slow, right?"

Says I, "Have a pleasant afternoon. Is all."

I grab a table solo.

Two minutes. I'll drink the Sprite as I paid for it and be gone.

Main door opens and John Wayne stands in the sunshine so bright I can't see nothin' but his outline.

He step inside and close the door.

"Abe," the barkeep says.

Light's brighter at the bar and Abe grabs a stool. He nods at the other fellers and swings his ten-gallon noggin my way. Lowers his head and stares for a better see.

"Yep," I say.

"Hey!" Abraham Church says. "Looks like you found a watering hole."

"A Sprite hole."

"Each his own. You ever hear anything about those girls in the car accident?"

Nod. Sip Sprite.

"What did you hear?" he say.

"It ain't good for the one."

"That's just too damn bad, isn't it?"

"What, you know her, something?"

"Not me," says Church.

"Hey, shit."

"What?"

"I got a question."

"Uh-huh."

"You seem the kinda feller… You won't know the answer, but you'll know the fella who does. Follow me?"

"I know people, yeah."

"Good. You know how some folk'll say, I'm asking for a friend, but you know it's bullshit?"

"I'm with you."

"Good — we ain't gone far. Well, I ain't askin' for a friend. I want to know myself, meanin' you got to keep it close."

"I'm not a talker."

"Good." No sparks nor juice. Here goes. "I want a new name and papers. Legit."

"You can't."

"What?"

"Not legitimately. There's only one of you and you already have a legitimate identity."

Man's a stickler for the truth and the knowledge of it is like a cool pine breeze on a sticky afternoon. Fella can breathe easy and enjoy the shade.

"Well not legit, but looks damn near."

"Understood."

"What's it take? Someone knows how to print a document."

"You know, I'll bet twenty or thirty years ago a college kid could've set up a basic print shop in his dorm room and made bank selling fake driver licenses. If he had a business sense, he could have charged a couple hundred each. And he could have nailed some of the girls for a twenty-dollar discount."

"You did that in college."

Grin.

"You still got the print press?"

Head shake. "No, that became the property of the State of Colorado. What you're talking about isn't possible without some high-tech equipment and I don't know what else. If you think about it, there's a lot of documents involved. Driver's license, but to get that you need a birth certificate. To do anything official you need a Social Security card. To drive somewhere, insurance cards. To pay for anything, bank cards."

"Or gold specie."

"Yeah. More and more. I don't know what to tell you, partner. I don't know anybody who does what you're talking about. I mean, you don't want a fake license. A cop'll stick the number in his computer and find out you're supposed to be an eighty-six-year-old woman. That means the number has to be legitimate, so you'd need a person who can put your picture on someone else's card."

"Or get a birth certificate, and use that to get a real driver license."

"And a real Social Security card."

"Yep."

"But I don't know anyone who can fake a birth certificate. It'd have to be an old one."

"Well it was good jawin' on it. I just figger it'd be pretty slick, use the regular driver license for the insurance, and give the new name to the cops every time I get a ticket."

He look at me like he got a bullshit sensor goin' off. I still ain't worth a shit at tellin' lies — and that's a virtue.

"Everyone has a secret," he say.

I guess it's gonna be Nat Cinder have to save the day after all. But that means me drivin' from Colorado back to Flag, in the thick of things... or callin' Mae on the phone and sayin' what I need and where to mail it while I lay low.

Noise.

Light cut in from the main door and afore I look, the curviest shadow I ever see jiggle up the wall. Like we boys said in school, I scrotate on the bar stool. Check her out.

Framed in the doorway there with the bar mostly dark and the sun a spotlight, it's so Hollywood the eye don't grab an image. They's motion behind and after a second or two, shit if this gal ain't got a compadre.

Pickin' up the Spanish lingo....

Second gal got a light gauge rack and seem tighter at the hips. Tough call. Six months back I didn't see a woman but once a month and that most often Mae. Or Kitty from the grocery — and from the top of Kitty's jugs I wouldn't want to see the bottoms.

But Skinny Tatas here... Fertile ground for a mammary connoisseur.

The ladies draw near and I shift my lean on the bar to accommodate them lookin' me as much as me lookin' them. They give the whole joint a scan and I suppose it's the fancy duds but when a woman flat out point at a man's heart and smile so her cheeks ball up, safe to say her mind's made and it's good to know what you know, else she'll have you knowin' somethin' else.

I don't poke the bar women, but if I did.

Damn.

Skinny Tatas shifts her hip while I take her in. Shoulders roll back a wee bit and the whole carriage adjust, end result is them jugs drift a quarter inch closer to the eyeballs judgin' 'em. Not an insignificant gain.

Got the denim skirt and bundled up wool socks in the hiking boots. Looks like a smudge of motor oil on the thigh. Perfume, maybe, these parts? Tiny jacket made of bubble gum wrappers and glitter. Tattoo on her neck — small and tasteful — says LOVE. Looks like a letter opener under the word. She wears the bubblegum jacket off the shoulders so skin from clavicle to cleavicle — or clavage to cleavage — glows like a strawberry milkshake. Woman's body's at war with her clothes and I'm on her side. Want her free. Pour this woman out.

It wasn't six month ago I'da felt compelled to tell this thirty-something young lady I got my female obligations spoke for. Now I marvel. Second girl, Skinny Hips is beside Skinny Tatas but now I get a look, I'll take the Tatas.

"We're lesbians."

"Settles that."

"What?"

"For a second there I thought I was headed down a certain path."

"Oh, we're still headed."

"We must ain't be talkin' the same thing."

"Don't think, Sugar. Feel. Listen, you're the only guy here who can help us."

She talks slow and I bet it's to give me more time to enjoy lookin' at her.

"How's that?"

"We just rented the apartment in the building next door. There's a Ryder truck right outside in the parking lot, maybe half full. Nothing a strapping man like you couldn't handle in twenty minutes."

She touch my shoulder, drag the hand half down my arm. Other girl gets close on the other side. Body tingles with the juice a wee bit. *Wee bit*. And back of my head I wonder if these girls ain't pattin' me down.

Strange thing, got a chub and the juice at the same time.

Skinny Tatas put her mouth at my ear and after a flicker of somethin' wet and warm says, "You notice I got a stud in my tongue?"

Try to figure how she got a breeding male or a two by four...

"Can't say as I follow."

She shifts her head in front and open her mouth. Got an earring in her tongue.

"See?"

Nod.

"Show him yours." Skinny Hips drops her jaw, rolls out her tongue and hers sparkles too.

"No, the other one."

She unbuttons her shorts.

"Ladies, uh."

Tatas smiles at Hips and she leaves off with the top button loose but the zipper fast.

"You know why a woman might get an earring in her tongue?" Skinny Tatas says.

"Sure makes your mouth purty."

The blood in my fingers and toes seeks greener pastures.

"We'll give you a blow job if you unload that Ryder truck."

Brain need an extra second or two. "Uh… What's in it for me?"

She smirk. "You ever have two girls at the same time?"

"I ain't entirely sure I had the one."

Skinny Hips lowers a hand to my leg. "What do you say, partner?"

"You prostitutes, that it?"

"No — "

"Yes — "

Tatas smiles big. Just the regular red and electric what's normal in a bar.

"We're not prostitutes. *Per se.*"

"But you want to trade my labor for your oral work."

"No money changes hands. We both get what we want."

More smile. Shoulders ain't back so far. She's more into skin than economics, maybe.

"No money? What you think labor is?"

Skinny Tatas pull back her head like the fella behind her sunk a meat hook and give it a jerk.

"Fine."

"Well shit, is all."

"Hunh?"

"It's economics."

"Are you a professor?"

"I profess on occasion."

"Then what are you, Cowboy?"

"That my name now?"

"I'm getting a beer," Skinny Hips says. "You buying?"

"You didn't study the economics neither."

Skinny Hips rolls her eyes and drops 'em on Skinny Tatas. Tatas blink and smile and raise two fingers. "You want a beer?"

"Nah, got the Sprite."

"Just two," Skinny say to Skinny.

"You not drinking tonight?"

"Dog made me give it up."

"Hey listen." She puckers the lips and stares at the far wall while I wait. "You know, we really need your help. Hey — how old are you?"

"I got a good twenty on you."

"So how about we show you all the sex that didn't get invented 'til after you quit having it?"

"We have a Ryder truck out there and all we need is some help with the big things. My brother loaded the truck, but he had to go to work. And we have to get the truck returned in six hours or else we're paying for another day."

"I'll help with the truck and all, that's just bein' neighborly. And truth told" — got to lean in here. Don't think I ever even confessed this to Fred — "couple things about the lesbians always puzzle me, maybe you could sort out. But we ain't tradin' labor for labor. Gettin' poked ain't suppose to be work and well…" I never seen hooties so perfect in my life. "Maybe someday we'll cross paths and if it don't feel like buying bulk hamburger I'll entertain the conversation."

"You're serious?"

"Yep."

"We said we'd blow you. Both of us."

Skinny Hips come back, got a Coors in both hands. The banquet beer.

"O-M-G!" she says. "Look at those boots!"

Lift the leg, push out the toe.

"Wow. They look super expensive."

"Nah. I thought so too. They's China-made fake snake."

She smiles and twinkles and I thought these trousers had more play up front.

"Let's go outside a minute. I want you to see inside the truck before you agree to help. You know… To see how big the job is. Especially if you're going to refuse payment."

"Don't need to see inside."

"Just look, so you know how much time you'll need. You don't want to be surprised or anything."

"You ain't but two girls. I be all right. Help you out and move along."

Skinny Tatas says, "Well, I actually wanted to show you something sexy. You know, what you'll be missing out on. Just a quick nibble."

"And I said I don't want relations like that, for pay."

"You dumbass."

"What?"

"I'm hitting on you."

Her eyes slink down like a cat stalked up on a bird. She reach for my timber and I don't got time to stop her.

Heh.

"Oh." Her smile gets wide.

My swaller's dry. "A nibble, you say?"

"Just a quick nibble."

CHAPTER FOURTEEN

Got the juice on my arms.

Could be anyone. I'm in a bar. Could be that fella throwin' darts hit the board sideways.

"You look distracted," says Skinny Hips. "That isn't good."

Skinny Tatas takes my hand off the table and peels loose the pointer finger. I watch her carry that finger to her mouth and stick it in. Slips the tongue out underneath and tickles the ball of my thumb.

"Can't see as how a nibble'd be wrong — long as I didn't deserve it."

She goes at my finder like a baby goat after an elbow and the fellers' eyes follow.

Hear boots on grit. Look right.

Abraham Church nod.

I nod back with my eyeballs, as the rest of me's engaged.

He repeat his nod and it look more like a suggestion.

I nod again, maybe a little less accommodatin' with my index finger about to procreate.

"Need a word," Church say.

"Shit."

"One more. C'mon."

I peel off from Skinny Tatas. "Wait," says I, content she knows my heart.

Abraham holds the door and I go in the restroom first. Got my elbow a little high so I can yank Glock and shoot if need be. But the restroom's empty — the shitters got no doors — and I pull up at the rightmost pisser out of three.

Church skips the middle and choose the left, one more confirmation he got his act together.

"Those girls," Church say.

"Yup."

He coughs. Swallows a couple times. Clears his throat.

"Afore you hacked that lung in two you wanted words."

I tap and tuck.

He zips and turns half away.

"Both of those girls... well, their reputations... Let's just say they're known entities. Wear something, all I'm saying."

Dip the head. Ole Abe lookin' out for Baer. Figured he thought with them girls being sweet on me, maybe I'd give an introduction. But in truth he's worried for my venereal health and though it go agin my grain, I'm —

Shit.

I'm a little touched and I reciprocate.

"I appreciate that, Abraham. Can I call you by your Christian name?"

"Call me Abe."

"I'm a little touched by your concern and I'd like to reciprocate."

"Oh! Well it's nothing. Those girls, you know. Fun times, but maybe not worth the penicillin shot."

"I understand."

"You said reciprocate. What do you mean — with some wisdom?"

"Yep. You don't want to cough like that while you're takin' a leak."

"What?"

"You never learn that?"

"You serious?"

"Hell, yeah. Hydraulic pressure blow your nuts off."

"You're fulla shit."

"Try it and see. Just make sure you stand over a bucket."

I come out the restroom and Skinny Tatas drops her head like a wolf found meat. She hips her way to me, stops a foot short and I hold my finger afore her mouth like a fisher hangs a hook.

Grin at Abe.

But she ain't havin' it. Tatas bring her hand to my trousers and with four fingers tucked behind the belt tows me to the door. Skinny Hips is after.

Outside they's a Ryder truck drove in so the front bumper's close the wire fence that got the slats wove through for privacy.

Stinky Joe sit up in the Eldorado seat and got his head out the window, snuggled in the bottom corner. Inside the bar they got the grease kitchen in back and the air smells like fried chicken and cow. Once I finish my business, I'll get him a burger and fries.

Skinny Hips stops at the nose of the truck. She smiles and Tatas go into the gap 'tween bumper and fence. She watch for me to follow. Gravel give out to dirt and weeds and I'm thinkin' I know a nibble don't mean a nibble. I'm thinkin' I oughta be bustin' Tat and Corazon out the hospital or findin' a fella knows his way 'round the fake identity papers.

But women got needs too and sometimes the neighborly thing is to satisfy 'em.

I ain't yet stepped into the gap 'tween truck and fence so Skinny Tatas tows me by the belt loop. Real easy I look back. Skinny Hips stands at the corner of the truck and alla sudden the juice hits my arms and red flares in her eyes like Satan ate grillin' beans and farted on the fire.

I lock up like a mule. Skinny Tatas grabs deep on my drawers and tugs. Feet scuffle on gravel. She latches aholt with the other hand too and throws her ass for leverage. Afore I look up and back I get the sixth sense says, *get low*; I drop to my knees while black boots and denim jeans come 'round the Ryder's nose.

Look up and some hairy feller got the baseball bat comin' down.

I keep droppin' and Skinny Tatas don't let go. I pull her along and she pop up her head while the bat comes down. She's too close to Black Boots for a home run so he bunts her to the ground.

Black Boots lifts the bat agin and me bent over and halfways concerned for Skinny Tatas, I launch while the bat's high. Plant my shoulder in Black Boots' sternum and drive him back.

Skinny Tatas moans.

I knee Black Boots in the groin and swing a crisp elbow to his mouth.

His eyes is stone gone so I press Black Boots to the fence with the left arm, cock my neck like a hammer and pull the trigger right after. Drive my dome best I can for his face and discover aimin' the noggin ain't like nothin' else a man'll aim.

Dunno what part of Black Boots makes the crack, nose, cheek bone, eye socket — I'm lookin' at the ground and kinda dizzy — but afore I lift my head and see, Black Boots' knees go slack.

Strong on pancakes and syrup, I pin him so he don't crumple. Got to put this animal out afore Skinny Hips back there — she still behind me I reckon — finds a knife or gun.

And soon as I think it a hand probes my ass holster.

Right elbow folded I swing the shoulder, launch the arm straight and the side of my fist connects with the Ryder truck and while the pain flashes hot Skinny Hips got the FBI Glock pointed three inches from my face.

"Don't! Fucking! Move!" says she.

Tatas moans beneath us.

Glock is said to have no safety mechanism, but they's one that always works. She didn't chamber a round.

I'll hear the slide mechanism if she does and meantime trust she ain't bright enough to brain me.

Black Boots require my attention.

Got him pinned agin the fence with my shoulder and I crush in hard and give my arms the freedom to punch his guts 'til he pisses blood soup. He goes soft and I'm still punchin', but now Skinny Hips learn how to strike a man with a pistol butt.

I let Black Boots drop and face Skinny Hips.

She got one leg on each side of Tatas and she's reared back for another head strike. I grab her neck and shove six feet.

Tatas is still on the ground but found her way to elbows and knees. Too close for a kick in the face so I knee her in the teeth.

Tatas is out.

I face Skinny Hips. "You was sayin'?"

She points Glock — and still ain't racked it. She backs out the gap 'tween truck and wire fence. I follow and study the lot. Nobody. She steps back. I step forward.

She stares me in the eye and positively beams. Skinny Hips turns toward the bar.

"Rape! Help! RAPE!!!"

She got the Glock in her right hand. I swing open palm and bust the pistol out her grip. Her arm swings wide and her body spins with it. Glock skitters on gravel.

I catch Skinny Hips.

Stand her up.

"Hold on, ma'am. You okay?"

She simpers, almost like the right smile's gonna put the game back on.

"You got yourself steady?"

She nods. Opens her mouth and afore she screams the poison words one more time, I give her the uppercut.

Skinny Hips drops to her back, knees up, head to the right so her knocked out eyes point at the bar. Blood drips out her mouth so maybe I cut some tongue.

I grab Glock off the gravel and slip it in my holster. Dust off the pants as Abe Church and another man exit the bar.

"Y'all better call the police, they's a man knocked out cold, other side the truck."

The fella with Abe Church trades a look and heads back inside.

Abe says, "Which one was yelling rape?"

"That's her."

"You knocked her out?"

"Indeed."

"You rape her?"

"That woman? Not possible."

We stand near the truck. Black Boots ain't moved and Skinny Tatas is back to her old self, groaning. Abraham moves for a better look.

Says I, "I guess they saw the duds and thought I was an easy mark. She got that tongue movin' and — "

"That's Frank Lloyd, back there."

" — them earrings in the tongue I guess. Shit, three seconds — "

"You did that?"

"Uh huh."

"He had the ball bat and the drop and you was already playing with your pecker."

"Was not."

Abe cross his arms.

"I didn't have it out."

"How'd you see the trap?"

"Just the country wiles is all. I saw the boots."

"Bullshit. There wasn't anything else that give you a hint... Nothing else?"

Somethin' strange in Abraham Church's face.

"Where you going with the questions, friend?"

"Something in your head maybe. A tingle or something?"

Hold on. Step back.

"You mean..."

I got a light head. Don't know about this. Don't — can't — what? All the black at the sides comes in. I'm standin' but that's about the sum of what I know.

I hear claws on paint.

Abraham says, "Hey, partner. It's all right. You're just a little wobbly."

Stinky Joe's chargin' in, head low like to cut a cowboy at the ankles.

Abe pulls his leg cannon.

"That's my dog. Gimme some room."

"Call him off!"

Abe swings his pistol arm.

"Joe! Easy!"

Joe skids and I hunker. He sniffs up my face and on accident nips my nose, then spins on Abraham Church and I can almost hear the growl under his bristling coat.

"Easy, Joe."

I reach and Abe grabs the elbow. Forearm lock and I'm up. He keeps a hand on the shoulder 'til I'm steady and I think on how I steadied Skinny Hips afore I knocked her out.

"What's your aim here?" says I.

"Just keeping it real."

"Well that ain't too hard is it? What're you after? All them questions?"

Another man come out the bar and all the men was in there

gawkin' and lustin' files out after. They fan wide as they walk and Stinky Joe rumbles under his neck fur.

The man in the middle who called the cops and brought the gang chins at Abe. Says, "You get the story?"

"It's like he says. That's Frank Lloyd back there, knocked out. Our friend got wise to him just in time and turned the tables."

"That's right. Uh-huh." My head's gettin' clear. Cops on the way. Bells is ringin'.

"I'll let y'all stand guard," says I. "I had that Sprite and I'll be needin' the facilities."

"No need to guard. These three are what you might call, known to law enforcement."

"How's that?"

"Frank Lloyd, Bunny and Bambi."

"Y'all knew the game when they came in."

Fellas glow. Juice up and down the arms.

"Not exactly," says the one in the middle.

"Meanin', you knew exactly they done this afore, but not exactly how they'd do it this time."

"Right. Not exactly."

Abraham says, "Men's room is inside. And what Will is trying to say is Frank Lloyd's been in all kinds of trouble, but you don't know what's next 'til you see it on the news. And Bunny and Bambi, they're just Bunny and Bambi. Believe it or not, they're car mechanics."

"Oh, I believe it. Perfect sense. I gotta piss."

I walk off and Joe follows. The men is fanned wide and fuck if I'm walkin' around so I stop in front of two 'til they step aside.

"Come on, Joe. Inside."

What's going on?

I open the bar door and Joe follows.

"They got the law coming."

Maybe we should leave.

"Joe, your brain's the size of a walnut. Mine's like a whole bag of 'em. Let me do my work, aright?"

Inside the bar I cut back the hall what leads to the men's room. Accourse the only escape there'd be through the window and that's more work. We go straight through the grease kitchen and out the side. Circle up front.

"Joe, you stay here. Pick you up in two."

He sits.

I walk straight to the road, follow the sidewalk 'til the line of sight has me on the edge of visible to the men 'round back. Road's straight ahead and maybe a couple hundred yards is the police. Got no time for finesse. I hunker low and scoot fast, hope the men in back stay more interested in the people on the gravel than the man who put 'em there.

Slip into the Eldorado, fire the engine and pull forward. In ten feet I'm outta sight of the guys in back. I reach across the seat and open the passenger door.

Joe jumps on the seat. Pullin' out I adjust the rearview and the cops swerve in.

CHAPTER FIFTEEN

Stay at the Lodge last night 'cause it ain't a quarter mile from the Glenwood Springs Hospital and got a hot tub too. Things settle down after bit, I bet a good hot soak'd be nice. In the day I had Farmer Brown's tub in the crick just below the still and I'd fill the tub with ten buckets from the stream, haul stones from the fire and that water'd get almost warm enough to nap in.

As it is, I shower and truth told, seems like more work 'n gettin' clean oughta require.

I get out still wipin' off the arms and legs. Motel like to soften the water, make soap suds feel like mineral oil. Any skin this slick oughta be pink.

Motel got a laundry and since I'm wearin' my skippy duds it's a good opportunity to wash what clothes I wore since Flagstaff. They been scrubbed in the Colorado River a couple time, come out half as dirty as they went in, but what dirt's left is new and clean from the river.

I open a white towel flat on the bed and cover it with dirty clothes. Hang my suit on a hanger and toss my shirt and t-shirt to the pile. Socks too. Ain't got the other unders and though I'd never confess it, I suspect any man cinch his nuts in underwear is a man oppressed by convention and never live a free day in his life.

Women on the other hand is free to wear silk skivvies and whatnot. Such things is encouraged.

Now I'm naked with my dirty clothes hoboed in a towel, I wrap a second about the waist, tuck the corner and roll it under.

Sometimes a man used to drink'll not know the difference — regular world's as frazzled as the drunk one and stone sober he'll look at it and not know what's real and what ain't. Condition like that, he'll toss the satchel over shoulder, fill his fist with quarters and strut past the tourists without a glance.

They come west to see the wilderness. Here I am.

Most these outta-towners got the same look. White or tan pants and windbreakers with company logos. People fight a daily war on hair. Clean shaved, nothin' in the nose. Prim and proper and got the underwear lines to prove it.

Glock in the ass holster don't work with the towel so I leave Stinky Joe armed. In the laundry room I drop six quarters in the machine slots and buy enough water 'n electric for one load. Stuff in the clothes and wait.

They put a chrome-legged chair with a plastic seat under the foldin' table. I get on hands and knees and drag it out. Pull down the towel as I sit. Head back agin the wall. Eyes closed.

Skinny Hips and Skinny Tatas. Bambi and Bunny. I bet Tathiana'd kick both them girls' asses.

Wash machine bang and wobble. I lift the lid, pull a soppy set of drawers and spot the problem. Most clothes is bunched on one side and I got a pantleg jammed under the agitator, spun into a three-inch rope. Make me recall Rapunzel or that little leprechaun. What was his name? Lilliputian?

Rumpelstiltskin.

Stole a girl to run a gold loom or some such.

I keep tuggin' on the pantleg. Spin the agitator back, pull, spin, hit it with the palm, look for a sledgehammer layin' handy...

Rumplestiltskin's troubles. Sometimes an idea'll get aholt and seem like it's the key that'll unlock every mystery.

Exactly the kind of thing I'd remember with a single gurgle of shine. No man recall sober what he learn drunk... 'Cept I don't suppose I was drunk in the grade school, so much.

A shadow cross the window — some weary traveler got his nose hair trimmed so he want to do his laundry next. Forget I'm only wrapped in a towel and wave, since they's only one of me and two wash machines and no wait on the other.

Rumpelstiltskin. All in all, that was a creepy fuckin' story for a kid.

The door opens.

I give that tangled pantleg a tug guaranteed to pop it free and shit if I don't cinch it tighter. And now I got company, I'm aware how the air circulates up in under the towel. Nethers don't often feel regular room air with another person near. Unless certain conditions is met.

"I'm usin' this machine and'll be done in twelve minute if you want both. But you can come in and use the other now if'n — "

I get a burst of juice like I'm strapped in Ole Sparky.

Normal lies about normal things, it's a tingle or I spot the red eyes. Most lies is simple misdirection and folk don't even know they do it. Next is the puffery and all puffers is self aware. Then on up through the serious lies, which is always about someone want me to put 'em in a different group in my head, as each means somethin' different, and these liars know folk'll give 'em leeway in one category they don't deserve in another. Folk like to look competent when they ain't. Smart when they ain't. Thoughtful when they ain't.

Here to do the laundry when they ain't.

Sometimes the juice carry a different sort of charge I bet no electrician could find. I wouldn't ask him how twenty volts taste and I wouldn't ask him why sometimes when a person mean me harm, the juice come with a cherry on top. I can taste the evil in it.

Standin' bare foot, balls loose and Glock sleepin' with Stinky Joe in the motel room, the body ain't cool and thoughtful. Response is dread, and me with my arms sunk in the wash, ass out in a towel and balls swingin' and the towel slit open clear to the hip… It's like I climb out the trench backwards and stand next the bobwire waitin' on the bullet, not knowin' if the Krauts'll be kind and put it in my head, or cruel, and somewhere else.

Man feel *exposed*.

A burst of juice like that is sometimes accompanied by a gun but not this time.

I let go the pantleg and skitter back hunched, arms wide and ready to grapple, ready to kill. But afore it even registers old Black Boots Frankie Lloyd is in the laundry room with me, he starts finishin' the job he start at the Ryder truck by the bar.

I'm smarter and faster'n Black Boots Lloyd but his ball bat works without wit and he can swing it faster'n I can disappear. Slugger catches my right arm above the wrist and the bones snap hard like when you tear chicken wings took too quick off the fire.

Frankie Black Boots winds the bat full circle up on his toes so he can get the whole body in on the rotation. He's coiled so tight his heels spin on the follow through. I watch half froze by the pain already in my busted arm, and shit if this ain't the clock tickin' down to zero on Baer Creighton.

Beat to death in a motel laundry room.

He's full swing and if I don't move he'll paste my brain to the wall. Close in, I sacrifice the arm and shoulder. Restrict his move, let him club me with the grip instead of the Louisville logo.

Though my right arm feels fit for cuttin' off, my left is just woke up. I got him close and the bat ain't so handy, I figure I'll put this son of a bitch down for good. Reach for my ass Glock and come up with two curly hairs and some words I ain't spoke since 1972.

Frankie Black Boots Lloyd shoves off, swings for my head. I lift my broken left to spare the right, take what impact I can and the rest deflects with the bat into my forehead.

I'm on the tile. Legs up like a dead dog. Towel flopped open, toes and fingers stretched into claws and nothin' but hope and luck to save me.

Frankie Lloyd's got one black boot on each side my hips, got the bat's fat end three inches over my forehead.

Lord, I am broken hearted over what I done.

CHAPTER SIXTEEN

Come to with eyes closed and the world covered in tar paper. I got a name but don't know it. I do recall a brain ain't suppose to feel like it's in a table vice. Sometimes when you're awake in one situation then realize you're awake and a new one — and don't recall the steps in the middle — and you didn't see the switch, some of those times it makes sense not to let on you're trackin' the swap. Not until any folk ain't announced 'emselves is afforded the opportunity.

And if they don't, that say somethin' too.

Last I recall I was in the laundry and that black booted slugger named — whatever — was swingin' a maple baseball bat at my arm. I thought first off the bat was ash but as he held it over my head for me, I saw the grain wasn't so porous.

Beep.

Beep.

This Tat's room?

Beep.

Roll the head. Feel the soft of a pillow and smell the chlorine.

Hospital.

Oh hell yeah I recall. Black Boots beat me silly and last I thought it was time for me to square things with the Lord.

Static on the arms...

"How long you been awake?"

"Who says I am?"

I know that voice — but the exact knowledge of the fella's name, that's squirreled deeper in the noodle 'n I can fetch right off. Starts with a C. Grab that name and pull like an earthworm still in the ground, easy so he don't break in two.

Worm breaks.

"You get a look at who did it?"

Ah. Abraham Church. Man in motion.

"Can you open your eyes?"

"Don't see why not."

But I keep 'em closed on account the noise. Somethin' squeak like can only come from rubber and linoleum. A loudspeaker ask for a doctor somewhere.

"So, I'm alive."

"Lucky twice," Church say.

"How you figure?"

"You survived two attacks. Did you see who came after you the second time? What you say now is real, real important to me."

"'Preciate you but I don't need the protection."

Open my eyes and swivel. It's just me and Church.

"Cops been here?"

"Not yet."

"I can tell 'em exactly who done it."

"Yeah?"

"Your town dipshit. Black Boots."

"Frank Lloyd." Church frowns. Try to use his tongue like a toothpick 'tween the cutters up front and quit after a tongue smack. Says Church, "I thought so. Puts me in an awkward position."

"Nah fuck that. Listen. Need your help on two things."

My brain hurt and shit if I don't have a cast on my arm. How the — been yammerin' three minute I didn't know I got a busted arm.

"How long I been in here?"

"Half day." He glance at his watch. "Twelve hours."

"Need you to take my room key to the motel and see about my dog. He'll need a couple cheeseburgers to communicate you're friendly. Tell him I sent you and he'll be fine."

"Ahhh. Sure."

"No, he talks. Honest."

Church turn and look out the window. See his face reflected on the glass as he say, "Where did you stay?"

"That lodge-lookin' place two blocks catty corner headed east of here."

"A lot of brown timbers, Tudor style? That one? Because I had it in my mind you was at the motel a couple doors down. The Caravan."

"Well shit. I don't know. But I doubt I'd stay at a caravan on account the name."

"You against commerce and trade?"

"I ain't one to complain, but you think they got any Wild Turkey about this place? My head's got so much pressure I'm afraid for my skull plates."

"Press that button there. See the cord? Press the button and the nurse'll hook you up with some pain killers."

I press like he say.

"So you're at the Lodge?"

"Okay."

"You got a room key?"

"Where they put my duds? Oughta be a suit 'round here someplace. Key'll be in the pocket."

"They brought you here in a towel."

"Oh. Yeah, well, a towel and my key, maybe?"

Church open a small cabinet on wheels next the wall Hurt to

rotate the eyeballs anymore, so I twist the head and it's like steppin' on the floor of a rat cage wired with juice.

Inside's a white towel with a credit card size door key.

"You'll see the Eldorado at the motel, right in front. That'll let you know."

Church study me and the hospital light ain't good for his face. Make him look pissed.

"You said two things," Church say.

"Second is I want you to come back here with Stinky Joe in two hours. I don't want him locked in a room no more, is all. You tell him what I said and tell him I said it, and he'll understand. He's likely smarter'n me and you both."

Church shake his head. Look at his watch.

"I don't think they'll let me bring him to your room, so what gives?"

"Have him with you out front."

Church's brow start dancing on his head… thinkin'.

"You'll be checking out of the hospital, is that it? Release yourself?"

"I got a busted arm is all."

"Likely your head."

"It'll heal and if it don't that'll answer some questions too. Nah, I got plans. Got some things workin'. Maybe take a trip to Chicago, see a lady friend."

Church shake his head and grin. "Amazing."

"Thank you."

"Whereabouts in Chicago? I got some friends there."

"You got friends in the physics department at the great University of Chicago?"

"You're intimate with a physics professor?"

"Well, it ain't gentlemanly to say if I was, but since I ain't it don't do the woman any disrespect to confess it. I ain't stuck her and way my head feels I don't think I could handle the fireworks. And my back's just healin' from the last gal clawed me up. Might be a short while 'fore I'm ready to take on the risk."

"Chicago University Department of Physics."

Can't help but beam, though his admiration ain't rightfully earned.

Church bends for the towel and key and both knees pop afore he gets 'em half bent. Puts his right hand on the counter for support and the left wheels bounce. It hurts the head to keep turned but I do, wonderin' if him hurtin' more'll make my hurt less. What you call a philoso-physics experiment so I can tell Chicago Mags.

Church swipe the key and lose his balance. Drop back on his ass.

"… damn… sonuva…."

Church finally twist so his belly face the ground and work m'self up hands on knees.

I smile and my head hurt. Results to make Mags proud.

"Like I said, Church, I appreciate you. Just tell Stinky Joe old bear —"

"Yeah?"

"Günter Stroh. Günter sent ya with the cheeseburgers. He'll know you's good people."

Church's eyes go skinny. "Bear?"

"Naked."

Church shake his head like I'm the problem.

My head aches. Arm too, even in the cast. Tat and Corazon flash through the mind — how I'm gonna get 'em outta here all busted up and hurtin' so bad I can't think. How'll I sneak 'em out? Tat maybe walk herself or I could drop her on a rope out the window. But Corazon? I don't even know how bad she is.

Yet.

"Hey, Church."

He turn at the door.

"How I get here?"

"What?"

"Ambulance?"

He wrinkle his brow like I peg him with a spitball.

"Uh. I don't know. Brought in by a good Samaritan, I guess." He nods. "All right. I'll bring your dog. Be in the lot out back, right? Two hours."

"Two hours."

Church leave.

I jigger the baby crib wall closest the door. Pain burst white like somebody shove a signal flare in my right ear and pull the trigger.

CHAPTER SEVENTEEN

Ain't decent to walk the world naked, most of us. Outta respect for the less endowed and fear of the ladies prone to ogle, I'll spare both the envy and desire.

Can't bust free in a towel and ain't decent in a hospital gown. Alden Boone needs some duds so he can become Baer Creighton in transition to the name I choose, since it's appointed somewhere I gotta have one.

I told Church to come back in a couple hour. While he's gone for Stinky Joe, I crawl out the bed, yank hoses and tubes and see one's got a rolly stand. Ain't no one in the hospital so legitimate as a bare assed fifty-somethin' dragging an IV stand. Likewise, they's no one less legitimate on the outside, hence the need for some passable britches and a t-shirt.

Hospital's dead as a graveyard. I scoot to my feet and drag the IV pole with me in case they spiked the juice with somethin' for the brain pain. Got to stoop and walk my good hand, the right, up my leg for balance and done. Feel a little light in the head, starin' at the bright spot on the wall — where they got a x-ray in the reader. Fibia and Tibula.

Nah, that ain't it.

My arm bones is busted 'tween wrist and elbow. Looks like a good clean break what'll knit up in no time. He musta clubbed my head too, hence the nonstop fireworks.

Clock puts the hour at a quarter after one AM. It's time to change floors.

I drag the IV stand. Elevator doorbell dings and once more with me inside. Brain goes a little light when the floor lifts in under me, but I catch the wall 'til the doors slide open on the critical care unit. Action all about. Light so clean and bright it smell of Ajax. These people got attitudes. Middle the night and they move about like it's a half hour past sunrise and they already squared away a second bowl of Wheaties. A man still got his baby fat zips by in his turquoise outfit, got those white strings hangin' from his ears and a dance in his hips.

'Nother man in dress pants and glasses read a clipboard while he walk, somehow got the sense to navigate and read gibberish — but what impresses is that he walk straight outta *Stayin' Alive* with the bell bottoms and lapels and maybe more swagger'n I'd want from a man with a scalpel.

Cut left fifteen steps then cut right. Round the bend and down the hall.

Other cop said Corazon was in surgery. I take it she's out by now. Accourse findin' her room should be easy as findin' the cops. If they got any handle on who she is, even her local work, they'll have sixteen men with flamethrowers mullin' the place, like Arlo said, veins in the teeth.

But they's no coppers loiterin' about, only just the nurses eyeballin' computer screens.

The lights is off in Tat's room and the door's open. Don't look more 'nough to see a different cop on duty.

Pass a couple empties.

Next door is open and a cop sit on a chair, head agin the wall and eyes closed, but after three seconds of me lookin', he cranks 'round and his elbow draws back. His eyes is slits.

Waren't expecting to find Corazon so fast. If that's her. Maybe Glenwood is full of riff-raff and the coppers got to guard every room. I give him a sleepy nod and move close to the door.

Lean forward and turn the head a bit, eyeballs twisted so they hurt, gaze crawlin' up the bed. Them mounds at the bottom could be a small woman's feet. Them hips could belong a girl — if she was young. Almost no chest and the shape of her gets more beautiful the closer I get to her face and know it'll be Corazon. Got to exercise care, as the eyeballs grow damp.

Hard to see.

I lean more and now the bandages come. Her neck's braced and her face's wrapped most the way around. They got a hole for the eyes and mouth but the pretty brown skin I expect is swelled up purple and the air sighs out my lungs and I couldn't hurt any more if it was Mae and her babies in that bed all beat to hell. Maybe it's the late hour and the hurt in my own head, maybe the busted arm, maybe the drugs. The scene got me about as broke a man can be, lookin' on a life in the balance and powerless to do nothin'.

All I know is love and responsibility, and the fact I ain't done shit for neither. I never loved like I coulda.

Look back at the cop and turn my whole face into a question mark.

Cop nudge his head sideways and his eyes drop and take in me and my IV stand from the ground up, and when his eyes meet mine he seem satisfied I'm a busted man, can't sleep and out walkin' the floors.

No juice nor red.

"Too bad," says I. "She the one from the news?"

He blinks. Nods.

"Rumor is she didn't do anything. I heard y'all arrest her and cut her loose next day."

"How'd you hear that?"

"My ears."

Smile big.

"One the nurses. One the people in the blue green outfits in the elevator said it."

I'm shootin' sparks and glowin' red in my soul. Never sits good to be a liar but with Corazon in the bed and me got to figure how to preserve both her life and freedom, and each one seem to exclude the other, I got to do what I got to do and I'll lie all night if it'll bring the right resolution.

The heart machine beeps. It's been every couple seconds but I hear it like the first. Got to keep that beeper beepin', then bust her out.

Cop looks at me studyin' at Corazon too long, like I care. Shake my head.

"These black hairs. Drive like assholes and get what they deserve. Stay strong brother."

I make the fist.

He wince.

Missed his M-O by a mile.

He make a square with his hands over his lap.

"This is a law enforcement arena, sir. Kindly move along."

"Yessir. Good day. Good night. We appreciate you — you men and gals what make up the blue line. Nothing else 'tween civilization and the wild."

His face don't register full enlightenment so I dip the brow and drag my IV stand. Pause toward the lady nurses and with me in the gown, my ass says hello to the copper. All stayin' in character, as the great actors do.

But soon as that cop slip outta mind Corazon slips back in. Keep on past the nurse station and swallow down a lump. Stare at the wall ahead but I dream Corazon's meated-up face six-foot-wide like it was shot out a film projector, froze at the worst frame, all her cuts and bruises so big I'd like to chuck a watermelon at 'em. Part of me says with the right ambition and surprise — and Glock — I could storm her room and she'd be free as fast as a cop drops dead in his law enforcement domain. An' I'd wheel Corazon's bed to the exit. But that heart monitor got a music to it and I like the sound of her livin' each second, beat by beat, a whole lot better'n I'd feel if that beeper quit. And the second I took off whatever wire's hooked to the machine I'd be frettin' I heard the last beat.

Way they wrap her face and top half, Corazon musta run her head through the windshield.

Non-seatbelt wearin' girl.

Keep walkin'. Blink and blink. Voices down the hall, quiet, urgent; old people voices got krinkles in the sound.

This might could be my clothing donor.

I shuffle six inch at a time. After I pressed the button Church said to press, I told 'em no meds, no painkillers, give me some water. But they give me somethin' anyway. My head's twice too big and fulla air — pulls the neck like a balloon pull the string.

I stand outside the room with the old people's voices and glance at the nurse station. Both faces still stuck in computers.

The krinkled voices belong to a man and woman. The man's is urgent but weak and I hesitate to call a syllable when I think I got it deciphered. But my guess is, man says he druther be dead.

I get closer and rest the back shoulders agin the wall.

"You should have seen what I saw. I can't wait for you to see it."

"You want me dead too?"

"Yes! It was so beautiful. And the Lord is there, like we always thought, just how we said. Except *not like we thought*. All the stuff I feared my whole life is false. I must have made it up. Look what cancer does to you."

Wait....

"I have nothing left for this world *and the other one is better.*"

"You can't leave me!"

Tiny sobs replace the woman's voice. Her face gettin' wet.

"It's a good thing… and I want it," the man say. "Death is where we get to see why we lived."

I think on Chicago Mags and even recollect Günter Stroh, him sayin' the things on the curtain ain't real. It's what behind throwin' the image that matters. I think on him sittin' with his head back and eyes closed, breath so soft a gnat on his nose hair couldn't say if he was alive or dead. How I'd imagine bein' in his head while his thoughts float off.

Is why I want his name — since the law make it that I can't have my own. And truth is they's so much attached the name Baer Creighton, so much evil I done fightin' fire with fire; back of my head I think if I ditch the name and start someplace new I won't do the evil no more, as no one'll know me to provoke it.

It's only me raisin' hell.

Why is that?

Me?

Hell?

Or all the folks oughta raise it with me and don't?

The solitary path is lonesome in the hospital, brain beat to meat and arm useless.

Least I know with Günter Stroh the name's clean as the breeze come up through the trees in the morning, cool and sweet, put a tingle on the skin and make a man feel they's nothing in the world so bad he can't knock it to its knees when he choose.

If I took Gunter's name, I might learn his peace as an old man like I learned his likker as a young 'un.

Twist back 'round. Nurse eyeballs me.

Her lips is movin'.

"I don't feel too good," says I. "Where the hell am I?"

"Fourth floor, ICU. Where are you supposed to be?"

"New York."

Joshin' don't feel so bad as lyin'.

She raise her brow — just the one on the right.

"Yeah, I got the contract for all the shine in Brooklyn."

"Huh?"

"Speakeasy." Wink. "Pretty girl like you know 'bout the speakeasy."

She elbow the other gal out her computer screen. Her lips move like to make words but she swallows instead of spittin' 'em out.

"Joshin' is all. I come up one floor on the elevator. Gotta find where they sell tobacca. Ain't had a chaw in hours."

"Sir, do you need help returning to your room?"

"I'll git. No tobacca up here."

Push the IV stand and skedaddle. Wonder how I'll find new duds in a hospital 'less they come from someone like the feller wants to go to heaven. Can't go in his room and dig in the cabinet while the wife sobs — though with her eyes clouded the feat is doable. But stealin' is stealin' and since it's rotten on the face, it's best to steal from assholes and not good folk that's dyin'. Or if I can't steal from an asshole, I want it someone I don't know one way or t' other, so they's a chance. Let the Almighty guide my hand and turn my evil into good.

To the elevator.

Right 'bout now I reckon Abe Church is feedin' Joe a burger.

Remind me of the responsibility I shoulder, though when I left North Carolina it waren't with the goal to see how many bags I could schlep, as Günter'd say.

A man choose his burdens each day. He maybe don't know, but if he don't pick 'em up they don't get picked. He carries 'em all day each and every, and when his shoulders hurt and his back stabs and his legs is weak he'll dream 'bout what he'd be without his lot, if he had someone else's. But truth is he's nothin' but his burdens. Makin' bags is all he's ever done. He stews on his past, walks to the door and sees he's had no life at all save the one he wants rid of.

And so I got the responsibility of Corazon and Tat weighin' on me, and just like the past is bags I got to shoulder, the future's where I 'spect the cool hemlock breeze to make things right, so I can do it better on the second go 'round, if I get one.

I got to bust out Tat and Corazon.

CHAPTER EIGHTEEN

Whooeee! I'm broke out the hospital. Couldn't go back for the towel but I expropriate from a man-nurse's locker some blue jeans with what they call fifteen twenty year back the acid wash. I got on new jeans look old and a shirt smells of deodorant, likely rain fresh 'nough it'll work for me too.

Played hell gettin' the polo over my arm cast and my head still feel like a bag of boiled taters, maybe mixed with somethin' cruel. Rat poison?

Down the elevator and cross the first floor, looks like a five-star hotel with a grand piano and fine art. Nobody at the reception station. Out the double doors, turn right and gander at the parking lots, climb the hill and they's a truck parked out back where none the security lamps shine. Ole Church don't enjoy the spotlight.

That's the man's character.

Guess that's maybe why I sense the kinship. He's always about and ready to help. You can't beat a feller like that. And I suspect he's frustrated with the untruth around him, same as me… yet somehow ole Church figure out how to roll with the world despite knowin' what it is.

Ain't ashamed to say I maybe could learn from the man. It's the social aspect I lack. Boggles the brain how a feller can talk to liars and not want to skedaddle back where he come.

Truck door open and the dome light show Church climb out. He's steady on his feet now he got somethin' weighs a ton to hang onto. He's a big somebody. Come around the front.

No Stinky Joe.

Raise the open hand.

"Dog?"

Church smile. "He's in the back."

Must be in the bed under the cap. Now I hear scratchin' claws like Joe's 'bout to dig out a Rhino bed liner.

"You said at the hospital you're going to Chicago?"

"That's right."

"When are you leaving?"

"Soon's I grab my dog and car."

"The Eldorado?"

"That's right."

"Haven't registered it in your name yet, Alden?"

"Wh — "

Stop talkin'.

Think.

"That's a nickname," says I.

"Interesting."

"Good. I didn't mention it afore, but I long ago decided I'd murder anyone who said it three times."

Church raise his hands. "Easy." Smile. "Just fooling. The name doesn't mean anything to me, Günter. And if you ask me, Alden isn't much of a name at all. Sounds a little pussified."

"Exactly."

"So why's it on your driver's license?"

"That's a fake ID you saw it on, is why."

He watch my face for lies and I watch his eyes. Fuckin' uncanny.

"Yeah, I can see that," Church say.

"Tell me, friend, how you come to study my license?"

"I thought you'd want your billfold."

"They must be six or twenty steps you're leavin' out."

He pulls a billfold and toss it. I got no balance and one arm.

"Shit," says Church.

"Stop." I lower to a knee 'fore Church get three feet. Grab my billfold. I look him straight eyeballs and get nothin' but a dark night and air that feels more December than April.

Shove the wallet in my stolen drawers. "I won't do you the dishonor of lookin' inside."

He give me a wisp of the shrug-frown. "Who names a boy after a pond, anyway?"

"Come agin?"

"Alden. Get it?"

"That's two. An' I ain't shittin'."

"Heh, yeah. You said your lady friend teaches physics?"

Stinky Joe scrapin'. His voice cry out. I march for the truck.

Church lurch. Cut me off. Put his hand on my shoulder and I get a lone spark. He pull away.

"Just a second," Church say. "Let me get that."

I stop. He's so big I'd need two of me to get around him. He rests his hand on the truck's cap door. Stinky Joe behind, whinin'.

"You planning on coming back to Glenwood Springs?"

"I'm planning on getting my dog in one single damn second. What the hell's going on with you?"

"Just help me out with one thing. Are you coming back?"

"Why is my whereabouts and whatnots so important?"

Church look a little coy but I got no more juice nor red to go with it. He shake his head, lean on the truck. Sigh.

"Well, you tangled with Frank Lloyd. I've had a hardon for that guy for years."

"I know what a hardon is. You must mean a kind I ain't heard of."

"I want the son of a bitch behind bars."

"Oh. That's good. Real good."

"I need to know if you're coming back. You're squirrely about your name and where you come from — and that's your right. But if I need you as a witness…"

"You a cop?"

"No."

"Lawyer?"

"No."

"Then what business you got with a hardon for Frank Lloyd?"

"I'm the undertaker."

"What? Like a joke?"

"No, I'm an undertaker. The thing you have to understand in any town, it's never the man himself who does things. It's the people the man knows."

"Sound like a riddle and I ain't got time. I want my fuckin' dog."

"Then let me solve it for you. I'm the swinging dick around here and I want to know I can count on you to show up in a court of law."

"Ah."

Stinky Joe scrapin'.

"Maybe let's see how Stinky Joe is, that good?"

Church twist the handle and the door elevate on its own. Stinky Joe jump agin the tailgate while Church pull the latch and drop it. Joe stumble half sideways and leap out. Land like his legs is springs and bound half across the lot with his ass low and happy. Pent up energy is all.

"Did he shit yet?"

"Four times. I was almost late."

"Any in the room?"

"None I smelled."

Joe lift his hind leg to a shrub.

Church say, "Why don't you give me your cell phone number?"

"Don't got one. Why in hell I wanna give up my right — "

"No cell phone?"

"Zip."

Church look at the stars.

"No offense, Abraham."

"It's just I don't know how I'm going to reach out when I need to."

"It ain't my way to have other folks know my plans, you understand."

"I understand, but … "

"But I'm coming back here come hell or high water and maybe with a battalion ready for war. Mark my words on that."

He look like he shit a porcupine, tail first.

"Who are you going to war with?"

"I said 'nough already. Now you been good to me and I appreciate it, but beyond what's been said I'll say no more."

"Yeah. Right. If that's what you want. Sure."

"You understand."

"Hundred percent. You'll look me up?"

"Count on it, my friend. I won't forget. Good. Alright." Offer my hand and he shake it. "I appreciate you, Abraham Church. I really do."

"No problem."

We get shook and he swab his brow with his forearm.

"C'mere, Stinky Joe."

Just raisin' the voice swamps the head in misery.

Squat careful since I don't got use of the right arm and Stinky Joe sniff the cast. I scruff his ears.

Who is this prick?

"Easy, Joe, easy. Let's get on."

Blood pressure build while I stand and time I'm back full height my head's 'bout to pop.

"You'll need this."

Church swing his hand back and first thought is he's goin' for the gun — but he got no reason and it's just my three AM nerves and headache and whatever drugs they shot in me. He gimme the motel key from his pocket.

"You want a lift to your room?"

"Nah. Appreciate ya. Druther walk an' clear the cobwebs. You know what drugs they give me in there?"

"Oxycontin."

"That a good one?"

"Lotta folks speak of its merits."

"Meanin', when it wears off I'll be hurtin' more."

"A lot."

"And the dog says I can't drink Wild Turkey." Wave at Church. "I'll look you up when I get back."

"Be safe. Chicago's full of crazy people."

"It ain't just Chicago, Abraham."

Stinky Joe walk aside me and we cross the parkin' lot behind the hospital. On and on.

"Puppydog... That a little weird?"

Stinky Joe looks back.

He's still there. Not going anywhere.

Chill in the air and now we've gone a hundred feet I'm a mite self critical on account I didn't swipe a wool sweater along with the polo shirt.

Why do you think he's still there?

"He watchin' us?"

Yep.

"Dunno. He's a good feller but every man's motivated by stupidity more 'n wisdom."

That include you?

"Accourse. Maybe I shouldn't speak for others."

The chicken leg woman. That's your stupidity.

"You wasn't there."

You talk in your sleep.

So now I'm dreamin' on Chicago Mags.

"Well, dreams is bullshit so don't go readin' too much in that. I want her views on a couple things weighin' me down, is all."

Joe stops at a McDonald's bag next the curb and tear at the rolled up end.

Cold out. I try and hug myself warm but realize my right arm's busted in a cast. Guess that pain killer's finally got to work.

"Go ahead, Joe, if you're hungry. Didn't Church bring you any cheeseburgers?"

No. But I smelled them.

"I told him to sweet talk you with some cheeseburgers. I think that's what I said. Did he tell you I sent him for you?"

Your friend doesn't talk to dogs.

"That is concerning. How'd he convince you to get in the truck?"

It was as simple as pointing his gun and dragging me with a rope.

Stop. "You fuckin' kiddin' me?" Turn around. "I'll kick his ever lovin' — "

Hold up. Think on it. Is that what you want right now?

Piece of cold hit me on the nose and it melt. Snow. One flake, like a miracle.

"I don't know at that. What you think?"

I'd let it rest. Like meat.

"Hmm."

Shiver. Cold out — and no one ask me afore the change.

"Either way I need some clothes. Let's get back the room."

Turn right at the corner and after a hundred some yards left at the 82 heads to Carbondale. Pass the motel Church thought I was at and after a bank and couple other joints, the Lodge. Couple men sit on coolers smokin' cigarettes. Joe growl. I nod. Wonder what I'd do if accosted without a firearm. Cuss 'em real good, I guess, and offer Joe encouragement.

Spot the Eldorado and good thing, otherwise I wouldn't know which room's mine. I got the memory back for everything I'd normally recall, but some — which room's mine — I wouldn't bother with anyhow.

Open the door and I got juice on my left arm and the right bein' under a cast, nothin'.

Step quick to the dresser and grab Glock, right where I left it. But holdin' with my left hand the gun feel light, though I ain't calibrated my left hand on the Glock, only Smith.

Need a Smith 'n Wesson.

Glock pointed, light on, I open the bathroom door and push back the curtain. Empty. Back in the main room Stinky Joe study me.

There's nobody here.

"I got the juice."

You're cold and taking dope.

"You think that's it? What's your nose say?"

There's no one inside.

Lower Glock and heft it side to side. Got my suspicion up. Close the door behind Stinky Joe and lock the deadbolt. At the table I break down Glock, seekin' what's missin'. Love to fire one into the bed so I know it works. Have to do it once I get on the highway. Reassemble and place the gun on the table.

That juice-on-my-arm tingle's gone but my suspicion ain't. I give the key to Church but that don't mean he was the only one here. Motel staff got keys and —

Shit.

Eldorado keys on the dresser by the television. I got a hollow in my stomach and a couple dry swallows don't fill it.

Better go check.

"You was here."

Locked in the back of his truck while he went through the room.

Swipe the keys. Unlock the dead bolt. Open the door.

Here's my dumb ass 'bout to go outside without Glock.

I tuck the firearm in my left front pocket on account I never practice pullin' a gun from my ass southpaw.

Go outside. "Come on, you black booted son of a bitch. I'll tell you how the cow ate the fuckin' cabbage."

Nobody near but the two gloomy fellers with the cigarettes. Wave Glock and they wave back, then the one on the left jab the one on the right. They nod and wave and nod and back step into they room. Good. Nobody need see this.

I rest Glock on the trunk lid and fetch the keys, insert and twist. Latch pops and I grab Glock and push the trunk up easy, a poker player checkin' his cards. But I can't see nothin' 'til the lid's high 'nough anyone on the floor above can see too.

Gold is undisturbed.

Slam the trunk, lift with the fingers on my good hand. Locked. Good. Now back to the task at hand. Inside the room I sit on the bed and look about. If I was seen they'd say I was puzzled. Seen by who? That's the question.

By and by the electric's gone and my left arm start to tingle sympathetic to my right. Whole thing maybe just the mind playin' tricks.

"Joe, when Church come for you, he do anything in here?"

He was in the bathroom.

"Oh? What'd he do in there?"

Number two.

"Shit." Shake my head.

Good one. Impossible to predict.

"He didn't say my name and he didn't bring cheeseburgers."

*I said he didn't **give** me any cheeseburgers.*

"Wait a damn minute. You sayin' he tease you with the cheeseburgers and don't give you none?"

That's what I'm saying.

"Don't sound like Church at all."

Can't get my mind around Abraham Church. I got to assume any man with the curse is gonna be a strange cat and after a life seein' untruth like a technicolor Picasso makin' the world fucked up ugly, he'll be worn slap out. Get to where wakin' up ain't a joy so much as a mild insult. Feller like that take an interest in a brother like me, and find himself maybe asked for more help'n he want to give, maybe get his nose outta joint and get a little testy. Good people sometimes'll treat other people fairly rotten and it ain't a surprise some of the people so treated is dogs. I don't like it, but without seein' the cheeseburger denial incident myself...

Chicago Mags.

Can't help wonder what the legs is like, and I remain baffled how the woman's wormed into my head without once even openin' her coat.

'Nuther thing. If them legs and tits ain't in order, I dunno. Woman's brain might be too much.

Look about to gather my things and here I see the laundry what was in the machine when I left for the hospital, all dried and folded neat on the bed.

"Stinky Joe?"

Here I am, Master.

"I like it. Hey, who brought the laundry in?"

A blonde woman. Strawberry.

"Cleanin' lady?"

She didn't clean. She brought in clothes.

"Mmm."

Glock on the desk aside me I drop my expropriated acid wash denim and smelly ass polo shirt. Grab a fresh set of socks and sit on the bed's edge in the raw, lift the right foot and give it a little help to the knee with my left hand. Wonder how I'll do the right with the arm in a cast.

I'll confess a flash of hate toward the black booted bastard busted my arm on account I busted his face while he was tryin' to rob and kill me both. One more thug someone decent shoulda put down long ago.

Lotta people like that.

Why don't the locals put down their shitheads? Oh, hell no. Leave it to the itinerant mass murderer.

You're rambling.

"Just a little torqued is all."

Sock half on the foot I whiff the armpit, accidental.

"Ah, hell."

Masterdog need a bath.

Snort. "Yeah. How the hell'm I gonna do that?"

I can't see Mags, me stinkin' like a gut wagon.

Arm cast locks the elbow at ninety degree. Don't want water down in under the plaster so I guess that arm goes high the whole time. That bein' the case, left arm's the only one workin'... how's a feller get the left pit?

Fold the left arm and the hand'll fit the pit. Son of a gun. I'da never thought.

Already nekkid I get the water adjusted hot 'nough to peel a tomato then cool it a degree, as I ain't cannin' Baer. Ma said a shower oughta hurt. I climb in and slip where someone use oil for bath wash. Scrub what I can.

Thud.

Look about. Pull the curtain a foot and poke the head.

Listen.

Nothin'.

"Joe?"

He nose open the door.

"That you?"

Head shake. *Outside.*

Think on it.

Glock's out there in the room and I'm in here balls swingin' like the last time I got my ass beat. That didn't give the results I wanted. Now I'm in the shower slicked up with body lotion, one arm ain't workin' and the brain's muddled on pain or killers or stupidity, one.

Both.

Yank the curtain all the way and careful of the oil slick on the bathtub floor, I climb out drippin'. Peek out the bathroom and Stinky Joe's hopped on the bed and curled 'tween two pillows. Leave water footprints on the tile and carpet to the dresser, grab Glock and though I recollect the status, check the chamber for brass.

Maybe that noise was someone poppin' an Eldorado trunk?

Open the door and a small gust whooshes the curtains. Feel it on the belly. Though I don't need to step outside to verify the Eldorado's parked unmolested, goin' from hot shower to icy outside predawn cold, every hair I got tingles tight and stands on end. First time in sixteen hours I got clarity.

I need to see Mags 'bout a feeling I got, maybe completely bassackwards what she intended. Grab a poke if she'll let me and come back for the girls.

First one thing…

Back inside I shut the door. Fish my wallet from my pants and out the bottom unfold a paper with a number. Press digits in the phone next the bed and wait. No answer. Voicemail.

"Pick up your fuckin' phone."

Dial again. Rings.

"Yeah?"

"That you?"

"Uh."

"Uh-huh. It's you. Listen. You runnin' for governor?"

"What? Who — "

"Girls is in trouble and I'm half busted up too. 'Less you're shootin' for the mansion get your ass up to Glenwood Springs."

"Ba — … — shit. What time is it?"

"Get yourself waked up?"

"Alden? That you?"

"Indeed."

"What kind of trouble are they in now?"

"Best we let that wait for the face to face."

"It's your… Alden."

"What?"

"I'm talking to Mae."

"She there beside you?"

"Yeah, right here."

"Nathan… Ain't you in bed?"

"I married her. I told you that. I asked your permission."

"Oh, shit. Right. Like I say, they bust me up good too. An' I suspect the hospital fed me some drugs."

"You said Glenwood Springs? Colorado?"

"That's right."

"Full day's drive. But I can't do it for two days."

"What you got goin' on?"

"None of your business."

"Fair 'nuff. You be here in two days."

"No, it's a full day's drive. Three days."

"Fine, if that's your best."

"Where do you want to meet?"

"Find a motel called the Lodge on 82. Look for the gold Eldorado."

"The Cadillac? That Eldorado?"

"No, the fuckin' Toyota Eldorado. Who the hell makes an Eldorado but Cadillac?"

"Easy, Grandpa. See you in two days."

"Good. Fuckin' cradle robber. One more thing. Bring ropes like we's going climbing. Oh, and I'd be thrilled beyond my limited capacity for speech if you was to connive a way to bring me a 44 Smith 'n Wesson."

"Forty-four? You been lifting weights? Or you want a sling and tripod too?"

"Eat shit."

"Fuck you."

"All right. Good?"

"Yeah. Good hearing your voice. I'll be there in three days."

"All right, Nat, all right. I appreciate you."

"I appreciate your daughter."

He grunts a laugh and a girl giggle come with it. I never hitched a woman legal with a ring, but I expect it's good to keep the sinful spirit in the fornication, so bein' married don't turn it into a plain old screw.

Now I'm cold and the soap I left on the skin's half dry. Shower's still spillin' steam out the door. I climb back in the tub, rinse what's been washed and figure the rest got wet too. Blow the nose. Chirp a weak fart like the gunpowder got wet and towel off learnin' each step new, now I only got one workin' arm.

Earlier I was thinkin' I'd shoot Frankie Black Boots Lloyd, but longer I deal with this arm I want to find a way to beat him to death instead.

Towel off best I can and since they's fresh clothes folded on the bed I don 'em and take special care not to upset the busted arm. Joe's eyeballs track every motion.

You leaving me here again?

"Nope. Now on, you come everywhere I go."

Yeah. Sure.

"I mean it."

This road trip has something to do with the cast on your arm and the bandage on your head?

"Directly in a roundabout way."

Don't have a hanger for the suit so I fold it loose. Gather what little items is about, a toothpick I been usin' since Albuquerque and a little piece of knotted juniper look like a horse head I found off the road takin' a leak way back outside Flagstaff. Coins, gold and fiat. Leatherman tool. Glock. Wallet. Do a final look about and take what's gathered to the Eldorado. Get Joe in the car and drivin' to the office to leave the key, learnin' how to drive with a useless right arm and the shifter on the right, I commit once more to killin' Frank Lloyd with as much cruelty as is meet and good.

Under the awning I fish a map out the glove box and seems no matter which route I take to Chicago, I go through Denver first. I'll figger the route from there. Mostly I want away from the motel and away from Glenwood Springs. From the map it looks a good thousand mile plus the zig zags, call it another hundred. Eleven hundred mile at a hundred mile an hour is eleven hour. Half that speed is twenty-two hour. Add half that speed back, figure seventy-five mile an hour, pissin' in a bottle and that adds half the time agin. Fifteen hours, plus stops to dump the bottle, as I don't want any extra yellow on the gold paint.

Four AM plus fifteen is nineteen PM on the twenty-four-hour clock or seven PM for us regular folk.

Looks like I'll need a motel agin afore I see Mags.

I showered for nothin'.

82 to the Interstate and I'm outta Glenwood Springs in five minute. No lights behind me 'til I'm five mile up the hill.

One thing I learned in all my hooliganism, as the mighty Clint Eastwood said, even the feller with no limitations oughta mind 'em. I try. Lord I try.

Joe seems all he wants is shut eye and for me it's the opposite. Keep thinkin' if I close my eyes with a concussion behind 'em, who knows if I don't pry 'em back open. Save the mortician some glue, I suppose. But I'm reluctant to blink, reluctant to lean the head agin the rest and I damn sure don't want to find a rest stop and kick off the boots.

So, I stew on what I think I know that don't add up and time I exit for Chicago I got a suspicion the situation in Glenwood Springs with Corazon ain't what I thought at all.

Not a damn bit. But I don't know why.

CHAPTER NINETEEN

The door's open but afore I arrive at the corner to look in and announce myself, part of me says it's time to head back the car, tell Stinky Joe the whole thing was a rotten ass stupid idea on my part and skedaddle back to Colorado.

They must be four billion ladyfolk in the world and I don't give a shit what any of 'em thinks. But this gal up here in Chicago — where the whole city make the point to tell you fuck off, go home, don't come here — got me so tangled I don't know what to say. On account my promise to Stinky Joe I got no likker to help ease into the situation and now I'm outside her door I realize how stupid my line is.

I come back for my coffee.

What kind of lame ass...

Well, I only got two lines and don't got the balls to risk askin' if she'd like to grab a pizza and screw. I'm tired of standing here like a fifteen-year-old boy dreamin' outside the girl's locker room, so here goes...

Step.

Phone rings.

"This is Maggie... yes... no... my office hours are almost over for today, so why don't we discuss the matter tomorrow at two? Good. M-kay. Thanks. Uh-huh. That will be fine. M-kay. Bye."

Now I really want to skip out back to Colorado. She says *m-kay*.

"How long are you going to stand out there?"

Shit.

"Uh." Try to recall my line — either — but she shook 'em both loose. Step into the doorway in my suit and rattlesnake boots. Got the bolo cinched up respectable. Suit jacket don't fit right on account my folded arm slung in under. Maybe fetch a little sympathy.

"Wow," Mags says.

"Thank you."

"You clean up."

"Ain't you supposed to say *nice?*"

"You clean up *nice*."

And now I see you got a rack like the Fourth of July…

Boom.

"You look sweller'n all heck."

She leans back in her chair and crisscrosses her fingers three dozen times afore throwin' her arms over her head and stretchin' her back.

And if that ain't a classic look-at-the-goods invitation…

"I'm stunned," Mags says. "You know, I really felt like we had a connection and I thought it might happen this way, you know? I knew you would find me."

She drops her arms, fluffs her blouse and after she catch me studyin' I know the right move is give her a deep look in the eyes, make her squirm. But I can't help lookin' at her desk fulla papers instead. A wall of books and folders is 'tween me and her. I sit I won't see them ta-tas but she don't look too unhappy I'm here so mebbe I'll set aside the finer survey work for later.

Mags flick her hand toward the chair. "Close the door, first. Or leave a crack. This is a college campus."

I don't get the reference but I swing the door touchin' and sit.

"Your arm! What happened?"

She just now notice. That's real good. No way in royal Scots hell I'm about to start off on the wrong foot with a lie.

"Well these two girls, you see — "

She hold up her hands. "Okay. Too much information."

"No, it was innocent. They didn't do anything. It was the feller with the ball bat come after."

"A man beat you with a baseball bat?"

Shrug. Grin. Maybe I'll buy Frank Lloyd a beer afore I beat him to death.

"Wasn't much to see. I was there in the bath towel on account I was washing all my other clothes — "

Mags is shaking her head now. Smiling too hard for ordinary life to get in. I seen women in similar states erupt into giggles, tears, even a little cluster fart.

"So, I'm there nekkid — "

"Okay." Hands up. "Okay. Enough context. I understand the broken arm." She smiles. Looks down at a paper and lifts a pair of glasses I didn't know she needed and plants 'em on her nose. "He didn't break anything else did he?"

"No, hell no. Everything else is solid. Rock solid."

"Good."

I stand. Point to the picture on her shelf with the knickknacks.

"What?"

"What the hell? That's Günter Stroh."

Her face don't move but her brow looks half past curious — on the way to I don't know what.

"I spent a year with that fella. What? How you get that picture?"

Don't feel the juice nor see the red but the spooky feelin' rise up quick about me. Got to reassess. Open the door and look both ways down the hall. Ain't practiced pullin' Glock from my back left-handed but I reach — and stop. No one in the hallway.

"What's going on? Baer?"

"This don't make sense. How you mixed up in this? Show me your hands."

Her eyeballs is round. She place both hands on the desktop, palms up and empty.

"What is this? What's goin' on?"

"I don't know what you're talking about. I don't know how you know my grandfather. But until we sort it all out, let me remind you that we already agreed this reality isn't the highest order and it's entirely likely your being here was orchestrated at a level so far beyond our capacity to imagine we'll only drive ourselves mad trying to understand."

"You said a mouthful."

"Baer, I'm not the bad guy, or with the bad guy. You came to see me, remember? And I'm so happy you did! Close the door and remove your firearm if it will make you more comfortable to have it accessible while we talk."

Dunno about all this. Woman's too damn smart, what with how a man get confused just lookin' at her. Hips like that wasn't built for carryin' stones. That's a jewel box. An' take a gander at them bodacious —

"Baer?"

"No, it's all right. I don't understand much any of this but it's like you say. I got this feelin' I need to see you and I don't know why."

"Not even a guess?"

"Well, no. I didn't even know your uh... purtyness... afore coming here."

More blush work.

"No offense, accourse."

"None taken."

"You want to get some coffee? Or maybe let's grab a pizza and screw..."

Lotta people inside. We're on the coffee house sidewalk, all the street people in they suits swarm by on the hour and the half hour. I had more coffee the last sixty minute than the previous million five.

"Baer, a man like you — any man, any person — he builds a life. He works and studies. He grows his wealth and his possessions and even a family. When he's old he thinks all of these things he built, the associations between them, the networks, the bank accounts — he identifies with all these inanimate things. He believes they are him. How could it be otherwise? That's where his thought-world has been. But history isn't identity. Those things aren't him. They're not his essence. His cells will disappear and the energy that animates them will fizzle back to empty vibrations in space."

Mags is excited. Leans in.

"Exactly right," says I. "Yup."

One more button, I'd see somethin' purty.

"Except it isn't empty because somewhere else out there is the real man."

"Real man. M-hmm."

"The real man isn't the image on the wall. The real man is like a slide in an old-fashioned projector. The real man is where the true identity resides. He's in the nonlocal."

"He ain't a union man."

She smiles pretty. "Are you following me?"

"Anywhere."

Rolls her eyes.

"You're saying the real me ain't in my brain. It's out there somewhere."

"That's right. Here's what you need to understand, Baer. Us — our bodies, this table, your coffee — are images on the wall. They are projections. Your thoughts and soul and all that matters about you, that all comes from somewhere else. The real you, the deeper you, projects it in."

"Sounds pretty neat."

"You see, the problem with materialism is that nothing real is material."

Things she's saying... back of my head I feel I known 'em all my life.

"Our neural pathways are inherited. We aren't responsible for our birthplace, sex, religion, economic status, or anything like that at all. Our minds are learning computers — but we aren't responsible for the program our brains are running when we're born. Those programs run along neural pathways created by the thought lives of prior generations. Next, you're not responsible for the experiences you have as a child, that inform your brain and rewrite the neural pathways in your brain. Last, we're born into an unobligated world that cares not whether we live or die. Nature is harsh and the people who are around us are just as confused. Everyone is prone to lash out. To lie, cheat, steal — and most of the time, they do it in a manner so subtle you won't even realize it when it happens.

"So if you're not responsible for any of the stuff that physically comprises you when you're born — the particular arrangement of chemicals that form your body, and if you're not responsible for the capacity of the brain you're running, and if you're not responsible for the program your brain is running at birth... and you're not responsible for the experiences that shape you... at what point do you become responsible for the wreck you now perceive you are?

"Because one thing is sure. Regardless of the fact that you didn't cause your birth, didn't cause your brain, or your early experiences and are not responsible for them, you alone reap the consequences.

"This means blame and responsibility are not the same thing, and it's a quandary that causes many people to never develop into full fledged human beings. See, if you can't embrace responsibility for things you didn't do, you'll never be aware of the miracle implicit in your makeup: the ability to cause yourself to be something different of your choosing. The two are inseparable. You have to accept responsibility for yourself in a certain situation to be able to muster proactive behavior, rather than reactive behavior. You have to reject yourself as you are born or you'll never actuate your true highest potential. I'm not talking about money or success.

"This is a profound point, so I'll make it again. If you embrace your nature as you were born saying this is what God made me, you miss the entire point of human existence. We were created as turds — and if all we do is embrace what we are, well, you've heard the saying."

Mags folds her hands together and watch my face.

"Can't polish a chunk of shit."

"I haven't heard it in that dialect before, but yes. Anyhow, how many people do you see that seem to have all the swagger and self confidence in the world, but all you really see is a shiny chunk of poop? Instead, we ought to think about it this way. All of us are born turds, so what are turds good for?"

"Fertilizer."

"Exactly right. Making things grow. Instead of polishing undeveloped potential, why not *become something* and polish what you become?"

"You're saying I'm no good as I am?"

"Are you satisfied with who you are? Do you know what you know and own what you own? Or do you sometimes wonder whether you have your values in the right order? Sometimes wonder why you don't live up to how you see yourself?"

"Uh."

"Yeah. That's the right answer. It's hard because we need to honor potential but not be satisfied with it. We need to love and embrace the turd, while not settling for it. All while the rest of the world is picking at us, probing us for weakness, calling us out for being turds, and ignoring that inside we're blooming into roses."

"What says I got to be a rose?"

"You don't like flowers?"

"It ain't that. Maybe I ain't somethin' nice."

Mags sips coffee. "I will confess that some things exist which are perfect, but which are not nice. Let's not get bogged down. The point is that your existence is not designed to be static. Being the rose is a metaphor. I'm talking about two planes of existence. One is animal, but full of potential. The other is human, consisting of the animal, but shaped by conscious will. Folks locked in the animal place don't tend to enjoy their lives because beauty always results from order and the animal resents order. The animal can't even see higher order."

"Blind to it, you say."

"Whereas people who shape their lives according to their best-conceived beliefs… those people own their minds and walk free."

"Sign me up."

She smiles. Stops. "Why did you come here?"

"Uh."

"Because that sounded like a smart assed challenge."

"Guess I'm sayin', how's a person do all that? I been around fifty-two, three year and ain't figured it out."

"You kind of figured it out. At least enough to be unhappy."

"Magnificent."

"The way you do it is by rewiring your brain. Remember what I said. Your thoughts follow pathways in your brain. You inherit the first of them, then develop the rest as you learn. As you think and stew on things, your brain is literally turning those thoughts into things. Clusters of neurons, like a superhighway of the same thoughts, over and over. Ever get a thought you couldn't let go of?"

"I'm familiar."

"You have to arrest the process. You have to, in the midst of your thought, say, this thought is untrue. This thought is not me. This thought is not valid, because I've mis-associated it with other things. I've given this thought the wrong value. And then you have to think of the right value. When you do this over and over, you break down the neural pathways that foster the thought. You literally change your mind. To take it to the next level, do you think God — whatever God you believe in — hates you for being a bundle of potential?"

"Wait. That's what you just called a turd."

"Right. Does God hate you for being a turd? A mind that isn't responsible for its birth, learning program, or initial experiences that feed the learning. Does God hold it against you that He made you?"

"Don't seem right."

"Of course not. Religion is up to you to figure out, but my two cents: I don't care for the Christian church, but Jesus gets it right. Limited, of course, by the language of the time. Honoring where we came from, striving to become holy and loving while seeing the best in others, that ought to be our ambition. And asking our creator's help in becoming fully actualized, and his forgiveness for when we err on account of our animal nature... it's all a loving, growing, nurturing thing."

"No fire and brimstone?"

"No, I don't think that comes from God. I think it comes from human beings who want to control other human beings. Remember, to a Christian the church isn't the building, it's the community of believers. Like any institution, it has the same competing forces as the individuals within it."

I nod. Wish she'd say it all three more times, from the start.

"And your thoughts about justice and killing are related. Just as you have to recognize the truth about yourself — you're born a turd and remain one until you deliberately become something else — you have to recognize it about other people. They're turds too — but with potential. And just as your creator doesn't hate you for being where you are and is always encouraging you forward… He's doing that for everyone else too. Even the people who hurt you."

Look at the ground. The sky. Got a balled-up jumble of underwear in my crack and alla sudden my throat's a little dry.

Thought I gave up underwear.

"That's what forgiveness is all about. Recognizing that even the most selfish or evil person you ever meet is just like you. Responsible for things he didn't choose, trying to make his way through a world that keeps screwing him. Trying to take care of himself and the people he loves."

"Even the thieves."

"Especially the thieves."

"The dog fighters. Kid fuckers. All 'em."

"All of them. If you can't let go of the harm they caused you, if you can't see them as working through the same plight as you, then you're clinging to the animal part of your existence. The selfish part. You're being the same thing they are. You're rejecting the higher plane of love, growth and forgiveness. You're wallowing in the corruption you claim to loathe."

I study my paper coffee cup and a gust knock it over.

Mags say, "That's why some people will tell you it's impossible to feel forgiven until you first forgive. Deep down we know we don't deserve it."

"You buy that?"

"Me? No. I'm a physicist. I think in terms of energy fields and equations, not signifying networks."

"What?"

"Another time, maybe."

"Good."

"Baer, listen to me. You came to see me because you want relief from your mind. Relief from your guilt. You want a path to atonement. This is what you must learn: your atonement is linked to your ability to forgive. Mercy toward someone else is the same as mercy toward yourself, but you have to get out of your own way. Forgiving others isn't an act of virtue; it's an act of humility."

"Don't ken your meaning."

"What is atonement?"

"Shit. Like from a dictionary?"

"It means," Mags says, "getting right with your creator. Break down the word. At-One-Ment. You can't be congruent with the Eternal while you're bubbling with anger, guilt and shame. You have to let go of all of that and accept forgiveness. Like you, the people you hate were born into circumstances they didn't choose and were programmed from their first sight that girls play with dolls and boys torture bugs. Their environments provided signals and their brains — taught by the people who shaped them, like giving them a map and saying, navigate life this way — their brains computed the scenes, sorted the disasters and chose a life path just like you did, without any divine road map or instruction manual telling them how everything works. You're the same as the one you hate — and since you refuse to forgive yourself, you refuse to forgive him. But he has the same birthright of forgiveness as you."

She's lookin' at me and I'm all clevered out.

"I'll say it again. Your birthright is forgiveness and you unlock it with genuine humility."

"That's the problem."

"Well, it has to stem from humility, from powerlessness."

"Ehhh. I dunno."

"No other forgiveness is real. You say you forgive and inside nothing changes. The person who harmed you has done nothing to make you feel better. He doesn't deserve your forgiveness. On the outside you force yourself to give grace, but inside you hold him accountable. This forced grace…you imagine it is a virtue. And here's where it gets suicidal: you can't even muster the same forced empathy toward yourself because you think grace needs to be deserved — despite *that* being precisely the ingredient that is excluded from the recipe. Broken people give grace because they want to cling to the idea they're better than the one they hate. Please don't mishear me. I'm not making a moral argument. My world is math and energy. To me, this is all a matter of whether you want to feel right with yourself and the world you live in or not. If you do, then develop yourself. Destroy the bad and replace it with what you value more. That's how you get right with the world. That's how you find atonement. Find the humility to rebuild something better."

We talk on and on.

CHAPTER TWENTY

People've cleared out. Streets kept fillin' up every half hour and now the shadows is long and the air ain't so comfortable. Mags and me drunk sixteen cups of joe and ate five bagels. Me, four.

"You're capable of talkin' more'n I'm capable of listenin'."

"I doubt that very much," Mags says.

We sit lookin' at each other. I got a new understandin' on things. Or maybe feel I'm at the foot of a mountain and know damn well the trail leads to enlightenment, if I got the gumption to walk it.

But this mountain I'm about to climb, I don't know if Mags'll think I'm headed at the right peak. That's where I'm about to disagree.

Long story short, if I wasn't made to be what I am then I can't fathom what I'm suppose to be. I don't know how you add up a whore mother, who was the best lady I ever knew, an electrocuted boy, a cursed and failed life — wrap it all up with a love of sacred truth and a hatred of all things lies…. And loyalty to justice. And the knowledge if I don't make it just, then it won't be.

I don't see how to get them ingredients to cook up another man but the one they cooked.

His name ain't Alden Boone and it ain't Günter Stroh, neither.

But me and Mags been touchin' fingers a couple times and the last she hooked the pinky on mine, I 'bout drug her to the alley for a standing romp. It's maybe time to stop the philosophics and loose the animals to the sheets.

"So how 'bout that pizza?"

Maggie stands.

Her head turns.

I hear the motorcycle engine like a buzz saw.

Turn.

See the flashes and hear the snap sounds, not even fuckin' manly bullets.

I spin and launch but Mags is already goin' down. Her head bounce on concrete and she got blood all up her blouse. She stares while red drip out her mouth and nose, until the stare go flat.

Mags says, "It's beautiful. Find me."

And I understand it couldn't happen no way but this, and the Almighty just put a big exclamation point after all she said.

CHAPTER TWENTY-ONE

I run at the Eldorado. I was lucky. Afore I met Mags for coffee I found a decent parkin' space on the road around the corner not but six cars away. Spot the orange ticket on the run. Yank it off the windshield and jump in the car.

Joe's 'bout to shake to pieces.

What the hell was that? A machine gun?

"Mags is shot dead."

Can't figure the gear shifter for thirty seconds. See the R for Reverse but Mags' face is blooded up and her eyes faded out like when I watch TV as a kid and the whole station shut down at night, and the tie with the rest of the world vanished just like that. I see Mags vanish and the eyes go dead.

Hit the gas and try to recall which road is which but all these buildings is exactly the same. Tall and square and ugly like a cancer wart. People like to jump out front the car. Keep turnin' left and though the traffic ain't what it was when I fought my way to the coffee shop, my nerves is jumbled.

"I said they shot Maggie. You got no wisdom on that?"

And you didn't shoot back?

"They was gone too quick. Cafe's on the corner there and they come around on a motorcycle shootin'. Time I was on my feet they was gone."

Joe got his face agin the windshield.

Are we hunting them?

"Sit back 'fore I send you through the glass. Accourse we're huntin' 'em. They was on a motorcycle. Come right by here."

What color?

"White."

You sure? That doesn't sound right.

"Was you asleep or guardin' the station? It was fuckin' white and the people on it was dressed regular. Blue jeans. Jackets. Helmets cover the face. Shooter was maybe a girl. Skinny with a pony tail."

I keep seein' Mags and after drivin' three fourths a square and almost turnin' back where I come, I drive another block and widen the circle. Turn left each time so I sit at the light and watch, but even with a moment stopped and brain space opened up for computin', it don't make sense. Shooters ain't circlin'. But it's a pattern I can hold and feel like I'm doin' somethin' while the disbelief waves through me like a cannon boom 'til the sound cut me down same as lead.

"I lost my temper, Joe."

I accept your apology.

"You're a scholar and a gentleman."

I keep the distance to the next car and let the buildings roll by.

I saw Mags die and I saw her happy in it. And I'm the most profane bastard in the world, as part of my mind is on her body and what I'll never see of it. We was right there and I already see her naked and hungry in the mind's eye. I go from that to red holes in her blouse and blood drippin' out her smile. Eyes sparkle but not lookin' at me, lookin' at the other side, and somehow she saw me like a ghost in the better world and she turn back to tell me, *it's beautiful. Find me.*

I can imagine all that as true.

But in this material world I adjust the rearview and check my eyes, see if I'm here.

Got Mags's blood on my face.

I was gonna mention that. Waiting for a better time.

"Right."

I rub Joe's shoulder. Leave the blood on my cheek where it is.

Sign point to the highway and it don't seem I can do nothin' here, plus the likelihood I stumble on the correct route outta this soggy fart of a city is nil, so I cut the wheel and get a bluehair pissed enough to set her bird a-flyin' and her horn a honkin'.

Still got Glock in my back and with the right arm in the cast and the left on the wheel, I gotta steer with the knees to fetch the gun. I do. I'm committed. But time I fish it out the ass of my drawers, the bluehair's braked and turned right.

Keep the pistol on the seat so the next shithead wants to share an opinion, I'll have a retort ready.

"Mags is dead."

Come barrelin' up the onramp and figure if I take the lane, the car that's there'll let me. He does and I recognize I'm the asshole in the equation.

Most wonderful thing in the world is a handful of woman.

"My mind feels kinda fucked, Puppydog."

You hide it... not so convincingly.

This whole thing's so big I can't ken it. How many days I curse the sky just darin' the Almighty to show himself real, even if he kill me to do it? And now he set up a batch of circumstances so perfect... it's like a set of straws all criss crossed and jumbled, and I shift six inches right and they's all lined perfect, or better yet, say somethin' like *Hey dipshit I'm lookin' at you.* Then you go back to center and six inches past and they's lined up agin and the words say *But you never even try to look at Me.* And finally back at center instead of a messed up jumble like it was, now it says, *Yours Truly...*

And they's no signature 'cause they ain't but One can do shit like that.

The act is the signature.

Mags is dead and I could bawl like a baby if it wasn't for the uncanny impossibility of how the whole show unfolded. Like it was staged the same day they stole Fred and put the wrecking ball in motion. Or they arrange the details when I kicked Larry in the nuts. Or maybe from day one, not when my father plant me in my mother but when Adam bent Eve over a rock and fucked not just her but all humanity after, when he plant the first seed outside the Garden.

Who shot Mags?

Dunno.

CIA? She'd talk physics to anyone and wouldn't look down on government people, even if they confess it up front. Who the hell knows? The University?

I bet the government's got all sorta people in caves full of computers and particle accelerators and radio tubes. They got the geniuses with IQs like bowling scores — the good bowlers — workin' day and night to figger how to use them quantum physics to murder men by the billion. I bet a bunch of somebodies like that don't much care for the love approach. Maybe Mags wrote a book.

What'd Eisenhower say when he pass the throne to Kennedy?

Ike says, "The business of killin' people is *big* business."

I know one damn thing. I don't care if it's some CIA spook or a soy-nut grad student had a crush on Mags and cut her down 'cause she told him *no*.

Whoever shot Mags….

I'm gonna cut his fuckin' head off and when I get to the land with the corpses in the trees I'm gonna fix it to a trunk with a nine inch spike.

Grip the wheel so tight it hurt the hand. Lookin' that way I see the speedometer and take the foot off the gas. Last thing I need's another entanglement with the law. When the speedometer drop to sixty-five I hold the needle steady.

Spooks killed Mags?

Mind's dull. Tired.

"Joe, listen to me. If I asked Maggie I bet she'd say her dyin' — she'd say it don't even matter. If what she said is true, she's already re-lived her whole time on earth."

Joe's speechless. He keep a lookout for the white motorcycle.

I drive and stew. Dotted lines attack the hood.

"Bullshit," says I.

No way in hell I let Chicago off the hook without I hunt somebody down. I cut the wheel and hit the brake. Rumble onside the road and throw up some dust. Gold coin rattle in the trunk.

Semi trucks blast by and shake the car, six in a row. One let on the horn. Ain't enough room 'tween the white line and the guardrail to park but I'm stopped and these kind folk'll give me grace on the park job or else.

No. Drive forward, this is stupid.

Look at Joe.

Do it.

I put the shifter in drive and scoot next the guardrail 'til it end and I can get off the highway. Lift Glock off the seat and hold it left handed then right. Can't bend the arm, can't extend it neither.

I got a solution.

Fetch the Leatherman off my belt and flip it open to the saw. It's the lower part of my arm that's busted so why lock above the elbow? I saw 'round the plaster just below the joint and soon spot blood in the white powder.

You want to open a window before I sneeze?

"You do it."

I keep sawing: Flip. Saw. Bleed. I don't care. I chuck the Leatherman to the console and punch the last two inch of the cast 'til the plaster snaps. I rip gauze, roll the window and chuck the sawed-off ring. Now plaster only covers what's broke. I flex the arm and my elbow pops.

You got it about worked out?

'Nother truck slams by so fast the boat seems to float.

"I feel like I gotta go back to Chicago and hunt down a couple dead men."

You can't.

"What?"

Tat and Corazon... their situations are time sensitive.

"You are a well spoken dog, a credit to your species. But I learned what I am. We're goin' back."

I look over the shoulder for traffic, figger I'll cross the median ahead a bit where it don't seem too rough. But they's a string of cars and I got to wait. Breathe. Try and keep the hate from makin' me punch whatever's handy.

Me.

Stinky Joe paws my right arm 'til I look.

Whatever you learned, I know it didn't make you disloyal to the people who are still alive and need you.

"You're a son of a bitch, you know that?"

You know I'm right.

Scruff his ears and let him slop my face. He ain't a woman but it's love and though I'm still so coldhearted I could shit a plate of iceberg lettuce, I take Joe's lovin' 'til I realize sittin' in the Eldorado next the highway ain't the brightest thing I done this year.

Break in the traffic, here's my shot. I engage the turn signal and gas it to highway speed.

I'm glad. I didn't want to ride five hours back to Chicago.

"Well, just so you know, we will go back to Chicago. That will happen."

God willing.

"I'll bet my life on it."
Your soul?
"That's where the life is."

Fillin' up at the Sinclair gas mart, I lean on the trunk and study Mags' face in the clouds.

"Hey there, you from here?"

I turn and look around the pump. Woman one over, got that sloppy blowjob look about the jaw. Eyes like pickpocket kids.

"Lady.... *Fuck* —"

Slam the door. Back on the road.

I got a idea on the off ramp to Glenwood Springs. Circle 'round and up into town at a cool thirty five mile per hour and hold steady down the strip. Pass the Mexican food joint and a bank. A pharmacy and grocery. Another bank. Some houses and a park and the next Mexican food joint.

Back a day ago I'd a found a new motel on account I need to lay low. But if I'm suppose to be what I am then what I am is hungry for a feller named Frankie Black Boots Lloyd to find me.

Pull into the Lodge and park under the roof. Leave the window down for Stinky Joe and mash the fists to the eyes — 'cept the right arm don't feel good even with the pressure it take to mash an eye. A little splash of water'd be nice but all I got is recycled Mountain Dew.

Go in bleary.

"Mister Boone... you've returned."

Nod. She ain't too endeared, from her look.

"I'm okay. Thanks for askin'."

She flat-smiles me.

"I got beat to shit in your laundry room."

She look at me and her face is dull but they's motion underneath like an idea comin' up she druther keep down. Must be why her eyes is pink.

"You saw me beat up?"

Shakes her head and I get a zap of juice.

"You saw. I see lies. You saw."

"I found you."

"You found me."

No red. No juice.

She leans. Looks back the hall to the office.

"Umm, I can't talk about this. I feel bad for you but I can't help you."

"Help me how?"

"With information."

"What information? I know it was Frank Lloyd."

She nods and looks away.

"That ain't the information. You just said that."

Frown. "I *can't*—"

"I bet you will… afore we's done."

She shake her head. Close her eyes. "I can't say." She clamps her mouth and talk through her teeth. "These people will *kill* me."

Study her long.

"Who else? Frank Lloyd and who else?"

"I can't say."

"Try and you'll find you can."

"I can't."

"I won't leave."

Her jaws clamp and her eyes get skinny. Cheeks red. Right eye spills a tear.

"If I tell you…"

"Dammit."

"If I tell you, *you are responsible for me*."

"Ahhh fu—. Fine. You're right. You're exactly right. I'll honor that. You tell me who was with Frank Lloyd and you'll never have to fear either of 'em again."

"Abraham Church."

Chicago Mags said she thought comin' to earth as a human being was like goin' in a pod.

They stick a soul in a baby and it's like goin' on holiday or sabbatical.

But it seem to me this place is a prison where the Almighty sends the shitheads for a time out. Shove a kid's nose in the corner. Some these people live a hundred five years, they was in big trouble in heaven and earn the longest sentence on earth.

Maybe as souls they was right bastards.

Then you got the babies that pass in the crib, or the stillborns and they get but a few days or even no time at all on this earth as sentence.

Easy time, a rap on the wrist. The Almighty called 'em home so's life in this world don't get a chance to fuck 'em up.

Mags works at the university where they puff each other's brains with nonsense and it feels like a vacation, all the wants supplied.

But most the people that ever is or was go hungry and suffer like fools.

Nah—hell.

This ain't vacation.

It's incarceration.

Don't matter if a man say somethin's right or wrong. Unjust or intolerable. Men tolerate the wrong and unjust every day.

A man can say anything he want about rights and what he'll tolerate.

Only matters if he's ready to bleed once he says it.

CHAPTER TWENTY-TWO

"Hello, Nat. Stinky Joe, say hello to Nat Cinder of Arizona fame and the future governor."

He hold out the hand and I shake it. He slap my back. Squeeze the shoulder like it good to see me. He's shift' shapin' into a politician.

Nat say, "I want to get something out of the way so we can make the best use of our time."

"Get it out the way. I don't care. Damn."

"Sometimes the only way to avoid a shitty outcome is to have the discretion to not participate."

"Well ain't that a hell of a thing? Then why you here?"

"I'm not talking about me. I'm talking about you. Sit this one out; I got it."

"Bullshit."

"You're still contending with your leg injury. Are you seeing a doctor for that? Leg's probably half rotted out by now if you haven't. I saw your step as you were walking to the van. And now you've got a broken arm and a knot on your forehead."

I'll confess the skull is more tender'n I'd expect for bone. But still...

"Bull Shit."

Cinder look past me like it's the decent thing; let me soak in misery 'til I think things his way.

"Won't work. I don't give two shits if you was the Green Beret Grand Poobah or whatever the hell you call it. I call you here for help, not to turn shit over."

"I told her you'd say that. Fine. I won't fight you on it. But you can be the one to tell her."

"Who? Ruth?"

"Ruth? Like she'd worry about you now that she has a steady man in her life. They married last month."

"Ruth married? In weeks? No shit."

"None. No shit at all."

"Is he? Does he treat her right?"

"Baer — don't look like that. She wasn't your woman anymore. You made sure she knew it."

"I said does he treat her right?"

"No. But I have an eye on him."

Step back. Got a flutter in the heart and that pressure start to come in on me like when I was at the bottom of Farmer Brown's house with the whole thing burnin' above, and I saw how the conspiracy was founded. How Ernie Gadwal and Burley Worley team up with Stipe and his lugnuts so the whole bloodthirsty cabal was set to steal my operation or kill it, which is what they done. I oughta go back and murder 'em agin is what I oughta do, 'cause killin' 'em the first time didn't kill 'em enough.

But now this situation is the same and it's almost a daily struggle how the shit comes a-flyin'. Almost like each day's got to provide the friction, the pain, else whoever's along for the ride in the pod don't get the show they pay for.

Mags said someone bought the jackass ride. Guess I oughta raise my hand or somethin'.

Whole situation's too funny. Rigged. Make a man think he's in a movie and the star of the show but he don't get the blowjobs and drugs like the movie stars. Now the actor's a work horse. You got the beginning, middle, end. Each scene the shit gets worse and worse and pretty soon it's insane-funny. Cosmic funny. You see the next drop coming. You know the bad guys'll show up on the mountain ridge and you even know the fuckin' drum music afore you hear it. See the white guy wearin' red paint with a plastic feather in his hair. You see the set, all the way through. The joists under how they tell a story, the studs holdin' up each level. What makes 'em laugh — your pain — takin' away the things you love — over and fuckin' over — but you see it from inside-out 'cause your life is the pod car these yay-hoos take on safari. The show must go on, right? Horseshit. What next? Mae's dead? The babies? Every show needs someone dead. Mags, yesterday, Ruth, maybe tomorrow. They got Corazon and Tat cued up.

Men fight men 'cause they can't fight the Almighty.

"They fuckin' killed Mags, Cinder. They fuckin' killed her and no reason other'n to fuck with me. That's it."

"Whoa. Easy. Who's Mags?"

"A woman."

"Wait a minute. What's up with your eyes? You been smoking the weed?"

"Naw, fuck that."

"How long's it been since you slept?"

"What? Why?"

"You were out of it there, a couple minutes."

"Didn't feel like I was entirely *in it* either."

"In what?"

"What?"

He look.

I look.

"How's Mae?"

"You'll have to be the one to tell her you wouldn't listen to reason. Look, Baer, I got this. I have the badge. I'm a Deputy US Marshall. I go in, cuff her to my wrist and sign a form."

"Which form? I'll sign it."

"You can't sign it. You're not the Deputy."

He hold up the badge hangin' by a neck lanyard.

"Well shit, Nat. You ain't a Deputy neither. It's a fake badge. I'm goin' too. Tat's mine. She's my responsibility — that way."

Nat hang his head. Well played. The whole thing kinda surreal. Sometimes I don't know and ain't sure.

Which world.

"Nat — about breakin' out Tat and Corazon, when I was in the hospital I notice each place I walk about the floor in the blue gown everybody's lookin' my ass. We can use that."

"You didn't tie the gown in back?"

"They got ties?"

"No. Baer, I said what I'm doing. If you want me to bring you along in handcuffs as a prop, I will. In fact, that's a good idea. But I got this. And what I said a minute ago — you're the one to tell Mae that you wouldn't listen to reason."

"Whatever. We got to move."

"She made me promise not to let you come."

"Now you're like the other fellas, promise what they can't deliver. Quit the bullshit. This is the plan. You wear the glasses. I know the room we can swipe a white jacket so you look the doctor. You play the doctor, right?"

Cinder shake his head. Look away.

"Now I got the Glock — you bring me a Smith like I ask?"

Cinder frown. Hold my eye. "You tell me straight. Your eyes are fucked up."

"Well shit, Cinder. Call a man out."

"Tell me straight. I'm not one you can play any other way."

"Dammit."

"Dammit what? Drugs?"

"Naw, shit. Is all."

"What?"

"You don't let up."

"Not when I care."

"I was fuckin' cryin'."

Shake his head. "Bullshit." He look close. "You sure? From the look of your eyes that was a hell of a lot of crying."

"Fifteen hours of it. I met a woman was about to unveil the whole thing, reveal the inner workings of the universe. What with the quantum physics. And she had tits like I dunno. I never saw 'em."

"Sometimes those are the best."

"Yeah, well... Not very fuckin' often."

"Probably not."

Cinder look away and I look away. Sky's blank. So numb I can't think. Bottled up. Beat down. So mad I don't even know if justice is worth the trouble.

I think I'm gonna kill for the killin's sake.

"Cinder, when all is said and done in Glenwood Springs, I'm goin' to Chicago, and I'm gonna say it, and do it, agin."

"Yeah. Maybe you need to. But here, tonight, this is how I'm going to play it. I have a Deputy US Marshall's badge..."

CHICAGO MAGS

"There is an eternal version of you on the other side that sometimes people think of as like a lower, more primitive consciousness. This is exactly backwards. Your brain has components that handle more and more advanced bodily functions, such as the medulla, or what you might call the reptile brain. But your subconscious isn't created in your brain, and fixing attributes to your consciousness based on a flawed theory of its design is... well... precisely incorrect."

"I see."

"In fact, the easiest way to understand it is by imagining that your subconscious mind isn't in your brain, but is somewhere far distant and is beamed in."

"Somewhere distant."

"The other side. The other dimension. Did you grow up listening to the Doors?"

"Ma was known to slam a door or two."

"The music group."

Head shake. "That ain't music. Now if they'd a had a banjo — "

"Anyway. Okay, we'll try it this way. You ever heard of people going on sojourns, to find themselves?"

"Hippy bullshit. They's right there."

"Baer, you're being ornery."

Hornery too.

"I'll stop. Promise. They's findin' 'emselves."

"The point I'm making is that human beings in every culture have different ways of expressing their sense that the most important part of their identity is somehow apart from them and mostly unknown to them. Even though it is immensely important in understanding what drives their behaviors. People all over the world have felt that not only is there more to the world than they understand, but infinitely more about themselves as well."

"You're a chip off the block. Günter talk like that."

"I wish I could have known him."

Have to explore that later, once we get through with the quantum... enlightenment.

"The other thing about the eternal self is that sometimes it breaks through into our conscious self to inform us, or console us, or even help us see the bigger picture. You see, the physical you is an animal. Your consciousness resides in the body of an animal."

"That's the truth."

"I remember a time when I was very young, barely conscious as I think of it now. I remember listening to a majestic song and being overwhelmed by feelings and ideas that I'd never had before, with words in English but so foreign to my way of thinking they might as well have been in another language."

"What song?"

"Fanfare for the Common Man. I remember thinking about my father. I was twenty something at the time. I remember thinking about how hard my father worked so I could have a safe place to sleep at night. How he worked overtime at a job he hated because his obligation to his wife — my mother — and me and my sisters was so much more to him than satisfying his own wants. The world is full of men like that. And women. And here's this song with soaring brass and booming drums celebrating all those people. I was overwhelmed and I sobbed."

"Uh."

"You don't see the whole picture, but it is this: all of that emotion and understanding came from a different me. An eternal me that lives in the nonlocal, that is steeped in love. She was introducing herself that day, and she has returned to teach me different lessons over and over throughout my life."

Mags study my face. I got to say somethin' intelligent.

"Uh… What she teach?"

"That all of life is not suffering and all of it is not useless. Sometimes the eternal self wants us to be aware that there is value and worth and reason somewhere, even if we don't see it. Reality is bigger and better than we can see or understand. Magnificent things are real and our true reality on the other side is what we can only think of on this side as magical."

"Like good sex. What? Don't look like that. I mean it."

Mags close her mouth while it fill up with air. Release it through a flat frown. "I wonder about you. I don't know what I'm thinking sometimes."

"Ain't a good poke just like you talk about?"

"You're serious. Not being funny?"

"I come fifteen hours to say hello."

"Okay, well then, yes."

CHAPTER TWENTY-THREE

Hands is cuffed at the back and Cinder put a cut on my brow next the bat circle where Frank Lloyd punch-drilled for oil. Caught a good study in the window reflection and I ain't been so cut and bruised since Larry and me was sixes and sevens. Got my jacket buttoned wrong and shirt pulled out. Cinder try to put mud on my elbow — on my new suit — and I said you know next Tuesday? I'll kick your ass to the next in after and Cinder relent, put the mud on my brow instead.

In the elevator I say, "You think you're gonna sweet talk this hardened lawman into giving up the biggest prize since Ted Bundy escaped the Glenwood Springs prison?"

"That true?"

"I'm sayin' it."

"No, about Bundy. He was here?"

"Well that nugget come from a gas station lady and most of them's about as no-bullshit as I ever see."

"Interesting."

"That's it? Nothin' on what I said on your plan bein' dumb as —

you know I was gonna say dumb as a rock but I better ask Mags if rocks is dumb as they seem."

"Thought you said she was dead."

"She's dead as Elvis. Dead as Jim, Jimi and Janis. And you still ain't answered how you intend to run this, since my plan ain't good enough. Oh, and Mama Cass, too."

"Baer, you're in cuffs. That's the plan."

Elevator dings. Doors close.

Cinder say, "Listen. Confidence comes from your ability to project the image you want your enemy to see. When you go into a tactical situation, no one has complete information. Every man's trying to accomplish his mission without missteps, but he never has enough trustworthy information. Today I lack information. So does my adversary. So I'll provide some noises that'll sound like facts. I'll add some intimidation to hurry a bad decision, and if the shit hits the fan, I'll try to keep in mind that God favors the bold."

Door dings and opens.

"Or we could just shoot some people," says I.

Cinder hold my arm and stop my exit. Put his boot in the door.

"It doesn't need to come to that."

"Well they got a suspicious copper up there when I come by the other day. Be ready for that."

"You talked to him? He saw you?"

"Yeah. That spoil your plan?"

"No, it means I caught you prowling around the hospital planning Tat and Corazon's escape. Which is why the Department of Justice decided to move them immediately. This works nicely."

"We're ten steps from *Go!* and you just figured out the plan. Remarkable."

Cinder pull back his boot from the door and lead me out the elevator. Next stop is the police, and Tat.

I bump Cinder as he walk too slow. He got the shoulders back and chest out. Brief case in one hand and on the other wrist, a chain from his to mine. Cinder wear the glasses that go dark outside and since we was just outside they's still dark.

Me in handcuffs led right to the law…

This is *stupid*.

Cold sweat roll from behint the right ear. Handcuffs chafin'. If I was ever cuffed like this for real I'd be in a fight to keep my innner freeman from mountin' a last ditch burn-the-camp effort to loose myself quick. And if they got me inside a jail with cuffs like this behind the back, and each step lead me deeper to a cement room I'd never leave for good and me livin' accordin' to other people's rules, state rules, prison rules, so I got no say over where I sleep or shit, nor what I eat or drink, and no say in comin' or goin' 'cause they ain't no comin' or goin', just sittin' and rottin', I might lay on the tile and die.

We come 'round the corner at Tat's hospital room and Cinder shove me agin the wall.

Tat's guard jerk himself upright in the chair.

Cinder say, "I'm Deputy US Marshall Tinson George and you'll address me as Deputy or Deputy George. Nurse, how long do you need to finish your task?"

She don't look up while she fiddles with a needle in Tat's arm.

"I'm done."

"What is your name?"

"Nurse Priscilla."

"Your last name."

"Bond."

"Nurse Priscilla Bond, please wait outside the room. I'll need you in three minutes."

She turn her head and throw a dirty look at Cinder but when she see his full form — tall and got that look the women dig, wide shoulders, shiny shoes and badge, looks like he could lift a house with one hand and rescue a broke-wing bird with the other — she wilts a smidgen and says, "Yes, sir."

Past her I watch Tat.

I only seen Tat make her private intimate face once in the daylight and she make the same face now, seein' me and Nat come to save her. Face says she wanna yell and buck but got to keep the voice low so we don't knock the Mustang off its jack stands and wake Corazon at the other side the garage. Seein' Nat and me dressed like law and disorder get her charged up. Her eyes sparkle like she saw magic but she keep the joy tamped under the same scowl she wore when Nat and me first come around the corner and into the room.

Cinder look at the cop in the chair and I think if I was that cop, if I had a problem or anticipate I was gonna do somethin' in response to the evolving situation, I wouldn't keep my ass glued in the seat. I'd get light on the heels.

Cop look at Cinder. "Uh. Was I supposed to do something?"

"Your command group received the order from Justice but if you're just learning of the transfer now, your superiors didn't alert you. When the process works like it's supposed to, your side has its CYA documents ready to go."

"I'm sorry."

"Officer — ?"

"Dugan."

"This happens often enough it's not a concern. I brought Department of Justice paperwork... we're the ones relieving you of custody... hence our forms. Any paper your side needs after the fact, we can fill those gaps by email or fax. Your people have upgraded equipment right?"

"Uh, no. Our computers are from 2003."

"Newer than most. We'll use email. For now, I've orders to remand the prisoner to federal custody."

"Uh, I don't know... I'm not uh, exactly...."

"You give'm hell, Dugan," says I. Cinder got the cuffs too tight — which grows clear as I gesticulate behind my back. "This *lawman* come in guns blazin', stompin' on the little man. He stomp on me and now he stomp on you. Tell him to go fuck hisself. I did. You're the law, these parts."

Dugan look from me to Cinder.

Cinder look from Dugan to me and his eyes got a glint, I don't know if its powerful actin' skills or a bonafide shut your piehole sign.

"His name's Baer Creighton," Cinder say. "You ever heard of it?"

"No."

"You sure?"

Eyeballs roll at the ceiling like the slow boy in math class. "Wait, did you say Creighton? Is he the cop killer from North Carolina?"

"The one."

Cinder pulls the chain and I come closer the cop. Cinder unfixes the lock from his wrist and tethers me to the cop's chair.

"Don't get up," Nat says, and I wonder if the silliness'll anchor the cop in place. "Your Jane Doe in the bed there is a co-conspirator wanted in seven states for everything from armed robbery to murder.... And I guarantee the whole time she's been in that bed it's been because she preferred it."

Dugan raise his brow but don't ask.

Cinder say, "She always keeps a hair pin next to her scalp. She could have dumped those cuffs within two minutes of deciding she wanted free. You're lucky she didn't cut your throat while you napped, Officer Dugan."

Dugan swallows. "Shouldn't the forms come from you guys anyhow? I mean, you have the forms. You're in charge, aren't you? Right?"

"Son, I see rapid promotion in your future."

"I mean you do this all the time, right?"

"Often enough, unfortunately." Cinder narrows his eyes and nods at Dugan like to welcome him to the inner circle of fraternal ... whatever. Virgin-sacrificers. "How long you been in the game, son?"

"Fourteen months."

"Ah now that's sweet," says I. "You count the months."

"Creighton — " Cinder say. He look back at Dugan. "Well you're doing fine work. Only thing I would draw your attention to is you are now interacting with the US Department of Justice. If you stay on the right side of only one institution in the world, you want that institution to be the United States Department of Justice."

"I understand."

"Good. What items did the prisoner have in her possession when she was brought here?"

"Uh, whatever's in the cabinet there. They didn't really tell me anything — "

"Do you mind?"

"Mind what?"

"Officer Dugan, get the prisoner's belongings out of the cabinet and place them on the edge of the bed. Prisoner Tathiana Domingo-Lopez, you will have three minutes in the bathroom to dress. I will search your person in the presence of a female nurse before and after you enter the bathroom. Do you understand?"

Tat scowl. I believe her. I could kiss her, she's alive and looks barely scratched up. I think of Mags and she ain't jealous. Love is always good.

Cinder shift around me to the door. "Nurse Bond, you are needed."

Cop Dugan slide off the chair and on his knees in front the cabinet. Suspect he's on the broke dick program at work, maybe got the back strain and can't write tickets.

"Nurse Bond," Cinder says, "I'm taking custody of prisoner Tathiana Domingo-Lopez. Looks like she's in your system as Jane Doe 1. From my chain of command I understand she is capable of travel, and because facts on the ground often get ahead of facts in the office in Washington, the Attorney General asked me to make specific inquiry on this case and ascertain if the prisoner is capable of travel."

"Um, what?"

"Can the prisoner travel?"

"Shouldn't we get her doctor for that?"

Cinder don't miss a beat with that grin. He lowers the voice like his next words is the ones she's been waitin' a man to say. "Why would we get a doctor when the nurses know more?"

Big smile. Cinder waits.

"Nothing's changed with this one. It's the other that has the problems."

"The other being Jane Doe 2?"

Tat lift her head off the pillow.

Nurse nods.

"What is Jane Doe 2's situation?" Cinder say.

"Critical. Multiple skull fractures and a broken neck. Brain swelling. Collapsed lungs. I don't know what else. There was talk of flying her to Denver early on but they decided not to. It's… um… a miracle she's still alive."

"I see. Well, I guess that's why we only have orders to move this one."

Tat's eyes is blank while tears run down her cheeks. I got to blink away the wet myself. Corazon… Ah, shit…. Corazon. I got the tightness in the chest agin.

Cinder move to Tat's bed and use a universal key to take the cuff off her wrist.

"Miss Domingo-Lopez, I am about to search your person. Please exit the bed and stand facing the window."

Tat move like a zombie. Cinder's got to keep the situation in hand, got to let on like he don't give a shit. Got to stay mean. But it wasn't five six month ago he and Tat drove to Salt Lake City to save Corazon.

Tat swings her feet out the bed and drops 'em.

I stand with my fingers agin the wall behind my back, rubbin' the tips to make sure I still got the blood flow. And alla sudden I want to scratch my head somethin' fierce. Want to find the last mechanic worked on that Mustang the girls stole. Or find the cops was there at the accident and didn't get the girls out the damn car. Or find the doctor treated Corazon and give him some fuckin' motivation.

Shit, Corazon.

"Miss Domingo-Lopez," Cinder say, "you are being transferred to the most secure federal prison in the United States, the Supermax in Florence — "

"Isn't that men only?" says the copper.

"They'll make an exception for this one."

Tat climb out the bed and her gown ain't fastened. Seem to be a problem 'round here.

Cinder and Dugan get a long study of Tat's naked backside, brown like country maple and lean, but meaty at the ass and legs like to run down a antelope.

"Hey, hey!" Says I. "Cover the lady! C'mon now!"

Nurse Bond jumps and ties the white strings.

"Y'all oughta be ashamed," says I.

Cinder steps behind Tat and runs a hand over her hips and thighs. Puts the hands up front where I can't see.

Tat don't move.

"All right. Miss Domingo-Lopez, officer Dugan has placed the clothing you wore at your arrest on the corner of the bed. Please take them to the bathroom and change. Remember, I will search you again when you come out."

Tat go inside and I ruminate on Corazon. Broke head, broke neck. If she wake up she maybe won't be Corazon and she sure won't be a pedophile slayer. I don't know what life she'll have, if any's left for her. As if we get one task and if we don't do it, they's no back up reason to be here.

Tat opens the bathroom door and steps out. Her face is set, like she use the bathroom time to put Corazon out her mind. No good thinkin' on her right now anyway.

"Please face the window, like before."

Tat moves.

Cinder take the handcuffs still attached to the bed frame and put 'em on Tat's wrists instead, behind the back like me. Nat Cinder's a lawman by the book. He search her body agin, and I shift closer the cop for a better angle. Nat's hands ain't but hardly touchin' her as he pats the hips and whatnot.

"Stay," Cinder says to Tat. He grabs his brief case off the floor. I never seen him set it there. He take out the Department of Justice transfer form with the pink and yellow copies. Press the paper agin the wall and with a pen from the lid of his briefcase scribbles and passes the pen to Dugan.

"I can't see what I'm signin'," Dugan say, jockeyin' between Cinder's arms and reachin' in for his scribble.

"Hit the line next to where I signed. The next block to the right."

"I see it, but this paperwork ain't Department of Justice. What is this? An auto lease?"

Just like Cinder put the brief case on the floor and I didn't see it, he fetched a gun and I miss that too.

Cinder swings the gun arm 'round like a lady softball pitcher so the pistol butt's goin' close to two hundred fifty mile an hour when it lands on Dugan's crown — and Dugan drops.

"Shit, Nat."

"Well he didn't leave much of a choice, did he?"

"Your auto lease? That was the plan?"

"I knocked him out. That was the plan."

"Well what was all the jawin' for? And me in cuffs. Take off the cuffs!"

"Can't do it. Now you both play it cool for two minutes, all right?"

Cinder drags Dugan to the bathroom. Don't close the door. He removes Dugan's right shoe. Sock goes in his mouth. Left shoe comes off and the sock next. Cinder try to tie it around Dugan's face to hold the other in his mouth, but it ain't long enough on account Dugan got short legs and junior feet.

"Hey."

I nod at the counter to an elastic arm jig used by nurses drawin' blood.

"Good." Cinder steps out and grabs it. In the bathroom he wraps and ties Dugan's head so he can't make noise and next ties his legs with his belt. Nat touches his ass pocket, pauses, looks, and comes out the bathroom to Tat and removes her cuffs.

Tat turns to me and wraps her arms over my shoulders and buries her face. I expect the sob or quiver, but she's silent like an acre buried in two feet of snow, deep in the draw where the wind don't blow. I feel her head agin the pocket of my shoulder. She ain't cryin' or shakin'. It's just the steady cold rage pushin' gentle agin me, maybe probe and see if the same rage push back.

We stand leanin' on each other, both lost, both found.

"Tat," says I.

Cinder puts Tat's cuffs on Dugan and close the bathroom door.

"You best leave my cuffs on, as folks out there saw you march me in," says I.

"Agreed. And Tat, you'd best keep your hands behind your back too. No one'll even notice."

Cinder unlocks the chain lockin' my wrist to Officer Dugan's empty chair, then nods at the door.

"Shall we?"

CHICAGO MAGS

Chicago Mags say, "That's worse than bad sex."

"If you're capable of bad sex, that's on you."

She looks wistful like when she was twenty some boy stomp danced on her heart.

"You know," she say, "with the right psychology — or meditation — a person can go to bed and make love all night long, be conscious for every moment of it and wake up fully refreshed in the morning."

"I read in a magazine I found on a park bench", says I, "that nobody thinks about the person they're sleeping with while they're, you know, in-fornicus."

"Making love," Mags says.

"Yep. Well, that... but you know. A little more raw."

She nods. "I have heard that most of the time people have mediocre sex, so they think about the best they ever had."

"That's what I'm saying. You got some fella you think about?"

She slash her eyes at me like the conversation is preposterous — and true.

"Yes."

"What's his name?"

"What? Why? I can't — "

"Shit, never mind. I don't want his name."

"Why did you want his name?"

"I took that back."

"You can't take something back. You're not five."

"Uh."

"Were you going to hurt him?"

Snort. "Yeah. His feelings. Next time he gets with you and asks who you was thinkin' about."

CHAPTER TWENTY-FOUR

Tat halts one step from the elevator. Her eyes got a mournful haunt. "I have to see my sister."

"Back the way we come. She's on this floor," says I. "Couple rooms past yours."

Cinder shake his head. "No time. Nurse Bond's no dummy. She'll find Dugan in minutes, if she already hasn't."

"Tat's right," says I. "She maybe won't get another opportunity."

"That's unfortunate," Cinder says. He steps around Tat into the elevator and hits a button. "But, no. We're not diverting to Corazon's room. Everybody in."

Tat turns around and marches.

"Better stick with her," says I. "The Almighty favors the bold."

"Better hope."

Nat runs twenty feet to get ahead of Tat and I shuffle quick behind.

Nat speaks low, "Okay. Stop. Play the part. All right?"

She nods.

Nat put a hand on Tat's elbow while she locks fingers behind her back. He's got the briefcase in the other hand, and to make things look official he take the chain from my wrist in his hand.

"We are about to make an avoidable error," says he.

"She's in the fourth room," says I.

Nat strides like a lawman for sure. Only thing stops the illusion is the memory of an F-150 lease. We follow 'round the corner. Pass Tat's room with the copper in the bathroom. Door's closed.

Second room, door's open but the lights is off.

Third room is open and the lights is off.

Fourth room is open and the lights is off.

Cinder step inside with Tat right next him. I come up on the other side.

Cinder turn on the switch.

The bed is empty and fresh made.

"Are you sure this is her room?" Tat says.

"It was."

"They moved her," Tat says, and I never heard a woman less sure of her syllables.

We breathe still and quiet.

"I'll check with the nurses at the desk," Cinder say. He backs out the room and I take my chain out his hand. He stops and with a tiny head shake turns back to the nurse station.

Tat stands lookin' at the bed and her shoulders got the shudder.

"She's gone, baby," says I, "but I got to tell you something."

CHICAGO MAGS

Mags says, "I was doing yard work last week and I thought of an analogy for another person, but it applies. Imagine you have a chainsaw and when you first —"

"You got a chainsaw? You run it?"

"Yes."

"Mmm."

"When you get the chainsaw, you're not accustomed to how it works. You can't get used to the throttle. The engine races. Imagine you know very little about how engines run, but you know the fuel is what makes it happen."

"Fuel and spark."

"You decide the best way to regulate the engine is to regulate the fuel. Instead of learning the throttle, you make the fuel less efficient. The chainsaw engine takes two-stroke oil. You don't have any of that, but you have some linseed oil handy and you pour some into the tank. What happens?"

"Won't start."

"Let's say it does start. How well does it run?"

"Shitty."

She look at me.

"What?"

She look more.

"Well, shit."

"Don't you see?"

"You bein' clever?"

"You are the chainsaw. It's an analogy. You are the engine."

" I know where you're going. I quit the liquor."

"Alcohol is just one of the things we all do to change the way our engines run when we don't know how to properly operate them. No one is born a mechanic. Human beings have figured out chainsaws a lot better than they have figured out human beings."

"What else is there?"

"All kinds of things. Music. I use music because most of the time it does less harm. Other people use drugs. Some people drive fast. Some people escape with sex."

Perk up.

"Other people. You know…Some people… kill people."

Perk down.

"The problem is none of this is actually making the adjustment that the engine needs. A good mechanic would have looked at that chainsaw at the beginning and would have discovered something wrong with the doohickey. A good mechanic would've stuck a little screwdriver in some slot you didn't even know was there and five seconds later the chainsaw would have been making sawdust."

"Good mechanic's the shit."

"Right. But you didn't have a mechanic, Baer. Did you?"

"Huh?"

"You as a boy with the chainsaw."

"Right, uh."

"Hypothetically. Stay with the analogy."

"Accourse. The chainsaw."

"In the analogy, you're both the chainsaw engine and the operator — "

"I saw that."

" — and nobody ever gave you a manual. That is what is so sad about the *human situation. Unless somebody reaches out to you, unless you accidentally learn the lesson that there are better ways to heal and fix problems and adjust engines, no one ever knows. So that's the point of the whole metaphor. Since we don't know where to apply the screwdriver and we do know that when we drink from the bottle or take the pill..."*

I close my eyes.

"And the more we self-medicate the more we believe we're doing what we need to do to hold ourselves together, while in reality the pills and booze and whatever are more akin to a hammer than a screwdriver."

"Like how you talk about tools."

She smiles. Furrows.

"What it all becomes, Baer, is hatred. No one wants to take a potion every day to salve over the fact he's broken. He resents the brokenness. Then he resents himself."

"You hit the hammer on the head."

"You ever notice that the people who hate themselves the most hate everybody else more?"

CHAPTER TWENTY-FIVE

"Are you following us back to Flag?"

"I got a couple pieces of business right here in Glenwood. Then people I got to find in Chicago."

"You know… if you go down that road, there will always be people to find."

"I know."

"You want that life?"

"No, I don't. I been hatin' that life since it was give to me six months back. But it's the one I was built for and it's the one I'm gonna live."

Cinder nods slow and seein' him seein' the truth of it make me sure I do too.

"Are you coming back for Tathiana?"

"I don't know. I'm comin' back. Soon as I cut off a head or two I'm comin' back. The *for Tat* part is for Tat to decide. And the part I get the say so, I dunno."

"Are you going to talk to her before we leave?"

"I will."

"Good. Take a minute. I mean don't hurry."

"Don't you got to get down the road afore they block the interstate?"'

Head shake. "We have a bird to catch about four clicks from here...." — he rotates and looks at the stars, then points at a hilltop — "there."

"A helicopter?"

"You didn't think I was going to drive the whole way? Besides, if they barricade the — wait. What was Tat arrested for?"

"I wondered that too. She wasn't with Corazon when she visit with the pedo from the website. If they didn't have enough to arrest Corazon, they couldn'ta had enough for Tat."

"So?"

"Grand theft classic Mustang."

"Yeah, well that's the sort of crime that merits shutting the highways down."

We shake.

I spot him comin' for a hug and can't git clear.

Cinder grab me. Back's stiff and my neck kinda jam back so I can git my face out the way. He slap my back and I hit his arm one time. He slap my back agin and pull. Leans away and fuck if my feet don't float 'til he sit me back down.

But he don't let go. I look right but that puts my face in his. I look left and spot Tat standin' by the Colorado River's edge on a boulder, that water spinnin' and churnin'. I cough and swallow and wriggle and Cinder says, "Stop."

And I stop.

I don't feel nothin'.

It's the first time since I grabbed that bare copper wire, the first time since I was a man of my own mind, that I didn't have the tightness in the chest of knowin' I was built for another sort of society. The first I see it's a good thing 'cause it makes me the outcast in mine.

He set me on the ground agin and now I ain't the boss of my

arms. As Cinder loose me I cinch that fucker close and let my head rest as much as a straight man's head can rest on another's. And I been so fuckin' mad so fuckin' long I don't know what to make of a moment without it. And like that a cloud pass and the day's prettiest sunbeam fall on my eyelids and I see Mags just beamin' at me through all the light, and she don't even got to say any words but I know her mind. She's here to make sure I understand when I get to the other side, it ain't a ass chewin', it ain't a secret courtroom, it ain't a frogmarch downstairs to the furnace room.

It's a hug.

I squeeze and slap and so do Cinder. I smell his cologne and shampoo. Back bones pop and feel better.

I count ten and next fifteen and Cinder loose me.

I loose him.

All the old women went to church and I heard 'em talk about it. They'd say a thousand times you'll be talkin' right there to Jesus and you won't even know it. Everyone meets him a thousand times. One day he's a baby and shit on your wrist. One day he's the boss who asked you for the overtime. One day he's your wife, when you look at the credit card bill. Every one of us spends a moment in turmoil with the Maker, and if we're lucky we'll feel peace and see a flicker like just now lit Cinder's eye as he back away from the hug and say, "I believe you're right about that. It's the life you were built for. Go talk to your girl."

CHICAGO MAGS

Mags says, "A friend of mine — not really a friend. But I know him because he's a searcher and we cross paths. He hosted a party and he had all these people in his loft. And picture this, you know, brick walls, tall windows, wood floor with burn marks from when it was some kind of factory a hundred years ago. In the middle of the room there's this rusty iron sculpture. It's a stick figure of a man, and he's dragging a cross."

"Jesus."

"Right. I asked him — the host — what the story was. He said, 'ain't it awesome?' I said, 'what's awesome?' He said, 'Dude, ain't it perfect? I fucking stole it.'"

Maggie's eyes twinkle.

"Come agin?"

"The image is the Christian savior, who saves from sin."

"They's a nugget comin'. I can feel it."

"He forgives — mind you, this isn't my religion. But the point is this man stole the image of the Savior, and what was awesome and perfect was that he was forgiven for it. Instead of a vicious cycle, it's a virtuous circle. You can't corrupt God. You can't outfox or trick him. You can't be more than you are and he can't be less than he is, and no matter how puerile or silly you are, his love is unfailing. That's the higher plane. That's the nonlocal. See, it has to be that way because God's love and his responsibility are different facets of the same entity. He's powerless to be one and not the other. We are all incapable of being what we are not."

"All the men I sent forward..."

"They don't jeopardize God's love for you. And here's something neat... They're in a better place. Here they were corrupt and broken — which is why you did what you did. Now they are reunited with the holy oneness of love: God. Whatever name you give. They are happy now. Happy isn't the word. They are complete now."

"Maggie, at what point am I responsible? If I never learn to be better, I never do better. I can't just keep on being forgiven forever."

"The animal in you will always be an animal, Baer. You can never unlearn it. That's why forgiveness is unearned and eternal. You are loved. That's all. When you arrive He's going to hug you. I swear to you, I know this."

"That don't sound like the God I heard about growing up."

"They didn't introduce you to God. They introduced you to religion."

"Same difference."

Maggie's brows pop back like her eyeballs is cannons and she fires a salvo.

"Men who do not know God and do not understand him at all claim him and reduce him to rules they can enforce. They put their little-G god in a box, package it as religion and it becomes another box to do battle with all of the other boxes that other little men have created. But people who experience God's ineffable qualities know their consciousness is but a drop of the infinite. They look in horror at the so-called religious people. There is no God in them. Only man, only man's rules. And it works for the godless because men on the whole are lawless, and they would rather subscribe to a hundred million man-made laws instead of the one law given by the God they confess: Love one other."

I let the air soak it in. Wait. She lifts her coffee and sets it back down.

"I close that subscription. All man's laws."

"Cancel all you want, the junk still comes to your mailbox. Like I said earlier, we're wired that way. You won't escape the animal until you die. But *when you do, you'll discover your existence never was solitary. You've always had a bigger, better informed and smarter you out there. One that's been through eternity so far and will resume eternity with you aboard when you depart earth. The more you learn about that other you, the richer your life on this side will be."*

CHAPTER TWENTY-SIX

Sit in the Eldorado on the street a quarter mile from the Lodge not exactly waitin' on the woman who found me in the laundry room to go home. Parked so I can watch the vista through the windshield and don't gotta slink low. I got a spooky feelin' like afore, with Fred when the whole shitshow start and the two men I thought was like witnesses out the Bible, the Archangels. They turn out lawmen but in the minute they was revealed as archangels, that's what they was. Possessed by good and immobilized by it.

I got the same feelin' now, like all these people drivin' by don't even know they's a gold Cadillac sittin' here with a smart mouth dog ridin' shotgun and a destroyer behind the wheel.

Mind won't stay put.

Mags.

Corazon.

I wonder if religion is like politics. People get the God they deserve.

I know a bit of peace for the first time, it seem, but sittin' here lookin' at the mountain I got to climb, the sum total of the people I got to send forward...

Glance about side to side and see the liquor store not forty feet off. Anything so close is bound to be deliberate and since the fates decided, I'll spare myself the drama. I want a bottle and I'm a man.

That's it.

"I'll be back in a minute. You see that white Camry go, let out a holler."

Stinky Joe yawns.

Hey what? Where are you going?

Close the door and feel the dog's eyeballs on my back all across the lot. Inside, I spot the Turkey right off and grab a jug. Adjacent the checkout machine they got the cigarette lighters and shot glasses. But they got the flask too, and I think 'bout the old Baer Creighton and I recall he carry a flask damn near everywhere.

"I'll need two of them hip vessels."

"Two?"

"Two."

"Up to you, I guess. But you could have one and fill it twice."

"Or I could have two and fill 'em half each, drink both twice and fill 'em four times more. Is all."

"What?"

"And have half as much space left over."

"I don't follow."

"Which'd be dumber'n fuck, as I wanted twice as much to start."

"I didn't mean to aggravate you."

"Or, I could fill each once. Like I want. *As the fuckin' customer.*"

"I am a little confus — "

"Two."

Back at the Eldorado, Stinky Joe shake his head. He don't even got to say a word.

"Joe, listen. I'm a man. In the whole hierarchy I'm at the pinnacle. If you was closer you'd know that word. As such, as a man, they's only one above me, and that's the Almighty. No government, no king, no general, no woman and no dog."

Twist the cap and I don't even got to inhale but I can taste the Turkey like the soul got taste buds.

Does the man at the pinnacle remember a promise?

"Bein' as how no two people agree on the Almighty, that leaves me at the top, with a silent partner. He whisper in my ear: 'All the things that's good, it fall on man to find and defend 'em. And what's evil, he got to root that out and kill it.'"

What does that have to do with your promise?

"Man at the pinnacle intend to break the promise, as it no longer represent the higher good. As is his will and duty."

Tip the jug and swallow deep. Feel the sparkle all the way down the pipes. Heat spread across the belly. I close the eyes and let the brain flatten out a bit.

Let the back ease into the seat.

Feel the toes tingle like walkin' in pine needles, then turn to mush and float off.

I see the men I sent forward in the trees, but the ones in the back is hard to make. Eyes is dim and lookin' on 'em I don't feel what I felt afore.

I don't feel nothin'.

But if I felt somethin' it'd be in the vicinity of work. The way a buck wantin' roots'll look at a woman's hips and sense the word pregnant ain't about babies so much as the yoke comes with 'em.

I look at the dark trees, 'most empty of eyes and the word comes to mind is *opportunity*.

One more gurgle of the Wild Turkle.

"Joe, if you was closer to the apex you wouldn't misunderestimate, as the former president say… you wouldn't misunderestimate man's friendship with the alcohol. You puppydogs is long been called man's best friend. But I'd wager W's left nut that man's *other best friend* been with him longer."

Hit the jug agin. Truth told I like the liquor more'n titties too, as I been a hell of a lot more intimate with it.

Time to fill a flask. Man at the store put 'em in plastic bags. Fish out the first and unscrew the cap. Blow it clean and blow the flask too. Stuff it 'tween the knees and unscrew the Turkey.

"Poise, Joseph, is the art — "

There's your woman.

Up at the motel a Toyota Camry with a dent in the back quarter panel and the left taillight out swing on the road headed at Carbondale.

Shit! I got Turkey splashed 'bout the thigh and already feel heat in the jewel sack.

"You keep watch which way she go!"

Dog roll his eyes.

I screw a cap with each hand while pushin' the gas and twistin' the wheel right across the bottom and out in traffic from the right parking lane. I finish screwin' the flask first so that hand git the wheel.

"That right there is pinnacle work. Dog couldn't do that. Nor a woman."

Then why do you love so many of them?

"Ain't possible not to, Joe. Just like you."

Put on the turn signal and switch the lane — though in ghost mode they won't see me anyway.

I hang back and she drive and drive. Couple mile out the road is empty save her and me. I drop way behind and let the woman disappear once or twice around the curves. The end is nigh. No worries this way or that. By and by I catch her single taillight cut a left into a community of houses and trees, each lined up like neither come out the earth natural.

She disappear and I stomp the gas on a half mile straight. Cadillac hauls ass and just when the nose floats high I aggravate the brake and swing the corner so the tires squeal and Joe got to peel his jowl off the glass.

But the white Camry's gone.

I sit with the gear engaged but keep a foot on the brake and take in the space 'round me. The trees and houses. Once I got a fix, I figure it'll take half the night, but I bet if I check every turn the next ten mile, and every driveway, I'll find a white Camry.

One hour and thirteen minutes.

Kill the engine. Got a flask in each jacket pocket, Glock in the ass and Smith on the hip. I slip the Glock under the car seat as it never was a favorite.

Walk up the door and knock.

Door open a crack and a man's beard come peering through. He steps back.

Motel woman let on like she had a run in with a criminal outfit, and somehow that mess of crooks is tied in with Frank Lloyd, and I don't know why or how it mighta happened, but she said Abe Church found me at the motel laundry. Which don't make a lick of sense, as Church said he thought I was at the other motel down the road. If what she said is true, Church lie to my face and I didn't spot it. But if it ain't true then the woman lie to my face and I didn't spot that neither.

I wish Stinky Joe was here at the doorstep with me as this is exactly what I was sayin'. Woman here — and got a man with her — she know wrong been done. He know wrong been done. But someone come along want to make right of it, he need a hammer and chisel to prize out what information'll let him do his good work. Almost like people ain't got a single ounce of fight in 'em for what's right and just.

That's what I was sayin' to Stinky Joe. World needs destroyers. Ain't pleasant and don't smell good, but truth is for all man's bein' civilized and high thinkin' it's the wild that keep him alive, and a man ain't fit to be civilized without he got a feral strain that'll never bend to the yoke. Without it he's nothin' but a slave. Just like the wolf seeks the weak and old and makes the herd stronger, the destroyer's the protector. He cut out the rot, 'fore it fester and turn good people bad. No man is good without killin' what deceit would make him evil.

Accourse Stinky Joe'd say if it's only good folk at the pinnacle then shit, you go from the Almighty straight to dogs. I see his point though he warn't here to make it. Destroyers ain't good people.

No, but I suppose they wish for it.

Ease out Smith.

Door open 'til the skinny chain stop it. Man's got long curly face hair like Santa afore the beard go white.

Santa say, "Are you the man my wife says is going after that son of a bitch Church?"

"No, I'm goin' after Frank Lloyd. So far."

The door close and the chain jiggle and the door goes open. Santa Clause steps back.

The house's got no ambient juice. I look behind me to the car and back inside. Step forward and the man close the door behind.

"You don't need your gun."

"I'll decide."

"Of course, be my guest." He put his hands together. "That's not a problem at all."

The woman from the motel sit on the sofa with her knees close as they can get. Her face seem kinda puckered but I don't know if they's a little Wild Turkification goin' on — though that error usually go in the woman's favor. She got a newspaper magazine open on the coffee table, picture of a man and woman lookin' stone cold pissed.

Some folks when they look at the wall you know the head's truly empty and they's not a single blue spark inside keepin' shit warm. And other people look at the same wall and the skin on they faces roll and shift like they got an air pocket needs let out. You want to push the bump to the ear.

All the turmoil, is the point.

Woman open her hand, want me to sit next her. "If you're here for information about Abraham Church, you have to know who he is in his heart."

"He doesn't have a heart," says her man, Santa. "You want coffee, Mr. — ?"

Nod. "Black."

"That's his coffee not his name," says the motel woman. "His name is Creighton but he goes by Boone."

"Baer Creighton," says I.

"I knew it, but it was hard to tell for sure with you wearing a suit and having that hair cropped so clean." She put her hand on my arm gentle as a mother with a sick child. "Am I — *are we* — okay trusting you?"

Her eyes is wet but it ain't fear of me that put the tears there.

"I don't know what Abraham Church is mixed up in, but as far as he goes, and Frank Lloyd and all his crew, I'm responsible for you and yours."

The man put a coffee mug on the table next my knees and sit on a recliner made half outta duct tape but he don't put his feet out. Elbows on his thighs, one hand tomahawks into the other.

"Tell me you're going to kill this man."

"Herman," the woman say.

"Lucy."

I nod. "Herman, Lucy. What'd Abraham Church do to y'all?"

The man picks up a photo from the end table with the lamp. Urn behind it. Picture's got some Mexican kid maybe, a girl like Corazon or Tat with the black eyes and hair. Herman got tears in his eyes and a tremble in his hand.

The girl's dead.

I swallow hard.

Picture's a fist in the gut. I see Tat and Corazon and this new girl, and the features blend so I can't tell which is which. All become one girl with pretty black hair and eyes so lit by hope and love I don't know how to see 'em defeated and dead. But two of the three black-hair girls in my head is gone and Mags is gone too. Got to look away and comport myself.

"Who is she?"

"She is my daughter," Lucy say.

"She was our daughter," Herman say.

I look at him and his brown hair. Look at her and the strawberry blonde.

"We adopted her when she was four."

"You love her," says I. "I miss a girl was maybe like her. How she pass?

"Car accident."

"She old 'nough to drive?"

"She was," Herman say. "Barely old enough. We'd just flown all the way to Arizona to buy the car for her sixteenth birthday. It was a super great deal on a used rental, but only if you go to them, kinda deal."

"He went to the auction, there," Lucy say.

"Big auction."

"Uh huh."

"That car is why he killed her," she say.

"You can't prove that," says Herman.

"I can prove it. It's the only thing that makes sense."

"I know it makes sense I'm just saying you can't prove it, and with a man of Creighton's, uh, *qualifications*…we shouldn't say things uh-uh-uh-unless we can prove them."

"Fine. We can't prove anything."

No juice other'n Herman stavin' off his desire to piss himself. At the woman Lucy I say, "You was sayin'."

"Gloria had friends. She was a very social girl and her friends, you know… they looked like her."

Says I, "Your daughter — Gloria? — was in the car."

"Yes, her name was Gloria. They were all out, you know, right after her birthday."

"Three days after her birthday."

"Thank you, Herman, three days. And that's why Abraham Church killed them."

"Three days?" says I.

"No, he killed them because they all had brown skin and the license plate was from Arizona."

Herman say, "No one would miss them."

I think on Tat and Corazon, the business of selling people. Is Lucy sayin' Abe Church is another Luke Graves?

"This agin. So how he try to take 'em, and end up killin' 'em instead?"

"We don't know. What? He didn't try to take them and then kill them instead. He just killed them."

Thoughts whirl in my head that don't compute. People got to be alive — for the most part — afore other people'll pay to screw 'em.

"I don't follow. Is Abraham Church sellin' kids for sex or not?"

"What? Oh — no. Not that we know. He kills them for their body parts — "

"So he can sell them... the parts."

"Yes, thank you, Herman."

"Uh."

Whole new category of evil. But on inspection all evil 'stills down to stealin' in one form or another.

"Why don't you maybe tell me what you know, and I'll stop interfering with questions."

"We don't know much. Four beautiful girls disappeared the way I said. Abraham Church runs a funeral home. And *Chester A DeChurch* runs a body broker business out of Vail, just up the road."

"Chester who?"

"He's the same man," Santa say. "Chester A DeChurch is the same man as Abraham Church."

The head swim. Water clear up to the pinnacle and Stinky Joe float by on a raft, grinnin'. Baer Creighton appointed to the lofty penultimate perch of civilization and bamboozled by common facts pilin' up in uncommon ways. Abe got a second name, and I recognize it. And what's this about... "You said some words I never heard put together. Body broker business?"

Woman say, "It's where they sell human bodies. It's legal — "

"But there's almost no rules — "

"Thank you, Herman. It's very unregulated. And that magazine article — " she point to the coffee table " — is what gave me the understanding. There are real businesses out there, Mister Creighton, legitimate businesses, that sell corpses to universities and different places like that. They convince people to donate their bodies to science and then they sell the bodies. It's a scam the way these people in the magazine story did it. That isn't what Church is doing."

Shake my head no. Wait.

"He's killing people too," says Lucy.

"Let me say it back. Sellin' dead people's legal if you use the right government forms."

"But Church isn't just talking to people and getting the forms signed, like you're supp — "

"He's killing them. He can't wait so he kills them and fakes the forms."

"Thank you, Herman."

"Pardon, and I mean this with all due respect. Herman, no more words. You're done."

"Yes sir, of course. I just keep adding things trying to be helpful."

"Herman. Stop talking."

"Of course. Whatever you s — "

Smith on the table, I put the index finger to the barrel and push 'til the revolver rotates sixty-seven degrees and the bore's sighted on Herman's nuts.

Herman frowns.

I face his missus. "So he wasn't tryin' to take 'em alive? That's where I'll be hearin' some details."

"This is all we know. I have a friend that works at the courthouse. You know that place. It's all one building-area. The sheriff and police and court and everything. They all know each other, right?"

Nod.

"I have a friend there and I will not name her — "

"Susan. Her name is Susan."

"Herman that was wrong," Lucy say.

"Complete transparency with Mister Creighton," Herman says.

Exhale. Tell myself not to kill Herman, though pointin' the barrel at his nuts was as good as makin' a promise, and now I'm welchin'.

Lucy shake her head and don't miss a beat. "Please don't point your firearm at my husband, even if the gun's only on the table. You're a good man and you don't need to make your points that way."

She leans across in front of me and pushes the Smith barrel four more inches so it'll mortally wound the bottom left corner of her television.

"Anyway, Susan told me she was talking to one of the police deputies — "

"It was a deputy," says Herman. "There's no such thing I've ever heard of in Colorado — "

"Thank you, Herman. Let me please just tell the story? Okay. God, I'm about to cry. Susan told me there were no bodies in the car when it burned. And she also said the accident didn't start the fire."

"Hold up. Herman, keep it shut. Now Miss Lucy, you said the girls was in a car accident. What did Abraham Church have to do with that?"

"I don't know exactly — "

"Tell me what you guess."

Herman got his mouth open. I eyeball him.

Lucy says, "Well I used to think Church and his people didn't do anything special. I thought they saw the girls in the car and decided right then. And they took the girls the way men always do. They gang up, tell lies, use guns, whatever. They get Gloria and her friends and then they... do... what... they... did. Excuse me." She pull a tissue from the box next her leg. "And what they did took time, because harvesting organs is like surgery. I used to think it was unplanned, and the girls just disappeared — but I don't anymore. Anyway, taking all the body parts from four girls is going to take time. I get clinical like this sometimes, you know? So I can deal with it. They had to get rid of the car right away. I think they burned the car to make it look like an accident, and when they were done taking everything from the girls they could sell, they sewed the bodies back together and burned them."

Herman say, "Then they put the burned bodies inside the burned car."

"How the police know they was no bodies in the car when it burned?"

"I hadn't talked to Susan in a week and all of sudden she sent me a text saying we had to get together for lunch. This was right after Gloria was found in the car, like a couple weeks later. I hadn't seen Susan since before it all. We're friends, but not bosom you know?"

"Uh huh."

"Well, at lunch she was like I was with you at the motel. I wanted to talk but I just couldn't get myself to do it. But she sends me this urgent text and then clams up and doesn't want to say anything? And I was like come on! You sent me the text. What's going on? And she gave me a look like *I'll tell you what's going on, but you really don't want to know.* But then she did. And now I know."

Herman look 'bout to blow a gasket. He raise his hand.

"Yes, Herman?"

"The science people can tell when the material is burned together or separate. One of Susan's friends works with the evidence and is right out of science school. Reaaally sharp kid. He told Susan and Susan told Lucy."

"What you got that puts Abraham Church mixed up in the accident?"

"The car didn't have any reason to burn. It had accelerant inside, but there was no accident. It was in a ditch."

"It was more like a cliff."

Stomach kinda in a knot. I see Tat's red Mustang ass up and smokin'. Coincidence put it in that precise moment in space and time so I can make sense of this accident with Gloria and her girlfriends.

The same exact thing.

"Okay, it was steep and deeper than the car was long. But not much, and not so steep the car should have blown up."

Herman raise his hand again.

"Herman?"

"That doesn't happen in real life."

"Thank you, Herman," says Lucy. "But that doesn't say why it has to be Abraham Church. The accident happened but it could be anybody, right? So, I looked up who was in charge of the crime scene at the police station. Guess who?"

"How could he know? Don't make him guess."

I say, "Some kin of Abraham Church."

"That's right. Mark DeChurch."

"Ah, see his lightbulb going off?" Herman say.

Says I, "Earlier you said Abraham was Chester too."

"Mark is his nephew. My friend Susan works in records. When I saw the article about the body business, I told her, and she did a search and found all of Abraham Church's businesses. He has the funeral home and the garage shop."

"That's your tie to Frank Lloyd," Herman say. "The garage shop."

Look at Lucy. "And?"

"But when Susan searched the system by the business by name

instead of owner, you know.... Looking for body brokers like I showed her in the magazine, then she found the Vail Body Brokers, Incorporated."

"That the real name?"

"It is. But I drove there and the sign doesn't say the real name. It's only a logo. There's no real sign. And the logo just says VBB, Inc."

Nod.

"Are you ready for this?" she say. "Abraham Church owns the funeral home. He bought it a couple years ago. Before that, he bought businesses under his first name, his real name."

Alla sudden the name Chester A. DeChurch come back to me from afore, like I heard it days ago not minutes. Too much time spent with no likker in me. Can't recall shit.

"His real name," Lucy says, "is Chester Abraham DeChurch. He never went by Chester because of all the jokes. You know, Chester the molester stuff."

"He's a pedophile," Herman says. "He's on the government registry. That's how we connected the two names together. Not that we really needed to at that point. I mean, the man has two names in real life. You go to the house owned by Chester DeChurch and Abe Church lives there. We don't have to connect the dots."

"It's the same fuckin' dot," says I.

"Yeah, exactly that. The same fuckin' dot."

Lucy look at Herman.

"Language, dear."

Herman bounce off the duct tape chair to a desk tucked in the corner. He push the computer monitor. "Here he is. This is Abraham on the Glenwood Springs Sheriff's department's website, you know, the pedophiles in your neighborhood. Chester was always Abe to the people who knew him, and he grew up in Carbondale anyway. All he had to do was drop the *De* from his name on the business everyone sees. And no one looks at these pedo websites anyway."

"One girl did."

"But on the business that isn't in the spotlight, he just kept the same old name."

"What, he change his name legal or somethin'?"

Herman shake his head. "No. We didn't look up the owner of the funeral home, how it's listed. We didn't know at the time it might be a thing, you know? A clue. We were just trying to see if there were any body brokers around here."

"What's this connection to Frank Lloyd and the car garage?"

"Frank works there."

"Used to work there. I think that's where Church found him and groomed him for the dark side. But I don't think he actually works at the garage anymore."

"Thank you, Herman," says Lucy. "The connection is this. I think they planted a small explosive on the car — enough to make the girls wreck — and were right there to grab the bodies, even if they had to kill them if the accident wasn't bad enough."

I nod. Keep noddin'. Stop.

"Why? People die all the time."

"No! That's just it. I read the mortuaries. I don't know if it's the water — "

"The obits. She means the obits."

"Thank you, Herman. I don't know if it's the water or what, but people just aren't dying as much as before. Plus, with regular dead people, you have family expecting bodies."

"Can't he just cut out a kidney and sew things back up? Put the body in a casket? Or cut out a kidney afore he run 'em through the furnace?"

"Yes, but he couldn't sell the entire body, and that's where the profit is."

"If the body business was relatively new and they had contracts to fill…"

"We're regular people," Herman say. "We don't know about stuff like that."

Ants love the anthill. Some folk love the rules and is happy they got so many other people handy, tell 'em what to do. Folk can't sleep at night 'less someone write a rule the sun got to come up. These folk see evil and think it's someone else's problem, right up 'til it knock on the door.

But that ain't these people exactly.

Herman's words stop me.

Regular folk don't understand the mechanics of it, the tools, how bad men work evil. Almost like Herman said, *so how we suppose to fight it?*

No one ever taught these folks to combat evil. They taught 'em to be meek. Go to work, pay the fuckin' tax, and go to work the next day. Keep the mouth shut.

I got a feeling Chicago Mags is lookin' in through the window, or maybe right through the walls from the other side of the material, the nonlocal, where she say things is real. Moment feel like it got somethin' to say but I wait and nothin' comes.

"Are you going to kill him?"

"Thank you, Herman," Lucy say.

"Who?"

"Abraham Church," Herman say.

Mags is there smilin' and the blood from her mouth is gone. All this shit goin' on is disjointed and the brain don't necessarily see it all or add up what it does. The ride's been turbulent but all my life I been in a cooker. Or maybe a cure shed with the smoke and I been cured for the work the Almighty prepared for me to walk in. I been preserved to withstand the sympathy or weakness that might detour another man off the narrow path.

Regular folk can't see the footsteps to follow, so I got to walk 'em alone.

"We'll see. Where's Frank Lloyd's garage?"

CHICAGO MAGS

Chicago Mags leans back in her wire chair. Sun's behint the buildings. She cross her arms at her chest and shiver.

"Human beings are at the apex of the material order, but they are not the apex themselves. The universe, all the matter, all the systems and forces, every single natural and biological microsystem was designed to operate in perfect harmony to support the existence of the creator's crowning achievement."

"But that ain't us," says I.

"No. It's something within us that we use or don't use."

"A riddle."

"Free will. Everything material exists as a playground for free will. Free will is how we learn the lessons we need to learn before we return to the nonlocal. Brains are designed as learning computers to process information from the environment. Brains are animal, concerned with things like heartbeat and how salty a drink is or where the lion is hiding. Brains manage the body, but their higher function is to serve as a vehicle for the consciousness that sits atop them assigning values, reacting, planning, eating, procreating, and most of all, becoming."

"You got to quit being fertilizer, is the point."

"No, we've moved on from polishing turds. I'm making the next point. To the animal, all value is assigned within the framework of whether something answers an animal need. Food is good so killing things and eating them is good. That doesn't require thought. But consciousness is the jewel sitting in the cockpit of the animal brain. Consciousness is separate, from someplace else, an ethereal hitchhiker crossing the material world. It has the power to lurk like it doesn't exist at all, or assert, so there appears to be nothing else. If it lurks it lowers. Asserts, it raises. When asserting, consciousness is literally the sculpture of the self-made man, hammer in one hand and chisel in the other, forming the legs that will walk him from the rubble when he is done. We are created to self-create. To finish the project. To sit atop the animal but resonate with the source, the divine. We exist to search for the underlying truth that created us."

"What truth?"

"Love."

"Love what?"

"Love. Like God said, I AM. The assertion is the proof. The answer doesn't need more words. LOVE."

"Don't fully cognitate your meaning."

"The material universe is a projection. Quantum physics has proven irrefutably that matter doesn't exist in a material form until consciousness looks at it and collapses possibility into actuality. It's like a mirror reflecting us. And just like there is a consciousness behind the eyes in your mirror, that, if you think about it, is more real than the image that houses it, there is a consciousness behind the universe that is more real than the stardust and molecules and vibrations that we call matter. That consciousness is God, and if you look, you'll find him looking back, swept away, lost in love for you."

"Fuck."

"Love."

"I can't ken it."

"He can, until you do."

"And if I don't?"

"Baer, there's nothing else. Love. The only alternative is evil."

CHAPTER TWENTY-SEVEN

Drivin' the Eldorado I recall standin' on the roadside with Abe Church lookin' at the Mustang accident and his surprise on seein' the law there.

I recall the truck behind him, haulin' horses.

The vehicle behind that was another truck with a man, two ladies and motorcycles on the trailer. I remember thinkin' these boys had with 'em all the stuff they love to ride. Trucks, horses, motorcycles and women.

That third truck was Frank Lloyd and the girls in it was Bambi and Bunny. Bet W's left nut.

I take a long simmerin' gurgle from the Turkey. Tool past the place where the car maintenance and monkeyshop's suppose to be. Got the windows down, seat way back and ass low like the cool kids but I grumble by the McDonalds and don't turn.

I just keep toolin'.

The garage ain't for cars, it's for motorcycles. Got ten out front for sale. Dirt bikes, a couple baggers, a tour bike and the rest is rockets.

After a half mile of noodling the implications of Frankie Black

Boots Lloyd bein' a motorcycle man the traffic's thin and I swing a U-turn. Next pass I go slow so I can make out the particulars. It's a gray-painted cinderblock building with a giant bay door on the left and picture windows wrapped around the right corner; glass ain't seen a washcloth in years. Little sign says *State Inspections* and behind the windows the inside is half dark, like they don't bother with the lights on that side. I pull over and watch the goin's-on.

Not a damn thing goin' on.

I bet he's behind the garage door.

"Right. And assumin' he's a shithead, for argument's sake..."

He's up to no good.

I think on all the work still needs done to set the world back on its axis. I got to go back to Chicago and find the pair on the motorcycle that shot Mags.

I got to rectify a little situation with Frank Lloyd.

Maybe put a hurt on them stupid ass girls he work with — Bambi and Bunny — though I'll confess the logic need a few stones added to the foundation. Frank Lloyd intend to put a hurt on me, but them girls in the simplest view only wanted to get me horned up.

I might give 'em a good ass chewin'.

But the biggest mystery is what the motel woman Lucy say, how Abraham Church was at the Lodge laundry room after Frank beat me with the ball bat. Her words don't reconcile with all I know 'bout Church and I got the paradox to work out. Abe Church see the lies — he said as much, and I got no juice nor red out him. He's a straight shooter and hates the untruth like me.

But...

In the hospital Church say some good Samaritan brung me in.... But I also got Lucy sayin' Church was at the laundry room when Lloyd was there, and she say Church haul me to the hospital in his truck. She wasn't shootin' sparks neither.

Only way to reconcile the two is if Church was the Samaritan but didn't feel the need to say so. Strictly speaking that ain't lyin'.

It ain't shootin' straight neither.

Last, Lucy said Church is a kid fucker. Showed me his picture on the website.

I ain't ready yet, but know I got to admit I gauge the man wrong entirely.

A man wearin' leather swings fast into the lot on a black Victory with no exhaust. Sounds like a pair of cannon mounted to a skateboard. Got a ponytail and he don't wear a helmet so the sunlight glitters off the earrings in his eyebrows real pretty. Bone-skinny and covered in tattoos, all in black ink. Dismounted, he raps the garage door with the side of his fist and after a minute the door lifts six inches and no more. He looks around. Glance right past the gold Eldorado 'cross the street. Adjusts his mess and from the look of the bulge he's hung like a light switch. He stoops and lifts the bay door and I wonder on that, how Frankie Lloyd do business... make a customer open the garage door.

Must be his kid.

"I was thinkin' that too, Joe."

With the door open a minute I see in the bay. They's a couple bikes on lifts with no one turnin' wrenches and looks like Frankie's on the side workin' some fabrication machine.

Light Switch parks his bike inside and while he pull the chains to close the door, Frank comes up from the back wearin' a onesie with oil and grease all over.

There he is, the fella try to rob me with the sluts then try to bust my skull with a bat. This is the famous two step operation: Kill him, then ask questions.

"I'm yankin' your chain, Stinky Joe. I'll ask the questions first."

Maybe you should wait a minute and see how the liquor's going to hit you.

"Likker don't hit me. It's more akin a kiss."

While I got nothin' to do but watch and wait I cognitate on the overall situation. Logistics and tactics. I'm willin' to step through the front door not knowin' what's inside, but if I was both lucky *and* walkin' a path chose by the Almighty I'd have a Abrams tank and drive right through the bay. Or a Panzer. They was nice. As is, Frank Lloyd'll be surprised to see me, but the surprise'd be loftier if I dropped the door with a tank, is all.

Another thing… be real nice if I knew where they was inside.

Sometimes with the curse, I feel the juice through walls and even know which room holds the liar. But I never got it quite so local as to know where in the room to look. The curse ain't like the x-ray vision.

I exit the Eldorado with Joe in the passenger seat.

"I don't know exactly what I'm gettin' into, but you're welcome to sit in the seat or come along and watch. I figger to ask some questions and fire some bullets."

No, thank you.

"You sure?"

We have to talk. This… behavior… doesn't fly. You gave your word.

I brace on the open window and study Joe inside.

"Joe, it's time for some instruction. Speakin' hypothetical… If you give me your solemn oath you was gonna be a man and walk on your two hind legs, and grow a couple thumbs, I'd have the sense to call bullshit. Wouldn't be fair, me acceptin' a promise you couldn't keep. Wouldn't be just, if I knew it."

Clever.

"I don't hold it agin ya. You ain't at the pinnacle like me and don't see everything as clear. But I got the crystal clarity and as such, I see I can't be what I ain't. Seems obvious enough. And since I'm on a mission here, and got Corazon and Mags to kill for and want to do it drunk, if you can't deal with that you need another best friend. I won't be what I'm not. Even if I could."

Joe says naught. Reach in for an ear scratch but he turn away.

I walk from the Eldorado glad I never taught Joe to drive.

I won't kowtow to a dog. Not this day. I sit at a fire writin' letters thirty years knowin' I was made different and not happy with it.

After all the killin' I had to think it through, had to judge my own evil self else it wouldn't sit with the moral sense. Had to plead sanity and call myself innocent, as every time I try to better myself, I only learn I was made right the first time. Is why every time I try to change, I go back the way I was.

Now I'm back to knowin' what I knew: I am what I am and things is rarely what they ain't. I'll drink when I want and kill when I got to.

Feel a little exposed huffin' across the lot to the garage run by the fella busted my arm and made me a short-term lefty. Keep the eyes peeled and the good hand ready to cross-draw Smith. If it wasn't for the street traffic, I'd have Smith on point right now and maybe I oughta anyway. But I push open the door without.

Buzzer go off.

"Right with you," comes the voice of Frank Lloyd from the bay.

Try not to sound like nobody. "Hooahh-yehp."

Inside's a wicked stink like bodies ain't been washed in a month, oil that's more grit than carbon juice and just plain old nasty ass men. Part of the stink is sweet, but the rest just piss me off. I live in the woods and got better hygiene. Now I got my mind in the right place for shootin' work, I yank Smith and the grip is still real good on the fingers... but the left fingers is twitchy and I don't know if the right, what's attached a broken arm, exactly want a handful of Smith & Wesson 44 Magnum recoil. Bust the arm all over agin, where'd I be?

Left it is.

Keep Smith at the door openin' but nobody come. Almost like this ain't a place for regular customers.

Almost like when anybody comes in the way I did, Frank Lloyd and his earring partner know he ain't with the program.

Step back outside. Buzzer go off agin.

"Yeah?"

Say nothin'.

"Shit," says Frankie Black Boots Lloyd. "Be with you in a minute."

I prop the door open with a coffee can of cigarette butts. Rap the outside garage door like I'm the IRS wantin' ten pounds' flesh. All I need is jump boots and a bayonet. Once the metal got fresh dents and the chains jingle jangle I scoot back to the buzzer door stuck open with the coffee can and swing into the bay with Smith in charge.

If I was more limber I'd slap the heel and dosey doe. They ain't got the garage door open but two feet and I don't waste time. Right up close is Frank Lloyd and the bony tattoo man — him with a wrench the size of a nightstick — and since I already know I'm gonna kill Frank Lloyd they's no sense leavin' him in a condition to fight back.

So I fire that Smith 'n Wesson 44 Magnum into his right leg and afore he stumble, his left too.

"You son of a bitch!"

Fire one in his foot for my mother.

"Fuck! Oh shit. Fuck. You shot me!"

Other fella — Light Switch — I ain't shot him yet. He hold the wrench like he played T-ball as a kid and started pitcher.

"Drop it."

"Fuck you."

Fire one at his ear — I was close. Keep ol' Smith on him while he dances.

He drops the wrench and I study Frank. On second thought, I wish I shot Frank Lloyd in the guts, as it's painful and a man might live a few days. Whereas, if I bust the leg artery he be dead in two minute.

And me shot him in each leg.

Frank Lloyd's on the ground and the blood pool grow quick. He flip from side to back and even while he got nothin' but cuss words for me his legs got enough motivation he'll be near any gun what's handy in no time. So I fire a bullet in his back... and out the three, the legs, stomach and back, I discover I like the back most on account the principal. Like sayin' to the bad folk, you got no idea when the Destroyer's a-comin'. That's the message. And now I shot him in the back I wish I could flip him over and reshoot the other three bullets, as when word gets about, how the Destroyer does rotten men in the back, rotten men'll know fear.

"Shoulda killed me Frank, when you was robbin' me with them dumb fuckin' girls."

"Those dumb fuckin' girls are ace mechanics."

"And you shoulda killed me in the laundry after you seen I'd bring the fight right back."

"Fuck you."

"You shoulda seen me comin'."

"Yeah, well you shoulda been in the car."

'Less they's a bridge in the cosmic fabric and Frank know I thought 'bout rolling the Eldorado through the door, I don't know what to make of him sayin' I shoulda been in the car. But a soul'll say anything if he's half bled out and face to face with the man gonna send him forward.

Look about the garage then back at the glitterin' eyebrow fella Smith been starin' down.

Kick Frank Lloyd's foot.

"Who's this?"

"Go to hell."

Flick the pistol back to Light Switch.

"Who you?"

He glance away and I follow the look. Spot a white motorcycle. Half turn the head.

A white motorcycle.

Almost dumb tryin' to assemble the pieces. That's the white motorcycle was in Chicago — I recognize the shape. The fairing and tank and bags. And that means this man's ass was like to be on the seat. And he got a ponytail like the shooter.

And if the man who try to rob me at the Ryder truck and try to beat me in the laundry attack me a third time, then Mags wasn't hit by someone aiming at Mags. Them bullets was meant for me.

Mags is dead on account of me.

I got this pressure in the head. Rush in the ears.

Light Switch jumps for Smith and with both hands wrapped about mine and him a little taller he push the barrel back at me and with my stupid assed finger locked by his in the trigger box I'm a half second from blowing my head off.

Poke out my head and kiss Light Switch on cheek. He turn his face with his brow knit for war and I clamp teeth on his nose and squeeze. His eyeballs piss tears and when he shakes and bucks and screams, I loose his nose and chew earrings off that bony brow like corn off a cob.

Spit out six.

This is the murderin' evil piece of shit shot Mags?

He give me the space for a good triple knee to the nuts and I oblige. As he slide down my arm and leg I ball the left fist to club his noggin, but he ain't with it and a sucker punch now, I wouldn't have the words to square it with the Almighty.

"Who is he, Frank?"

Light Switch curls on his side and though his face is hamburger he's more concerned for his mushed-up nuts.

"Who is he, Frank?

"Fuck you."

"It was you two on that white bike over there in Chicago. You come for me. Who is he?"

"Fuck you."

"Don't matter, I guess. Boy," I kick his stomach and he holds my foot. Yank my leg and bury that boot one more time. "Boy — you shot a woman meant somethin' to me. If I had five years to peel your skin I would but since I don't, roll over on your stomach."

He's on his side, arms folded at the belly for protection. He's quiverin' now and somewhere inside his brain all he learned from school and society and whatever art he soaked up, all that shit's out the window and the only signal sparkin' his noggin is fear.

Love to see him shake.

"There you go."

He don't roll so I ease him on his belly with my boot a few times.

"There it is. Stretch out a little more."

I fire two forty-four slugs at an angle into Light Switch's back thinkin' the ricochet'll come up through his head, like billiards. But his head settles with no bounce.

Light Switch is off.

Reload.

"You fucking bastard. I'll murder you."

Frank Lloyd's bled out. His words is weak.

"That was your boy, right? He got the same chin as you. Easy to see with enough blood.

"I'll kill you," says Frank, "I'll murder you."

"Listen. Your breath's short on account all the blood spillin' out your body. That makes words expensive. All I want to hear from you is what Abe Church's got to do with this?"

"Fuck you."

"He part of the cabal? He write the marchin' orders?"

"Go fuck yourself."

I stand over Frank Lloyd's ass while he bleeds out and sucks in tiny breaths. Musta shot him better'n I thought. If I don't do nothin' more, from his sputterin' and shakin' I bet Frank'll greet his maker in under ten minutes.

"Tell you what, Frank. This is how things work. I know on account the woman you and your boy killed. She taught me the physics of heaven. Anyway, your dead boy's already floatin' around the happy land where it's flowers and love all the time. Sunshine and Karen Carpenter songs. Grew up with a fucker like you, I bet he don't know what to make of it."

Frank Lloyd stares. His shakes is weaker. The blood about his body covers a space two times his size.

"You're bleedin' out, Frank. You'll join him soon and when you get there, I hope it's in time to see the Almighty boot your boy's ass over the side."

He's weak. Almost gone.

"That ain't actually how it works. The hell you get it is the one you made. If we had more time, maybe."

"*You shoulda been in the car.*"

"Well, good talkin'. Guess it's time for me to push off. Did you know that's a naval reference?"

I put a slug in the back of his head.

CHICAGO MAGS

"Now we're getting to why you came to see me," says Mags.

"I got a confession."

She leans. I lower the voice. Look about. Her eyes sparkle too eager, but I trust her like no one ever afore.

"I been kinda fucked in the head. Only way to say it. I can't think. I give up the drink, but I still know I done wrong. All those men I put down; each deserve it better'n most people who die. I know they deserve it."

"What do you think is the problem? If they deserved it?"

"Well like you say. What if they was on the path they was suppose to be on? What if they was someday gonna be better, and I cut that off? Maybe I wasn't the one suppose to give 'em what was due."

She smile like I'm a little boy just peed his first time standing up.

"I been kinda sidin' with the dead men," says I. "I see 'em in my dreams, like they was stapled to trees. They eyes glow and they legs and arms hang. I been seein' 'em and thinkin' I stole somethin' from 'em, and become just like 'em, almost like fightin' fire with fire just burns everything good too."

"Sounds like a breakthrough."

"Sound like bullshit and I know better. It's just a feelin' I ain't been able to shake. I done what I done and I'm responsible for it. Nobody pull that trigger but me. And the day comes I'm afore the Almighty and got to explain myself, the words'll be there. The men I killed needed dead and the whole world's better off without 'em."

"You're willing to speak for the whole world? For all of humanity?"

"On that score I sure as hell am."

"There is a difference between being the physical cause of an effect and being responsible for the effect. Did you know that?"

"No and I still don't. You do it you done it."

"Baer, I've spoken about free will.... But you don't have it yet. Not fully. Your decisions have followed a channel because you've never learned to reject yourself and all you think you know."

"Why would I do that?"

"Because you don't know where the information came from. Listen to me. If a politician tells you he's going to spend some money on a program just for people like you, what do you think?"

"He's a lyin' piece a shit oughta be strung up by his nuts and shot in the kneecap first. Maybe add some honey and ants to the equation. Maybe a cattle prod."

"Why?"

"Some dynamite. Fishin' hooks."

She smile.

"And broken glass."

"Okay. Why?"

"Because he'll say anything to anybody to get what he wants."

"He wants something."

"A vote. And he'll lie to your face to get it, and all the other sonsabitches call him an esteemed colleague 'cause they's a bunch a rat fuck liars too."

"He shapes what he says to get what he wants."

"A fuckin' liar. Exactly."

"Would it be fair to say that you distrust everyone?"

Tilt the head. I'd like to say I'd eat cow feed out her hand but somehow this don't seem a flirtin' moment.

"I distrust everyone. That's fair. But only 'cause most all I ever met was liars and I knew it."

"Okay. Who gave you your first thoughts? Where did they come from, when you were a tiny boy and didn't even know you were you? Where did all of your ideas come from?"

"Hell if I know. Ma?"

"Certainly her, but also from your father, through your genes. And his father, and his father, and his father. They built up thought patterns based on what they wanted for themselves in the world presented before them, and you inherited all those thought patterns. Not the thoughts, but the patterns. The neural connections that function like roads and highways in the brain, for thoughts to travel on. Did you know that?"

"Uh, nope."

"All of those thought patterns are good for one thing only: they are a starting point. Your brain has to have a starting point, but the art of being human is about discovering which of those thoughts you should reject because they aren't true for you and replacing them with ones that are true for you. You won't be your own person until you disavow everything about your thought life that has an uncertain provenance. It's the only way to be certain that you can defend whatever is left."

"You're saying all my thinking ain't mine? Sounds like bullshit to me."

"I know who you are, Baer, and a little about what you've done. I can handle the truth about what you think."

"Okay. All my life I been thinkin' every wakin' fuckin' minute. How's all that not my thinkin'?"

"Have you ever done anything you knew you shouldn't do, but you did it anyway? And even while you did it you were thinking it was a bad idea?"

"All the time."

"Those are prime areas to search for inherited beliefs. Something deep within you compelled action, even while your conscious mind was aware the action was... unenlightened."

Nod.

"My question for you is, why are you living someone else's thought life? You wouldn't just slip into someone else's clothes. They wouldn't smell right. They wouldn't fit right. They wouldn't be worn thin in the right places. Stretched in the right places. So why would you wear someone else's thoughts?"

...stretched in the right places...

I sneak a peek at her jugs and feel positively... enlightened.

"I dunno. Stumped."

"You've lived in a narrow channel your whole life, with walls formed by beliefs that were appropriate for your ancestors, but not for you. These inherited beliefs do not apply to you, but you try to conform your life to them anyway. Is it any wonder you are confused? Or that we are all confused, sometimes?"

Raise the hand. Want to reach and touch this woman but I also want to listen. "Expound on that, maybe," says I.

"Here's an example. Throughout your life, there have been certain thoughts that you've never entertained about yourself. Have you ever applied the word astronaut to yourself?"

"I never been one."

"But have you ever imagined you were, or could be if you chose? Or has the word always applied to other people?"

"Other people."

"Right. See. Here's another: Rap music fan."

"Nope. Never."

"Doctor, Lawyer, Police. All of these words can only in your mind apply to other people, not you. Am I right? You've lived deep within the known territory of what is possible because you've never conceived of yourself on the margins, cutting new territory. It's a shame because you have gifts and could be any thing or person you choose."

Close the eyes. Been talking too long. Throat's hoarse and I ain't the one movin' most the words.

"Earlier you said you were surrounded by liars. How did you know?"

Long breath. Almost wanna get outta here and skip chasin' the lay. Talkin' to this woman's the strangest thing and if I'd a had a drink of likker in the last week I'd say the whole thing was made up, dream, illusion like she say. But this woman's truth rings like mine, though the words ain't the same. The feeling behind is dead on the money and if all this is true, I got some decidin' to do.

Yet her truth ain't one hundred percent. It's maybe ninety-nine, and the one percent she's missin' means the whole deal.

"I was in a fight in high school. Fella called Ma a whore. Anyhow, I was suspended and walkin' home with Larry my brother, he called Ma a whore too. I kicked his ass and he try to murder me later, by electrocution. Ever since, I know when people lie. I feel electric and sometimes the liar's eyes glow red."

"Okay. Really? You're being honest?"

"Sure as shit."

"I'm hungry for potato salad."

Red eyes.

"Lie."

She sits back. Studies me. "I drive a Toyota."

Red eyes.

"Lie."

"I eat pistachios when I masturbate."

Wait.

Wait.

"I'd like to see that."

CHAPTER TWENTY-EIGHT

Lucy from the motel say Abraham Church ain't really Abraham Church. He got another name, Chester DeChurch, and how he got tangled in all this I don't know. Part of me almost want to forgive and forget. Or not so much forgive as put Glenwood Springs justice behind me. The girls from the bar with Frank Lloyd, maybe let them off the hook. Lloyd and his son killed Mags, not the girls. And Lloyd's dead.

I didn't cut off his head neither. Another broke promise.

But this Abraham Church fiasco aggravates the shit outta me.

Lucy and Herman said he runs a body sellin' business and was there when Frank Lloyd help me with my laundry. Abe Church was good to me and all, but he held somethin' back at the hospital room and at the parkin' lot. If we was lifelong chums maybe I'd owe him, but with Corazon dead and Mags dead I broke out with the fuckits. Like a rash all over I don't give a fuck about the social lubrication, what the old folks call manners.

Justice is the bigger principal.

I'll force the confrontation and whatever shakes out is what it's worth.

Funeral home is two streets back off the 82 in Glenwood, down low on the west side. Outta town a good half mile.

Drive by with Stinky Joe ridin' shotgun. He got the window down, grill out huntin' bugs. Keep drivin' past; get a sense of the lay lookin' mostly left, on account I'll see the right comin' back. Ahead is a gravel spot aside the road and I swing 'round and like I thought, everythin' out the window's different. This time I spot ground broke open for a new building, some commercial job with a big sign out front on account the world demanded an announcement. They got a half acre scraped flat, workin' two levels to boot.

Wonder what… sorta… earth movin'…

Lookin' past the shoulder I spot a Caterpillar D6 bulldozer, what with the diesel engine you start with the gasoline engine runnin' first.

That Caterpillar's a tracked vehicle and when a man need to make an impression, any sorta tracked vehicle's real nice.

No one loiterin' 'bout the construction site — sure seem like a sign to me.

'Tween here and Church's mortician service is a grove of thin trees and grass. A double track runs the middle and I swing the Eldorado on it and park. Anyone on the 82 lookin' this way'll see, but I come to believe I could soak Godzilla in gas and light his ass in the Walmart parking lot and not one in ten thousand folk'd notice on account they was seekin' truth in the cell phone 'stead of what they can kick and punch in front of 'em.

Eldorado's safe, is the point.

Grab the jug of Turkey in back the seat and enjoy a snurgle the size of two. Return the jug and nudge Stinky Joe on the shoulder.

"Wanna tag along? C'mon, Puppydog."

I think I'm going to rest my eyes.

"What? Your eyes? What the hell work your eyes done?"

They were out the window.

"Ahhh — bullshit. I'm callin' bullshit."

Leave Stinky Joe with the vehicle and head thirty yards deeper in the rough. It ain't field and it ain't woods. Way up ahead is a fold of Rocky Mountain, wooded and low like a mountain youngun. Can't look more'n a second or two but I hear the call.

I cut parallel the road and at the funeral home steal quick to the back wall.

Left or right?

Fuckit.

Right. Come 'round the corner and ease up low to the first window. Room's dark. Next window I slink up and find the same. Third is lit but it's a room with chairs and flowers and no people yet. Next corner, turn 'round and shit, this side's visible from the road. Any number of folk might see, but they won't know if I'm suppose to be here or not, so long as I don't tell 'em by lookin' the crook.

Around the corner, dosey doe. Pass the viewin' room, keep goin' and stop at the next window. Look up the road and no cars so slow and cautious I look inside.

Abraham Church sittin' with his back to the window at a big ass wood desk. I guess with the chairs out front that's so he can sell to folks when they need a casket. I turn 'round and it's a straight shot across the grass to the paved entrance.

Must be a while 'til the next body showin', as I can hear the guitar and drums off the radio through the wall.

Doobie Brothers.

Some tunes is writ to play loud. I dig the Doobies too and try to square the music with the man listenin', and can't. I look at Church a long minute, shape of his back. In another world he'd be a sailor hoistin' ropes, a farmer chuckin' bales. He's a big somebody up top. Sits with the knees splayed like his nuts is six inches wide. He works at the desk and just like his body don't look too comfortable, I bet his mind got the same issue. He's a brute force man, I see now. He'll use the paper and pencil — he taught himself the tools of the world he chose — but his natural habitat prefer the most basic instrument a man can wield.

Force.

And the whole time I was so taken with his lack of deceit and pretend give-a-shit, I miss the omitted lies and his general life lived in the pursuit of evil.

They's no way to add up what I know about Abe Church without him deservin' a couple questions. And if I know a fella got the ability to lie and me not see it, and the propensity to cause harm to get his way, and a past of animosity despite my best and most accommodatin' good nature, well fuck him. I'll ask the questions my way, in the manner I see fit.

With good fortune that'll be assisted by a Caterpillar D6.

Head back and if I walked any faster they'd think I was trainin' up for the Olympics now that walkin's a sport.

I'd like to check in on Joe, but I won't.

That gimme the thought I ain't had a swaller of Wild Turkey in longer'n I've been countin' by at least thirteen minute. Cut to the car and under the front seat pull a flask, as I'll take it along. But the flask is a pain in the ass to fill and if I want a swaller right now I'd best, for simplicity, take it from the jug.

"I'm back, Sir Joseph. Last chance. After I git a pull a Turkey I'm a tear some shit down. Wanna come?"

Joe shake his head.

Open the back seat and swipe the jug. Spin the cap and with the first splash past the teeth I'm jazzed agin and tinglin'. Another couple swallers for good measure and other nonsense and I tuck the jug back safe in the Eldorado.

"I'll be back. Don't go and get nice on me."

I'm in snakeskin boots and a suit bottom with a shirt suitable for ironin' if I was the type. That and a jacket looks real smooth. All total I'm a man no one's like to expect to see runnin' through the scrub havin' a giggle fit so I temper the enthusiasm. But as of spot-tin' that Caterpillar I'm feelin' positively righteous about my life and station. Sure, back of my mind I'm about to weep and brood on two girls I wish was still in the world. But they's work to be done and I'll visit memories in the privacy of a campfire tonight and the next two hundred.

Construction people left the Caterpillar near edge of the site, next the only big tree on five acres where some other folk left a few trucks and a couple porta potties.

"Hey."

Kick the porta door. Nothin'.

Take a leak and shake thrice.

Outside I ease up to that Caterpillar slow. She's real purty but she'll be less so if she know it. Meanin' if whoever owns her left a chain and lock I only know two ways to bust a lock open and one require tin snips and a soda can I ain't got, and the other — Smith — is too noisy for applications this close to the road.

Slip out a hand and drag it easy 'cross her track.

"Hey, girl. Like your lines."

She got a fresh coat of yellow paint but nobody sanded smooth what was chipped out beneath. From the road she's all bright and shiny but up close I see the scars of fifty years' work movin' earth on account of men's ambitions. Somethin' noble in a old machine, what's been beat and used and still got a soul for toil.

Though I bet she's less susceptible to flattery'n she was in 1960.

Some of these D6's got the roof front to back and some got none at all. This one's got a roof over the driver, though it ain't but wire mesh that wouldn't cast a shadow edgewise. The way these D6's is situated you got the main diesel, and right behind on the drivers' left is the gasoline starter engine. I climb up her track careful not to muss the suit, and squat.

Check the cockpit for chains...

Looks like I got me a Caterpillar.

Let's see... Been a lotta years.

Decompressor point at me, throttle halfway, choke out, bam... Power button down.

Gas engine fires right up.

This switch and that, one two three and the big diesel engine smoke-farts herself awake too. I kill the gas and the diesel grumbles low and moody about how I like. If she was a singer she'd be hunched on a stool and each word'd come with a half lung of Marlboro smoke, and though she maybe don't got another sixty years in her, she's rootin' and tootin' for the night she's on the stage.

Smack the seat clean and drop a load of Baer in it. Throttle's the short lever on the right. Clutch is on the left. It all comes back natural.

Brake on each side, stop the track. This one lifts the blade. I give it a foot.

Time to ride, and hope them Doobies still sing at Church.

That diesel don't lug nor chug but keeps the same grumble no matter what I do. Pull this lever and that. Maybe if I was pushin' ten tons. Reverse and brake left, that points the nose right. Figger I'll run parallel 'long the road and drop straight in on the driveway, afore it swings to the main entrance for those that come to view their dead.

Wave at Stinky Joe, crossed over to the driver seat to watch the commotion. Caterpillar don't move but ten twelve mile an hour but on tracks and knockin' over scrub it feels a heady fifteen, easy.

Out of abundant caution I look back and see no one's yet at the construction site and no one on the 82's payin' me no mind neither.

Look forward agin and someone put a tree right in front, tall and skinny like a birch.

The blade shears the stump at the earth and the top drop back on the cage with a snare-rattle boom. A branch stripped white of bark and jagged at the end shoves through the metal mesh. If I was lookin' I'd a lost a eye. Instead I brake right then left and though the tree wobbles, it's stuck on the Caterpillar like a small cannon tube. I lift the blade with the hydraulics and the tube rides up. Someday when I'm a grown man I'll see 'bout buildin' a howitzer on top a Cat D6. For now, this birch log's in my line of sight and I'm a stickler for safety. Nearin' the funeral home entrance I brake the left track and the right keep grinding.

Release the brake. The turn stops and the sideways motion jolts into forward and dislodges the tree over the side. I'd like to throttle up but time's short so I boresight the D6 along the hood and draw the bead on Church's office window. While the Caterpillar grunts after the bulwark I know in the heart this man ain't innocent.

He ain't a friend.

Deep down I'd like to see Abe Church is a good man. I'd like to know other people got the curse and figured out how to live regular. But that ain't Abe Church.

I'm on the window. Church is still in his chair. The blade smash through aluminum siding, glass and two by fours. Metal scrunches. Wood snaps. Glass shatters and dust blow out every crevice so the air's thick as the guts of a grain silo.

The building give so easy it don't even bounce me in the seat.

Church spin on his chair then bounce like a cat saw a cucumber.

A little brake on the left track...

Church jumps to his feet but a section of wall takes out his legs while I drop the blade to the concrete pad and drive him back. He get a hand over the top and I keep chuggin' at the wall. He get the other hand up, and just in time his noggin too, and I stomp both brakes and pin Abraham Church to the wall with his head above the blade and his belly pressed agin.

That's fuckin' dandy work there.

Blood spill out a hole on Church's head and his eyes ain't leveled yet but by and by he spot me and his brows pucker.

Hands go below the blade.

Somewhere under the tracks is a radio. "Howdy, Abraham. You turn off the music for me?"

He look at me so blank I bet he ain't got the words he'd need to cry mercy. He stares and I stare back.

Through all the dust I see Corazon like she was in the garage, lookin' at me across Jubal White's Mustang, disappointment in her face on account I was drunk and half out my mind. Her likely rememberin' sweet innocence and wonderin' why so much of the world can choose somethin' else. I hate how things is ordered so I'll never see her agin 'til I'm dead, and I hate how she'll never see me live to a better standard. Lookin' at Abe Church's beaded eyes I ache for Tat's broken heart, now her sister's gone. And I ache for Chicago Mags. Sometimes loss comes so quick and heavy it's like fat raindrops from a clear sky, and every which way you go, zig or zag, it don't matter you just get hit more. Death and loss and destruction. And deep down like Mags say, it's all connected in the nonlocal, and they call it that 'cause they's no such thing as space or time, and it's a big ass place — big as everywhere else — and each and every point is both the center, the edge and all in between.

And here in the middle is Abraham Church.

"HHHHGgggggt."

"Too much blade?"

He's pinned at the neck 'tween steel and sheet rock.

"Was you carryin' a pistol, Abraham? I'd hate to come aside and have you fire a bullet in me."

"No. Hhggghhtt."

"Lotta dust in the air. I didn't anticipate that and I'm sorry. Tell me the truth about the gun."

"No gun."

"You swear?"

"I swear. Hhghgtt."

No red nor juice but with this feller that don't mean squat.

"You should let the spit build up in your mouth a couple minute. Save it for one good swallow, clear the throat. You do that while I talk a minute. On the one hand I bet you wonder how it come about

I wreck your joint with a Caterpillar. That's the D6 — you maybe don't got the best view up front behind the blade. I think this's a sixties model. And on the other hand, you know what all this's about more'n I do, and part of you's thinkin' how do I say what I need to say to keep me alive, and not say enough to get me killed. Right?"

"Ugh."

"Just say right."

"Hhhght."

"Or don't say nothin'. Just save up your spit like I said. I come from Frank Lloyd's motorcycle garage."

"I ... can't... "

"You can breathe if you don't talk so much. Now listen, Frank Lloyd didn't want to say your name, but he did tell me I shoulda been in the car. I know it was him and his dipshit boy shot Maggie in Chicago. He musta knew I was parked just a couple spaces down. But it don't make sense he'd want to kill me in my car, see? Open your fuckin' eyes! Now listen! Frank and his boy killed Chicago Mags — "

"No..."

"I know that for a fact it was them."

"Nhhgggghttt de — "

"And I'll tell you another thing. That woman at the motel's under my protection, and told the truth. You kill her daughter and her friends so you could part 'em out. Ship 'em UPS."

Ghhhtt.

"I thought as much. Church, I heard enough. I'm here to kill you. That'll be the end and I got more to say on that, like to make you feel better. But afore I do, they's things I want to know."

Cghghttt.

"You don't tell the truth, I'll fill your nuts with 44 slugs and watch you bleed to death. That's the proposition. Keep the answers coming. Or don't. What's your truth sense tell ya?"

Ghhhttt.

"Ah, dammit."

This prick can't say shit. Exhaust is buildin' up quick, but if I back out this Cat I got to figure another way to secure Church while I extract some answers. So I tilt the blade; give to his neck and take from his knees, as he don't need 'em for talkin'.

Church's head drop down and it's just Kilroy and me. I kill the diesel and look about the smoky office. He got one wall made of window and I didn't even see but they's a woman out there steppin' back slow and cautious like she spot a grizzly.

No one else.

Church's too fat to get his belly out the bucket so even though his neck is loose he ain't a risk. But that woman is.

She see me lookin' and turn and bolt.

I swing Smith and fire two through the glass and past her head. She halts with her hands up and head tucked low.

"Stop, lady." Point Smith at Church's head. "Abe, what's her name?"

"Delma."

"DELMA! You listen, woman. I'm here 'bout Church and his illegalities. You'll be free to go once I kill him. But you got to wait, understand?"

She's shakin'.

"Delma, listen, Dear. This is justice, and since you ain't done anything wrong — " Wait. "Abraham, what's Delma's role in all this? What she do here?"

"Telephone."

"Delma, listen. Once Abe's dead you can go. Well, a couple minute after. They's always things a fella wants to do, you know? Police his brass. So you go back to that desk there like you was, and pull that seat 'round so you're on this side the partition, where I can keep an eye out. Sit a minute and I'll give you the all clear. That fair?"

She's shakin' agin. Women.

"Delma, I got to pay attention to Abe here, 'fore the police come. You do as I said and if you don't I'll shoot you."

She backsteps and nods, hands out front like to swat a bullet.

"Now Abraham, Lloyd says I shoulda been in the car. Why?"

He clear his throat.

"You do that thing with the spit?"

Church nod.

"So why he say that 'bout the car?"

"So you would have died."

Uh.

Brain just shrunk twelve ounce.

"What? What car?"

"The girls in the hospital."

"What girls in the hospital? Chicago?"

He close his eyes. Open 'em.

"What girls in the hospital, Abraham?"

"The day we met."

I kept the thought tucked as far back in the brain as I could, but when I realized it was Frank Lloyd and his sluts in the truck... I knew they done Corazon too.

"What the hell you got to do with that? You was what? You knew Corazon afore I was in the hospital and got to see her? You and me never talk 'bout Corazon. You was there at the accident..."

And I see sixteen worlds spin backwards and suck up together in a single piece outta what was broke. Chester A DeChurch. Corazon went to kill Chester Abraham DeChurch. Church was there at the accident, watchin'. He owns the motorcycle place so he had the people with the knowledge of nuts and bolts and dirty tricks. He was there at the bar when Frank Lloyd and the girls lure me in with titties and sin. Beautiful titties and sin. And he was there when Frank come back for me at the motel laundry. And in the hospital parkin' lot he was real interested in where I was headed... Chicago University to see a woman named Mags.

I see it.

And same time I see it I see the sweep of... Me... the lay of my life's peaks and valleys. How I got the Eldorado on account of my instinct to be on my own — and it accidentally save my life. And how I went to Chicago to learn the depths of the universe while lookin' at Mags's rack — and that accidentally save my life too. The whole dance set up so I both see the jewel and the misery, always enough of the one to keep me chasin' the other. Always enough motivation for the sin to keep me agitatin' for the virtue.

Without life's miseries I doubt the titties would be so lovely.

That's all of everything. The big wide picture.

And if I look at one inch of the big picture and ignore the rest, reality resolves and I see the only two scenes that matter.

Abraham Church killed Corazon and Chicago Mags.

"Been you the whole time."

"I am what I am."

"Things is rarely what they ain't. The motel woman tell me about her sixteen year old daughter, Gloria. You killed her and her friends."

Church's head bounces small, like you got to look to see each jiggle. I bet behind that dozer blade he's beat to shit. He rest his head on the metal edge and don't answer.

"And you try to do the same with Tat and Corazon. See the black hair and you figure — "

"No. Nghhghghgt." He spits. "No. She came after me. She was going to murder me."

"That's on account you're a pervert likes to fuck kids. Entirely justifiable and got nothin' to do with what you did to them other girls."

"That's what the FBI told me," Church say. "She chose her victims on the Internet and that's how they picked me to wait for her. They had guys like me in six towns. Stakeout in each house every night for a week."

"Ambushes."

"So they could arrest her in the act of attempted murder."

"And when they didn't you decided to kill her back."

"It fit."

"It fit what?"

"Me."

"Say more."

"There's a market for bodies. I sell them."

"Sold."

"A distinction with merit," says I.

Rolls his eyes. "She would have come back for me."

"That's true. You don't poke a stick at some people. You see that now, accourse?"

He float his gaze to my face and I bet if I was inside his head the world'd be lookin' pretty fuzzy.

"Was risky, you goin' after her. FBI and police was trackin' the whole thing."

"She said she knew everything," says Church.

"What everything?"

"Everything I did. My whole operation. She looked like the other girls. I thought she was with the others, somehow. Looking for revenge."

"Well I guess she was at that. Just she was with the girls you rape and not the girls you tear apart and sell. It's real good we're havin' this conversation. So that's the whole business. Make people into bodies and sell 'em. What they call the vertical integration in the business books."

He look at me.

"I read."

"That's not true. Most of our bodies are sourced according to the rules."

"What rules?"

"The Organ Procurement and Transplant Network has a rulebook. It was on the wall you drove through."

"I guess it's real good someone wrote the rules." Spit, and too late realize I coulda spit on Abe Church. Next time. "How you do it? With Corazon and the car?"

"I knew the FBI didn't have what they wanted on her and that they'd release her without charging."

"How you know that?"

"The way it went down. They had agents in the back while your girl was trying to be smart with me on the couch up front. One of the agents sneezed and your girl ran. She never did anything illegal. They had to cut her loose."

Fact she's dead and at the hand of a man she didn't do nothin' illegal to... kinda grab me by the short hairs.

"When the police released Corazon my nephew called Frank on the cell. Bunny and Bambi waited up the street. Frank watched from his truck with binoculars and followed while they stole the Mustang and when they finally parked it for the night, he told the girls where."

"And that's all."

"He had Bambi put a tracker on it, and a small charge of C4 on the steering column."

"C4. How the fuck you get C4?"

"I can sell you some."

"Un fuckin' real. Bambi does C4 work."

"Her dad raced cars and she grew up in the shop. Have her tune your Caddy before you kill her."

"We talkin' the same girls? Them skanks from the bar, led me out to the Ryder?"

"Uh-huh."

"They play dumb real good." I let the explanation settle out and fill the cracks.

"You know Baer, you don't have to play it this way."

"Pretty sure I do."

"No, listen. We can work together."

"Well let me say somethin' I just thought of. If Frank Lloyd says I shoulda been in the Mustang, that means you and them was gonna sell my body too."

Abraham look down but his gaze bounce back. "The fact is still the fact. Did you kill Frank Lloyd?"

"Yes."

"Of course you did — you're a thousand times better. He had the drop on you twice and failed. You're exactly what I need. So back this bulldozer off me and we'll explain this whole mess easy enough. The Caterpillar brake didn't work. That's all. Then we form a partnership. Legitimate and legal. Papers drawn the right way — "

"One more thing I'm curious 'bout."

Broke him out the dream where everything turns out okay.

"What thing?"

"Where you get bodies to sell? The ones you don't kill."

"Regular people."

"You just take 'em? Ain't no use lyin', Abraham. You know it and I do too, so let's just say everythin' truthful the first time."

"Most folks we just tell them they get a free cremation if they donate their bodies to science."

"A free cremation for donating their body to — you mean donate the ashes? To science to study the ashes?"

"No. Their body."

"And you sell the parts."

"I sell them through my other company, Vail Body Broker. I run it out of Eagle."

"You run Vail Body Broker out of Eagle, Colorado?"

"I couldn't name it Eagle Body Broker. Eagles are protected."

"That was good thinkin', but you don't see the bullshit?"

"What bullshit?"

"You never cremate the body. You offer the free cremation but folks got to get their parts sawed up and shipped out first. You only cremate what you can't sell."

"So?"

"It's a fuckin' lie."

Woman in the other room hear me raise the voice. She look up.

"You're good. Just another minute, sweet Delma."

Shit!

Church got a pistol up over the dozer blade — but he can't get the wrist bent to aim it. I back away the other side a hair and level Smith.

"You want a bullet in the wrist? Or maybe just drop the gun?"

He open his fingers and the gun slips out his hand. Clang twice and no more.

"You know, Alden, it's a hell of a lot easier to get what you want when you're willing to see the world my way."

"Almighty didn't make the world for lies. You see 'em like I do. How is it possible in the fabric of the sensible world you and me ain't allies in the good fight?"

"Why?" Church says

"Because you see the truth."

He smirks. "It's a hell of gift. Get anything you want."

I don't comprehend. It's like he said the dragon soup is purple not four. He sees the love and respect and choose the hate and mayhem.

He *choose* it.

"I can understand a man does wrong and don't know it. You call him out and he'll feel like shit and mend his ways. Maybe backslide and maybe he don't change at all. But at least he knows he fucked up and done wrong. He don't change but he don't escape the guilt neither. That's the way it's suppose to be, doin' wrong. But you do it knowin' full well. I can't get the brain around it."

Blood from a cut on his noggin finally start flowin' down his face, now his head rest on the blade agin.

Abraham Church says, "Good men do good things because they look like good men doing good things. They feel good with their honor all bright and shiny. But a man with no honor to begin with…"

"Why do good things?"

He nods and his chin hit the metal so he stops.

Church says, "Why is taking care of other people a higher value? Why is it worth more than taking care of myself?"

"You don't know?"

"No. And you don't either."

"But I got time to noodle it."

He let the wind out his lungs. "Yes you do."

"Abraham, I need one thing. Them girls, Bambi and Boobs."

"Bunny."

"Ahh. Where I find 'em?"

Church smiles. "You aren't persuaded by my other points?"

"Where I find the girls?"

Church shakes his head like to deny me but the Almighty moves his mouth and pushes air through his pipes and the words come out agin his desire.

"They live in the trailer court you see on the way to Carbondale. On 82."

I climb back up on the dozer. Fire the gas engine, then the diesel. Exhaust fumes is still heavy inside and it's time to back this beast out.

But first I push the hydraulic lever and the blade tilts forward. Church twist his head and barely get his chin over the blade agin and for two inches that's a good thing. But the blade keep tiltin' farther and pressin' Church's neck agin the wall. Meat and bone give and after a second the flesh rips — gash fills with blood so fast I all but quit watchin' 'til Abraham Church's head rolls over the blade and a single squirt of blood hits the wall afore his body drops behind and his neck paints the blade instead.

I meant to say some nice words to give him comfort, but I suspect he's already over his disappointment.

CHICAGO MAGS

I fold a leg. Realize both hands is cupped over my mess but if I move 'em that'll draw more attention and she'll know I was a pervert the whole time.

"Your brother, the one who tried to kill you — have you spoken to him lately?"

"Day he died."

"Oh, I'm sorry."

"I sent him forward."

"That's almost how I think of it too, but not forward in time so much as forward in experience. Do you think your brother deserved to die?"

"Don't know. Use to."

"What changed?"

"You."

"How so?"

"You got me thinkin'. Ever since you hitch a ride. I wasn't thinkin' right afore that night, let alone since. The day my brother Larry try to kill me I kicked his balls so bad they broke. He was a mule and knew it was my doin'."

"Okay. Go on."

"The stuff he did later…"

She crosses hands. "I'm not going to finish the thought for you."

"I set that in motion. I killed my brother 'cause he did shit I set in motion."

Mags frowns and spends a good fifteen count studyin' clouds.

"What did Larry do before you kicked him?"

"That's when we was fighting after school. He said our mother was a whore."

"Was she?"

Nod.

"What do you think about that?"

"I'm glad. We ate."

"Your brother provoked you?"

"Some. Yeah, that's right."

"Isn't he as culpable in his death as you?"

"Logical."

"And the others...."

Tilt the head like I don't know whether my left ear weighs more or the right. It ain't a revelation. "I know what they did. But they didn't make me do what I did."

"Then why did you do it?"

"I chose."

"How?"

"I thought."

"You thought? You questioned whether or not to kill? You reviewed the reasons pro and con and arrived at a studied opinion?"

"Well shit."

"Baer, is it possible you thought about how to kill them, not whether to kill them?"

"It was a fairly creative moment."

"At what level of consciousness did you arrive at the decision to kill them?"

I'm blank. The sidewalk don't got the answer.

CHAPTER TWENTY-NINE

Feel bad 'bout leavin' the dozer at the funeral home but it's a chance for someone else to do good. Just a couple more positive things I want to see about.

I roll down the window. Man in a white jacket lockin' the back door of the Vail Body Brokers Incorporated. Sign say VBB Inc.

"You the manager here?"

"We're closed for the day, sir."

"I got a special delivery."

"I'll have to ask you to bring it — "

"Chester A. DeChurch."

"What? What about Mr. DeChurch?"

"Mister DeChurch the boss here, right?"

"That's right."

"And you do his biddin'? Or does he run the day to day operations?"

"What does this pertain to? I'm sorry. I didn't get your name."

"I'm Baer Creighton. I need to hear something, but I didn't hear it."

"Just who are you? Do you represent somebody?"

Well shit. I'll be —

"Might say I do."

Alla sudden I feel scrappy like I might invite this skinny dipshit for a donnybrook here on the blacktop. But with the busted arm I got to play it safe.

"I'm leaving for the day," says the manager. "You can take up whatever issues you — "

"Chester Abraham DeChurch got a *severe* issue. Let's see what he got to say."

Exit the Eldorado and pop the trunk. "Can you see? Or you need to come closer?"

"What? Where is Mr. DeChurch? Are you saying you have him? You mean you are in physical possession — "

"Right here. Now I need to know afore you get to talk to Church, how much of the day to day 're you responsible for?"

"Mr. DeChurch? Are you in there?"

He come stompin' now like he found his nuts. He ain't yet seen Smith on my hip and as I shift the right side away to protect the broke arm, he won't either. Got the holster slung backwards so I can cross draw with my left.

Manager's at the trunk.

"Oh, God! Is that him? WHERE IS HIS HEAD?"

He turn away from the trunk and see Smith in his face.

"How much of the day to day you do here?"

"Mister DeChurch does everything. He doesn't trust — didn't trust anyone. He said you never know when someone's lying… and so he did everything himself. And I only just started. I started two weeks ago and I think I'm going to quit. Better opportunities in Portland. That's where my mother is from. And my wife and children. Three small children who would grow up fatherless. On welfare. Oh please mister — "

He's throwin' so much juice and red I'm like to make fruit punch. And it occurs, that electric don't sting at all like it useta.

"Surely that ain't all," says I. "Don't you support your disabled mother? Veteran of the war?"

"No, my mother wasn't a veteran. But I do help her out with cash."

"I thought so. Otherwise who's gonna make all them apple pies?"

"I don't understand."

"Sounds right. Folk lie all day and you call 'em on it, they don't understand. Nobody suppose to call out the bullshit. Well, I got a lesson for you. Not *you* in particular, as you'll see in a minute. No use. But I got a lesson in general. From this day on you might expect your lies to be called. That or a bullet in the back."

"What's that mean?"

"It means shut the fuck up. What your name?"

"Richard."

"You sure?"

"What? That's my birth — "

"I think your name's Dick."

"Dick is fine. Perfectly fine. I go by Dick all the time."

"Dick, none of this shit's real. Don't worry too much."

"What?"

"What I said. Now listen. Chester Abraham Church DeChurch, this fella here in the trunk with no noggin, says he wants you to sell his stupid assed body all over the world."

"I... uh..."

"You uh. Here's the deal. I know the corporate structure of the Vail Body Broker Inc. You see that bucket of gold by Mr. DeChurch's — "

"Did you trade his head for the gold, somehow?"

"Dick, you ain't impressin' me."

"I promise to be more nuanced — "

"Maybe try the truth instead."

"That's a great suggestion."

"Now I already had the gold and like I say, I'm gonna own this

VBB Incorporated in a couple day. I need DeChurch's body to go away like all the others, and I want to profit from it. You understand?"

"I... think so..."

"Keep thinkin' 'til you get an answer your nuts feel good about."

"My nuts? Oh, I understand. You want the *visceral* answer. You want to know if I ran the operation for DeChurch, and if I would be capable of continuing to run the operation under new ownership. Is that the size of it?"

"That is exactly the size of it. Perfect size."

"I can."

"Your nuts feel good?"

"My nuts feel excellent."

"And just so we's clear. You got the connections to sell Church's liver to one country and his kidney to the university, right. You know the ins and outs, what I'm sayin'."

"Mister Creighton, did you say?"

Nod.

"Mister Creighton, Mister DeChurch knew almost nothing about the business. I approached him with the vision of what it could be and he bankrolled my vision. I've been at the center of this wheelhouse since day one. I am irreplaceable. Without me there is no Vail Body Brokers, Incorporated."

"Center of the wheelhouse. I like that."

"Thank you."

"If you're irreplaceable, who else works here?"

"No one. The receptionist, Viv. Vivian. Vivian Mancuso. She lives in the green house on Crestwood — "

I pull Smith and blast one piece of lead into his nuts.

He go down on the pavement screamin' and I leave him a minute while I fish Church out the trunk. Now I'm here I see I coulda likely done the whole thing without Church's body and that blood's gonna be there 'til I yank out the carpet and hose the metal. But at the time, hell, I didn't know if I'd need the corpse or not. So as the general rule, I figure I take the corpse. Maybe rethink that, goin' forward.

Almost slip a disc but the headless bastard's on the pavement.

"Hey, Dick?"

He's cryin' and gruntin' thirty feet off, crawled all the way back to the metal door he come outta. But with half his blood stretched across cement they ain't much in his veins to do the work of livin'.

I walk to him. Look back at Stinky Joe in the passenger seat. Ain't even interested enough to get out the car.

"Dick, you see why a minute back I said the general lesson wasn't for you?"

His eyes is beady and don't move off front 'n center. His breath come in quick little pulls.

"It's 'cause you're soon to die. Now I also said all this is bullshit. None of this is real. I want to put your evil ass mind at ease. You ain't here now and you never really was. It's like your brain's a television set, see? The picture comes from... They got this place the unions can't organize, right? That's how I remember it. It ain't the local, is all."

His breath is fast and his eyes don't fear me.

"You think death'll get you off the hook, but for fuckers like you, death *is the hook.*"

He stares forward like I ain't even talkin' at him.

"You think you just disappear? No, Dick. You got the confrontation with the Holy, comin' next."

He's lookin' forward to black space and nothin', but that's on account he's a materialist, and like Mags say —

"Dick, here's what you don't understand. The problem with materialism is nothing real is material. Dick? ... Dick?"

CHICAGO MAGS

"You aren't responsible for being a man, or hailing from North Carolina, or for experiencing the lessons that taught you what you think you know. You've done things, though. You've caused other things to happen. You're definitely in the causal chain of your reality. But responsibility for the causal chain doesn't reside in a single link, somewhere in the middle. Does that make sense?"

"More and more."

"True, maximal responsibility lies with the prime cause and that's the chain's creator. The divinity who set everything in motion. That's why it's important to love all. We are infinitely forgiven because God is just, and he knows the highest responsibility for creating evil lies with the one who created good. And that's why we are to love others the same way. He loves us and gives all for us. He died for us — whether you take that figuratively or as a fact of history. He did that for you and me. But also, the other people, the ones you sent forward. God loves them the same way and forgives them the same way. And you think about how unlucky some of them were, in how they came to be the people they came to be, then maybe the most wonderful thing you could hope for would be that they would have the same forgiveness and freedom as you enjoy. Truly good people, I think, are those who spend so much time aware of their own lack of holiness, they see other people as brothers and sisters in an epic struggle to be good, instead of seeing them as failed human beings whose destruction would somehow bring about a better, more just world."

I never been so convicted.

"I went off the rails when my brother give me the curse. If I want to live like you say, I'd need to go back to the beginning somehow."

"Your ten-year-old innocence is still in you. You just have to expose it. Our best never leaves us. It always resides within, even if we can't find it."

Says Chicago Mags:

"Nietzsche said good and evil are false constructs. The world doesn't work that way. The world is about advancement, about living, about embracing power. And he's right. The animal world is all about power. But the non-material — the higher reality we glimpse in our eternal selves is all about love. Here on material earth, the false dichotomy of good and evil is just another structure that's used by one group of men to enslave another. The men who don't believe in good and evil enslave those who do — and they bind them with their beliefs. But consciousness is eternal. It's everything, and it's full of vibrant love, and when you glimpse it you want to share it. Love is bigger than good and evil, so much that when you experience it on a cosmic level you want to share it with everyone, regardless of what they believe about this or that. Good and evil. Little things. Everything is a little thing compared to God's love."

"The evil people get love too?"

"If you still think they're evil you've missed the point. They need and deserve as much love as you or anyone else, and they've probably gotten less. We're all evil. We're all good. Remember, it's a false dichotomy designed by people who know they can control people through fear and guilt. Have you ever noticed the people who enforce the rules always seem to carve out an exception for themselves? Ever notice the police are allowed to speed and politicians trade stocks on inside information? They don't care if they break the rules because they know there's no good or evil behind them."

She's moved on while I'm still stuck.

"Bullshit. The dogfighters. The pedophiles — you sayin' that ain't evil?"

"I'm saying broken people need love, and good and evil are labels that allow us to hate, instead."

Shake the head so the last nonsense falls back out. "All the rottenest bastards get the love too?"

"Don't you want them to?"

"Nah, shit. That's great."

"What?"

"Yeah, hell. Love it."

"You're being facetious. The men you sent forward are better off where they are now. Dysfunctional people here aren't going to be dysfunctional there. It's just like, I don't know. Remember before when I talked about coming to earth and being empodded in a baby?"

"Uh-huh."

"Someone has to buy the jackass ride. Not everyone can buy the Roosevelt ride, or the Ghandi ride, or whatever. Some folks have to be the assholes. There's only so many rides. But we all go home when the ride is over. All of us."

"Wait a minute. You mean I done this world and them a favor?"

"I suppose you could frame it that way. Yeah. We are all going to cross the same bridge, or sequence of experiences from this state of consciousness to the next."

"How you know?"

"Because doctors have interviewed thousands and thousands of people who medically died and then were revived, to find out what they remembered."

"Oh."

I tell her 'bout the old folks in the hospital, what the one that passed said, and why I couldn't steal his duds to break out the hospital. Then I tell her 'bout the polo shirt and why I thought to glance at her rack. Which I still adore despite her nonsense.

Chicago Mags smiles. Mouth all bent up.

"Let me put it to you straight. Each of the men you killed crossed a tunnel of light and at the other side, were greeted by an all powerful, loving force that reviewed their lives with them. In a timeless instant they understood how they harmed you with their words and actions.

"They felt what you felt, experienced through your body and emotions. They cried on your dog's grave with you because they felt your pain and knew their viciousness caused it. They carried that hurt with you while other men hunted you and tried to kill you. They felt your reluctance to use force — but they also knew that tickle of happiness the killing created in you, Baer, because even though you are trapped where good and evil seem real, within that world you are good and good men do not tolerate evil. They knew you, Baer, more intimately than you knew yourself. They loved you more than you loved yourself in that moment or any since. They received total understanding of the harm they caused, then from that newly informed position, the wrongness and selfishness in their hearts was healed. They rejoined family and friends and others who arrived before them. So, instead of you feeling bad for the men you sent forward, and aside from the dead people not actually being harmed for being murdered, you're still judging yourself harshly. You still forget your victims provoked you endlessly until you meted out your best version of justice. Out of all that you still don't understand despite your flaws you're the only good man in the crowd."

CHAPTER THIRTY

Frankie Black Boots Lloyd is dead.

His son with the glitterin' eyebrows who held the machine gun and filled Mags' chest with lead... He's dead.

Abraham Church, kid fucker and body thief. Philosopher murderer.

'At fucker's dead too.

And the man — all I got was Dick — set up the body sellin' business. He's both nutless and dead.

How 'bout Bambi and Bunny...

Church said I'd find 'em at the trailer park visible from 82 afore Carbondale. I sit in the Eldorado at the park office and watch. Dark out. People need a upgrade on the security lights.

No one pay attention to a car with no one inside, so I slink low in the seat and watch over the hood. Recall it wasn't ten hour ago I wipe Mags' blood off my face so I could talk to Cinder and not look the madman.

He seen it anyway.

But not ten hours and the last of these people killed Corazon and Mags is 'bout to die too.

I got Frank's blood and Church's blood on my hands, maybe equal to what I washed of Mags' blood. I think on that. The blood spilt's already equal. Like I get the cue from on high: proportion.

I made the proportionate response. Time to move on?

But that don't sit. Man don't kill evil bein' proportionate. He got to exterminate that shit. Murder it. And since civil man can't risk all his other obligations, he got the Destroyer circlin' the herd with his gaze pointed at the dark beyond, watchin' for red eyes.

"Don't get out the vehicle, Joe. When I come back, we're haulin' ass for the next. You hear?"

Joe look off to the pine .

I leave him with the windows down and step out the vehicle with Smith in hand. Pull Glock from under the seat and take it too, since Bambi and Bunny is girls and with all them tits, I might get confused.

Out left the trailers look tinny like enough sun and wind and the paint just evaporate. Must be the half dead streetlight. On the right they's no light at all.

Pull the flask from my jacket pocket and press it next my ribs with the arm cast. Twist the cap and take a long gurgle. Alcohol go down like lava mixed thin. I gulp a couple more, one for Corazon and one for Mags. One for my mother and one for Fred. In no time I got the flask empty and wonder why I didn't just work the jug at the car.

Adequately fueled for judgment work, I go rightward into the dark.

Tromp like I got a purpose but with all these trailers I still don't know which has Bambi and Bunny. If I don't find it, these Jezebels live another day to help murder another girl or woman or man. Or sell body parts. Or whatever else they do. Spread the syphilis.

Women got to have honor too.

Use to be noble. Woman knew her place and you could spoil her and she'd stay there, honorable and decent, even if most often ornery and mean. Some rare women'd treat you even better for the spoilin'.

Them days she got the respect back so she give the respect due. Man and woman as them natural selves.

And a boy never beat a girl 'cause no man near'd tolerate it, and no woman'd leave her man ignorant. They's a fuckin' team. Plus, half the women was as strong as half the men and could stamp that shit out on they own. Life was hard for both but they knew who was who.

Where?

Thought it was past but maybe it's the world to come. But right now men ain't men so it's no wonder women ain't women. Can't expect a woman to be a lady when her man's got a pussy too.

Nowadays, some of these piss flaps use the biological advantage agin a man's noble soul — what few's left that got one — and take advantage. When they do, they give no quarter. Like any evil man they'll use the best tool they got, tits, a pistol in the purse, another man with a club, whatever. They'll beat a man to death and throw him in a Ryder truck. Sell his pickled parts.

I heft Smith, cinch the hand tight on the grip. Nice to have a gun don't fit the small my back. This 44 Smith almost need the *big* of the back.

Thinkin' of the back give me an idea, on cue.

These girls maybe know how to turn the wrenches but they wasn't at the garage. Maybe they got another way to generate the cash flow.

First trailer I come to I circle slow, listen for the sounds of money-paid love. The bangin' moanin' rattlin' yellin' sounds any pig'd make ridin' them sows.

First trailer got a granny with her eyes pressed agin the television. I doubt Bambi carries on like she does under the nose of her mother, but the thought occurs a woman's age don't say shit about her willingness to do wrong. So I circle the trailer and when they's no sounds but what's coming out the idiot box, I leave the idiot to it.

Next trailer light's flat out, no car... Circle it and nothing.

On the gravel roadway I scan the line. This joint's the Taj Majal of trailer courts. On and on. Kinda purty with the lights in a row and the fuzzy glow halos, but big enough I'll likely need 'til dawn to find the girls.

On to the next abode.

A man and woman on the couch. Young black haired and scruffy — both his face and her legs.

Next trailer got the front light on over the cement block pile makes the steps. Closer I get the more the drums and bass shake the pantleg. Feel that bullshit in the chest. Can't get close on account the front light so I keep on the gravel and once past cut left across the dirt to the back wall. Next trailer beyond's dark inside so I got the right climate for surveillance work. Slip along the wall of the party trailer to the gap of light coming from the first window.

I get the right angle and it's a woman's arm but more burnt tan than redneck pale. She move out the way so another dark skinned girl can come by.

"Hands in the air you pervert! I said *now!*"

Voice of a man, low pitch and frayed at the edge. Liar.

Still watching the glass, says I, "You didn't say *now*. Not earlier. I mean you said it just now, but not afore like you said. Follow?"

"Uh — "

"Friend, I understand. You saw me here and got excited. Truth went out the window. You're under a lotta stress I bet."

I turn. He got a pea shooter, looks pink like a lady's purse gun.

Since I already got Smith in hand, I turn the wrist ninety degree and give him the profile. Ease the arm out the shadow.

"Friend, I want you to hear me. I'm the Destroyer. I circle the waters protectin' the fleet. I circle the herd and keep out the wolf. You fuck with me, you're fuckin' with the one who put his ass on the line to keep softies like you safe in your dream world. And I assure you, if you want, you can shoot first. But in none of the six hundred million universes Chicago Mags told me about, in *none* do you shoot last."

He lower the pistol hand.

"Chicago Mags?"

"Philosopher, deceased. You wouldn't know her. Get on back to your party and I'll get to mine."

"Uh, yeah. Uh, thank you?"

He turn.

"Hey! I'm lookin' two white girls. One's got a rack like — "

"They're not on this side of the park."

"Very kind. Their place… Any landmarks? Car? Paint?"

"There's always a black Ford Explorer parked in front."

"Always?"

"Most always. They each have one."

"Perfect. Good night, sir."

"Uh, yeah. Good night."

Back the way I come. Stop at the Eldorado. "I got information she's up this way, Stinky Joe. Be along shortly."

Stand by the door.

"You still ain't talkin' to me?"

Nothin'.

"Or on account I'm a free man and I'll drink when I choose?"

Stinky Joe hold his tongue.

I bend and look inside the Cadillac.

No Stinky Joe.

Guess he heard the mountain's call too. Or maybe he wanted some privacy to dump a load, and wander off.

I keep walkin' 'til I spot the black Ford Explorer. Turn 'round the bumper and six feet afore I reach the front door it open. Man got his back to me, maybe just paid one these girls.

Scoot fast; yank the screen with my broke arm and shove the man back inside with my good. One the girls screams and jiggles back the hall. Other's on the couch pullin' up her undies. The man swipes a paw at my broke arm but he don't know the Almighty put a stink on him to protect my path. He miss my arm. I hook my left boot behind his legs and shoulder-stomp right through him. Swing Smith in his face, now he's on the floor lookin' up.

"Stay down. Take off your belt."

A knife flip-wobbles past in the air and bounce off the wall. I shovel Smith in my holster and grab the blade off the floor. Chuck it back where it come so fast the dipshit on the floor ain't looked up and Bambi's still dumpin' boobs in a bra.

But that skinny-hipped Bunny is stuck in the guts.

"Leave it there," says I.

Aimed too low... still, I'll work with the results.

Hand and Smith meet at the hip and in zero seconds the 44's back in the carpet man's face. "Move! Gimme that belt. You — Bambi — get your ass down there with 'im."

She moves.

Bunny pulls the knife out her guts and looks at it like she can't decide if throwin' it agin makes sense.

"You want another hole? Or to die from the one you got, maybe a little farther out?"

Bunny ain't bled much yet and part of me thinks it's likely she's got very little blood in her. Or soul. Just a whisper—no more'n a image on the big screen.

Five steps I kick the knife out her hand. Bring the Smith butt to Bunny's crown and drive through like to snap her neck on the first try. I don't feel the bones give but she's light's out.

Step back to the other demon snatch. Barrel in her neck I shove her toward the hall. Talk low-voiced at her. "You take that feller's belt and tie his hands good. 'Cause here's why. When you're done, I'm gonna put this gun to his head and count to forty. Tell him if he can get his hands free, he lives and I shoot you. Understand? Nod if you understand."

She nods.

"Oh, and one thing. You say a single word to him while you're doin' his hands, I'll judge you for cheatin'."

Her eyes wander. Brow draws tight.

"That means I'll shoot you for cheatin', too. I'll shoot you for most anything. All right. Git to it."

I shove her and she trips on her man's feet. Lands on him. I toss the belt with my busted arm and keep Smith pointed at the girl 'cause the man don't give off the hero vibe. Imagine that. Meanwhile Bunny's gurglin' and squirmin'. I lean agin the wall and shift a boot to her neck. Grind it a little so the sole is flat and don't irritate the ankle.

Bambi shakes as she works that belt around her john's wrists. She jerk the belt and he flinch and wrench his arms, but with her workin' behind his back he just squirms.

Bunny wiggles under foot. I press more.

Bambi's done with her granny knots. She falls away from her john and got the legs up missionary showin' off the goods. Knees get farther apart.

She say, "Why don't we work something out?"

She move the right hand at her undies but it's the hooties I notice, and alla sudden I see Chicago Mags. I bet hers was the same as these, if it woulda been my lot to see 'em. Bambi's writhin' like a sex serpent and I see Chicago Mags loving on me through the conversation we had, sometimes laughin' so much I smell her coffee breath. Like the sex was built into everything else we did, and I had her every which way just listening to her talk and soaking up her curves. Mags come to me through the death haze like she walked all night in the woods. Mags come from where I sent the men forward and her face is so full of love I could cry for her and me both right now. For all of us. Mother, Larry, and her other son. For Fred. It's like all the love in that other place wants to shine right through her and fill me up, but afore it all spill into this world she whoosh away and I see her dead face agin, that godawful smile drippin' blood.

Some kind of cosmic interference. Static. The shiny happy Mags from beyond look at me and say, "This is not you and this is not a thing you are compelled to do."

Lower Smith to my side.

"You aren't a killer," Mags says.

Her eyes flicker.

I got a boot on one girl's throat and a 44 Smith N Wesson on the other's heart. These women is rat fuck evil and any justice in the world at all — *any justice at all* — they'd be dead.

But Mags look at me with love and I don't have the wherewithal to hate. All I want's the love. Church is dead. It was his mind thought up the evil. And Frank Lloyd and his boy is dead. They drove and pull the trigger. They's dead. I even got the body sellin' man.

Ain't that enough killin' for the day? How much blood these pod jockeys need in one go-round?

But the vision is gone and Mags smile got blood out the edge agin. I see Fred curled in his diesel turbine crate, eyes scabbed and a hole at the top his head drawin' flies. I see my mother sprawled out reachin' a busted shotgun already let her down once. I see Mags bloomin' blood from holes up and down her chest.

And I think of Corazon, lookin' at me from across Jubal White's garage, her head slunk low and her eyes steady, like she hides but don't need to. I think on her wonderin' what kind of man I am, whether even after all she'd seen of my loyalty, her life so far taught her she'd never see a man she could trust. So she look at me not knowin'.

I hope she saw enough to hope, is all. That one day she'd be free. I hope she saw enough to think the world don't gotta be shit even if sometimes it look like that's the general plan.

I hope she saw a man'd love the truth and the right enough to look past what she got 'tween her legs and on her chest.

I hope she saw a man'd kill a woman if truth and right command him to do it.

"All right Bambi. Same deal. Take the belt out your jeans over there and do his feet. Same deal's afore. You understand?"

She close her legs and sit up. All business, now the sex gambit fail. She crawl to her jeans and draw out the belt. Wrap the feller's feet.

"All right, back on the couch."

Smith in the air I let up on Bunny's throat. Aim at the man.

"Fella, you got 'til I count to forty in my head. You won't hear me count so you won't know if I'm a-countin' quick or slow. When I get to forty, if you're still in the trailer I'll put a bullet in your head. Forty seconds — give or take — for you to untie and get out. One... Two..."

He flips. Wiggles.

I credit the man's effort but they's no way in hell he's gettin' on his feet, let alone free.

Tits thought it was her or him.

I don't count in my head like I said, but I watch and when he's flopped about enough I spot his pissy drawers, I say to Bambi on the couch, "You recall a red Mustang?"

"What year?"

"Sixty eight. Had the four twenty-seven."

"That wasn't us."

"Wasn't you?"

"No. They made us do that."

"Made her? Or made you?"

"We were both there."

"How you do it? When?"

"Frank and Abraham...They made us. We followed the girls all day."

"When you put the C4 on the steering column?"

"They went into a hair salon. It only took a minute."

"How you do it? Since when's a woman know shit about cars?"

"I grew up in a garage. My father raced — "

"Ah, hell. Shut up. Where you put the charge?"

"On the column."

"Where?"

"Right after the firewall. What, you think a woman can't turn a wrench?"

"No. I just hoped you bein' a woman, you'd have better judgment."

Bunny squirms under foot. The man can't get free. I got what I want so I stomp her head with my boot heel 'til the crown bust open. Don't take two more for her brain to shit out on the floor.

"No!" Bambi lurch forward on the couch and I swing Smith at her face.

"Oh God! We didn't have a choice!"

"Uh-huh. Don't move."

Holster Smith and figger here's as good a place to send a message as any. I been carryin' a FBI Glock a month. Don't like it. I fish the law enforcement pistol out my ass holster and bend knees to the floor. Press my hand in blood and wrap palm and fingers on the Glock.

"NO! Oh, please, God, no!"

Walk to her slow.

Man rolls and kicks but he won't reach a phone 'til long after Baer Creighton's down the highway. Step 'round him.

"Please don't kill me," says he. "I'll do anything."

"No!" Bambi screams. Her eyes cross while she watch the tube hole get closer and closer. Fat tears spill out and I can almost taste the salt.

It was stronger in Maggie's blood.

"If it was only what you did to me at the bar, you know, the trick, I'd let things slide."

"Please, I'll do anything—"

"Shut up. Your stupidity breaks my heart so I'm doin' you a favor.

Now when you go to heaven, it ain't a bunch of pillars and clouds, see? You get to live all the good stuff agin, and the best things you did, you'll do 'em agin. The people you loved in your earthly life, you'll be with 'em agin. That's what I told the sister of the girl you murdered in the red Mustang. I told her you get the love from both sides. The love you give and plus you feel it comin' back, as you feel what you created in the other. Heaven's just swimmin' in love, but they's a catch."

"What? What catch?"

"All that love is what you made on earth. If you didn't give much…"

She shed a tear out the right eye.

"Yeah, you see. That's a pretty nice heaven, ain't it? You see all the good you did and the love the people felt. But that ain't where you're goin'."

Now she spill a tear out the left.

"There you go. I think you understand. See, in a minute your whole everything's gonna get nicer'n you deserve — but only for a minute. You'll pass through the white tunnel and after that, you'll see your life from the eternal side. Stop cryin' and listen. This is important. Stop. You good? Okay. Once you're there you'll see your life from the sight of the people you wronged, too, not just the people you loved. You'll see all the hurt you caused and you'll live all that sufferin' with 'em. Eventually, you'll've seen your entire life, intimate with every hurt you made."

She's afraid but that fear is wholesome as apple pie.

"If you loved in your life that flashback's gonna stretch eternal, and that's the stuff of heaven. And if you done evil, you're gonna suffer mightily, feelin' all the pain you cause everyone else. That's the beauty. Any hell you get is what you made for other people."

"That's horrible."

"I expect that depends on whether you was a selfish piece of shit or not. Anyway, soon enough you'll be right back here, livin' each moment up to the one you die. And when you come back through the next time, you'll know what I'm thinkin' right now."

"I don't want to know."

"I don't want you to wait. It's 'cause I'm doin' you a sincere favor."

She search my eyes.

"For your sake, I hope the pain destroys you."

I fire one bullet into her face. Drop Glock.

Leave john on the floor in his shit.

EPILOGUE 1

Flagstaff.

I lean on the side as the pump fills the tank. Passenger window's open while me and Joe talk.

"You gimme a scare, Joe."

I couldn't leave. I wanted to.

"I couldn't drive off. I told you I wasn't leavin' you agin."

I didn't think you meant it.

"When you decide to come back the car?"

When the police came and you were still sitting there waiting for me.

"Yeah. Well I don't think they can see me anyhow."

Joe's lookin' 'cross the gas station bay.

I recognize that woman. The big one with the blonde.

"How?"

She tried to drown me. She drugged me and tried to drown me.

"You want I should put her down?"

No. Let them be. She has a completely different vibe.

"Looks harmless enough. What about the skinny blonde? You see the tits on that?"

Stinky Joe curl on the seat.

EPILOGUE 2

Nat's on the step and Tat's lookin' out the window. I let Joe out to do his business while I lean on the grill.

Tat come out.

Cinder wave and go inside.

She come to me and when she's on the porch her face is flat but each step closer and the muscles start movin'. Cheeks get tight. Eyes narrow. Tears and shudders. Tat wrap me in her arms and press her head agin my heart.

"The people did that to Corazon... they ain't no more."

Head still agin me, she nods, and don't pull away.

"Once you're ready, how 'bout you and me go murder what people needs it?"

"Which people?"

"They'll announce 'emselves. They always do."

"I thought you found a conscience."

"I did."

"Don't you want to go someplace quiet? What about the law?"

I take Tat's shoulders in hand and ease her back a foot. Eye to eye.

"Tat, no other man'll do it. I AM the law."

TWO THINGS...

1. **What's next?** Good question! The Baer Creighton universe currently includes nine novels, with more on the way. Visit the Baer Creighton Universe to see all the books and the best order to read them. Or for the next in the series, click here: Destroyer.

1. Do you have a moment to leave a review on Amazon? It is one of the most beneficial ways you can help an author. Every review helps — even just a few words! **You can leave one here.** I appreciate your help. Thank you!

ABOUT THE AUTHOR

Hello! I appreciate you reading my books—more than you can know. If you've read this far, you and I are fellow travelers. I suspect you sense something is not quite right with the world. It's not as good as it's supposed to be. We human beings aren't as good as our ideals. Yet, we prize and want to fight for them.

I do my absolute best to write stories that portray the human situation with brutal transparency, but also I strive to tell stories that are not as bleak as the human condition sometimes seems. There's no limit to the darkness. Light is rare. But it exists, and I hope when you complete one of my novels, you find your values validated.

I'm grateful you're out there. Thank you.

Remember, light wins in the end.

Printed in Great Britain
by Amazon